D0058002

Happily Ever Now

Happily Ever Now

Nicole S. Rouse

URBAN
CHRISTIAN

www.urbanchristianonline.net

URBAN CHRISTIAN is published by:

Urban Books
10 Brennan Place
Deer Park, NY 11729

©copyright 2007 Nicole S. Rouse

All rights reserved. No part of this book may be reproduced in any form or by any means without prior consent of the Publisher, excepting brief quotes used in reviews.

ISBN-13: 978-1-60162-945-6
ISBN-10: 1-60162-945-1

First Printing September 2007
Printed in the United States of America

10 9 8 7 6 5 4 3 2 1

This is a work of fiction. Any references or similarities to actual events, real people, living, or dead, or to real locales are intended to give the novel a sense of reality. Any similarity in other names, characters, places, and incidents is entirely coincidental.

Submit Wholesale Orders to:
Kensington Publishing Corp.
C/O Penguin Group (USA) Inc.
Attention: Order Processing
405 Murray Hill Parkway
East Rutherford, NJ 07073-2316
Phone: 1-800-526-0275
Fax: 1-800-227-9604

For my Angels who continue to protect and guide me:

Bernard Jerome Rouse Jr.

Rev. Lula W. Rouse

Rev. Bishop C. Rouse

Acknowledgments:

To God be the glory! For loving me, and for continuing to bless me when things seem so far out of my reach.

For their love and support, I'd like to thank my family: My mother, Linda B. Rouse, the next published author in the family, thank you for allowing me to dream big. I love you more than words can say. My nephews and niece, Russell, Rayven, and Bernard, I thank God for you everyday. My grandmother, Mary L. Booker, I don't think I fully appreciated your love and guidance until I became an adult. Thank you for your 'tough love.' I love you.

I'd also like to thank: The Booker family—my Aunt Ivy and uncles, Wayne, Kenny, and Lloyd, my many cousins, especially Kenneth Jr. AKA, Ken-Ken (I love you like a brother), Tangika and Emery. The Rouse family—Although there are many miles between us and we don't talk everyday, when we're together it's like we were never apart. Rev. Trenell and Alexis Felder and New Faith Baptist church. Zeta Phi Beta Sorority, Inc., especially the beautiful ladies of Eta chapter, my sorors from Mansfield University and the brothers of Phi Beta Sigma Fraternity, Inc. My home girls: Chairese Smith and Heather Gunter, my Goddaughters, Kamille, Jholan and Jhayden, Sheila P. Miller (my writing buddy), Sydne, Janeen, Ramona, Ayanna, Kim-Shawn, Sharon and their families. My little sister: Kleanna Virges (I'm so proud of you) and her family. My friends in the publishing world: National Geographic School Publishing and Scott Foresman, especially Suzanne Belahmira, Marcia Tokich, Christopher Kammer and their families.

Last, but certainly not least, the UC family. Joylynn, my editor, I believe there are no coincidences. Thanks for taking a

viii ACKNOWLEDGMENTS

chance and believing in me. Kendra, and all the wonderful authors at Urban Christian, this has been an incredible journey and I look forward to what lies ahead!

For those who were not mentioned specifically, please know that you are not forgotten in my heart. God bless you all!

1

Renee

Renee shut the door to her personal bathroom and took a deep breath. Slowly, she closed her eyes and counted to ten. Still quiet. Opening her eyes, she immediately noticed a hand towel out of place. No matter how many times she told the boys to stay out of her private room, they always found a way to invade her space. Renee walked over to the towel and fixed someone's feeble attempt at folding. Carefully, she removed the towel, then folded it the way a fancy hand towel was meant to be displayed. Now calm and relaxed, Renee was pleased until she noticed a faint black hand print covering the flower embroidery. The print was too large to be one of the boys. This time, the guilty party had to be Jerome, her husband of seventeen years. Renee didn't have the energy to yell. She just crumpled the towel and threw it in the hamper.

Now slightly annoyed, she took off her blouse and sat on the edge of the bathtub. Why she let something as simple as a dirty towel upset her, she didn't know. What did she really expect living in a house full of boys? Lately, little things like that were getting on her nerves. She turned the knob and watched the water fill the tub.

As the water adjusted to a soothing temperature, Renee looked into the full-length mirror behind the bathroom door, a gift Jerome installed for Mother's Day. He was sure he and the boys had finally thought of a gift Renee would like. Evaluating the excess body fat hanging over her belt, she was reminded of her husband's lack of thoughtfulness. How many women over the age of thirty actually want to see their layers of fat each and every time they got out of the shower? Renee's eyes left her mid-section and focused on her facial features. There was a time when her face was full of life and expression. Her eyes used to sparkle and a permanent smile used to dominate her face. The image that stared back at her today showed very little signs of life.

Her creamy tone and flawless skin that used to turn heads of many men seemed different now. There were wrinkles in her forehead; one for every year Jerome struggled with alcohol, and small bags forming under her eyes. The bags were compliments of late work hours and being a personal taxi for her children. She forced a close-mouthed smile. The mole above the left side of her lip used to be sexy. Today it reminded her of an old maid. Though still in her early thirties, Renee was beginning to look and feel old; one of the reasons why she spent more money than she should on expensive clothes and accessories.

Steam from the running water covered the mirror and Renee tried to remember the last time she felt happy about life. She couldn't even remember the last time she and Jerome had laughed together. Renee inhaled deeply and took off the rest of her clothes. Memories of the "good ole days" seemed so far out of reach.

Under the sink, an assortment of bath oils overflowed a medium-sized wooden basket; a much appreciated gift from her mother. She fingered through the bottles and chose oatmeal and lavender. With the water at a suitable level, Renee dropped a few oil beads in the bathtub then turned the knob to off. She could hear the boys downstairs talking in raised voices but ignored them. Jerome was home and could handle whatever was going on, she thought. She lit a few candles and then reached for a comb next to the basin. Maybe doing something different with her hair would change the way she felt.

It had been almost two years since her last haircut. Minus a few split ends, Renee felt her hair was strong and healthy, but she wanted a change. She *needed* a change. Pulling her hair back into a ponytail, Renee frowned. *Too drastic!* The roundness of her head made her look even heavier. She let the ponytail fall then lifted her hair to her cheek line. Still, not satisfied. Close to giving up, Renee glanced at her magazine basket. Halle Berry was on the cover of the latest *Glamour* issue. Halle's long and wavy tresses intrigued her.

"I may not be as skinny as Halle," Renee said to herself as she looked in the mirror, "but curly hair may be what I need." She made a mental note to schedule an appointment at the salon then put on her shower cap. Just as she lifted her leg to settle in the bathtub, there was a bang on the door.

"Ma, Reggie won't let me watch *Sponge Bob!*"

Renee rolled her eyes, grabbed her favorite terry cloth robe and wrapped it around her before snatching the door open. Jerome Jr., her seven-year-old son, stood still, forcing tears to flow from his eyes and mumbled about not being treated fairly. Renee tried to be careful when handling him. Her husband claimed she played favorites and was turning their youngest into a momma's boy. She couldn't help herself most times. Jerome Jr. looked so much like her—same pie-shaped face, button nose, and deep dimples. Although he looked like Renee's twin, his butterscotch tone was a mixture of her French vanilla and Jerome's caramel complexions.

Letting out an enormous sigh, Renee walked to the stairs, "Reggie, you know it's his time to watch television. You have the TV at eight o'clock."

She could hear her oldest son suck his teeth and complain. Unlike Jerome Jr., Reggie was her complete opposite. He had long legs and a high, round butt like his father. At fourteen, she prayed Reggie still had some years to grow a longer torso. She didn't want him to look as ridiculous as his father.

"See, Mommy, he never lets me watch what I want. It's my turn, Reggie!" This time a few real tears actually escaped Jerome Jr.'s eyes.

Renee let out another sigh and raised her voice. "Reggie, turn the channel!"

"Mom, he's been playing with his Game Boy. He's not even watching TV," Reggie snapped.

"I am too watching TV. You just want to watch them videos. I don't want to watch that," Jerome pouted.

"You're a big baby," Reggie bounced back.

Renee interjected before a shouting match started. "Okay, that's enough. I'm trying to take a bath." She walked down the steps and looked around the room, then toward the basement door, becoming upset when she noticed that the basement light was off. "Where's you're father?" It was 7:00 pm on a Wednesday night. Where did he have to go without telling her?

"He went to the store," responded Reggie, knowing what was about to follow.

Renee's tone escalated to a higher octave. "He went to what store?" Both boys studied the floor, knowing any answer they gave would upset their mother. "I'm sick of this! He's never here to control you two. I have to do everything around here!" Renee yelled to the air. She noticed Reggie's jacket hanging from the stair railing and grabbed it. "And, I'm sick of this bickering! There are five televisions in this house and you mean to tell me neither of you can find *one* to watch?"

"The ones in our rooms don't have cable," Jerome Jr. replied harmlessly. "I can't watch Nickelodeon."

"Too bad!" Renee said, then came up with a solution. "Reggie, you're father isn't here. Go watch the one in the basement."

"He gets on my nerves! He always gets his way," Reggie sulked. "I don't like sitting in the basement. It smells!"

Losing her cool, Renee threw the jacket toward Reggie. "Go hang this up. I keep telling you and your father that I'm not your personal maid." She started walking back up the stairs. "If I have to come down here again, I'm gonna whip your tail and send you to bed early. You either go in the basement or wait until eight o'clock! Do you understand me?" Renee didn't wait for an answer. There was a warm bath calling her name.

Reggie threw the remote and hit Jerome Jr. in the arm. He began to wail. Reggie laughed at his younger brother, "You big brat. That didn't even hurt."

"Reggie, get in the basement! And Jerome, stop whining before I really give you something to cry about!" she shouted from the top of the stairs.

Reggie moved from the sofa and stomped his way to the basement, dropping his jacket on the back of a chair in the dining room along the way. As Renee approached her bathroom, she screamed at the top of her lungs, "And, for the twentieth time this week, stay out of my bathroom!" She slammed the door and sat on the toilet with her head in her hands. She was too angry to cry this time.

At thirty-four, she was beginning to regret marrying so young. If only she had listened to her mother, maybe her life would be different. But, when you're eighteen, your mother's wisdom doesn't count.

In high school, Renee was confident Jerome was "the one." Holding tight to her religious upbringing, Jerome was the only boy who didn't pressure her into sex. He was willing to wait for marriage. Although Jerome hadn't been a faithful member of any church, Renee still believed this was a sign. Thinking back on those days, she grew angry. How could God let her walk into a marriage obviously doomed from the start?

She stood up and pressed the power button on the radio stationed in the windowsill. A song from Chante Moore's debut album was playing. Still standing, Renee closed her eyes and let Chante's smooth and soprano-pitched voice relax her for a moment. As Chante crooned about a troubled relationship, she wondered if her life would've been different if she'd never met Jerome. When the song ended, she walked to the tub and let her robe fall to the floor. She tested the water with the tip of her right toe. It was still warm. As she stepped in, one tear rolled down her cheek and she wondered if she would ever be happy again.

2

Taylor

Sweaty and out of breath, Jerome lay flat on Taylor's bed. "Dang, baby. Why you do this to me every time?"

Taylor pretended to be naïve, "Do what?"

Drained, Jerome pulled Taylor closer and wrapped his arms around her. "Put that thang on me, that's what."

Taylor was nestled on his chest about to respond, but the sound of faint snores silenced her. She lifted her head slightly and kept her eyes open long enough to get a glimpse of the clock on her nightstand. 12:22 am. *Mission accomplished.*

As Taylor listened to Jerome's heavy breathing she smiled. Finally, after two years, Taylor knew she had him. This was the first time Jerome stayed past midnight. For her, this was a sign that they were one step closer to making their relationship official. All Jerome had to do now was divorce his wife.

The right timing was crucial. Taylor knew that. Jerome wanted to wait until his youngest son was old enough to understand divorce. If Taylor was ever going to have a positive relationship with her future step children, she had to play her cards right. She didn't want them to view her as the enemy. Still, being patient wasn't easy.

Throughout their affair, Taylor worried about Jerome's true intentions. She was taking a big risk. Being involved with a married man usually didn't have a happy ending. Tonight, Jerome's presence next to her comforted those thoughts. Building their relationship had been a slow and gradual process, but she had a feeling that after tonight their relationship was going to soar.

Two hours later, Taylor felt Jerome leave the bed. He quietly made his way to the bathroom across the hall. His release was longer than usual and steady. Not the rapid squirts that left splashes of urine around the rim of the toilet bowl. Out of respect for Taylor being asleep, he never flushed when he was finished. At least that's what he would tell her time and time again. But she knew better. By not flushing and possibly waking up Taylor, Jerome could easily leave her apartment without looking into her eyes to say good-bye and feeling guilty.

Taylor listened as Jerome turned the faucet on a low pressure to wash his hands. When he finally walked back into the bedroom, Taylor prayed he'd get back into the bed, but he didn't. She lowered the sheet that was covering her just enough to see Jerome putting on his jeans. A wave of sadness moved through her and she sat up, covering her body with the sheet.

"Baby, I don't think I can handle this much longer," she whimpered, determined to make him stay. She needed just this once to feel first in his life. "I mean, you are supposed to be *my* man, and *my* man should be with *me*."

Jerome continued dressing. "Taylor, you know I have a responsibility to my kids."

"To your kids or their mama?" she asked sarcastically, knowing this would set him off, but tonight she didn't care. She was tired of sparing his feelings.

Jerome stopped buttoning his shirt. Taylor could see the fire in his eyes, though he remained calm as he spoke. "Must you ruin a perfectly pleasant night?"

She was trying to fight back the tears, but frustration had already taken its course. She left the bed, still loosely wrapped inside the sheet, to join him. She was crying now and begging him to stay. Unmoved, Jerome fastened his belt. This frustrated Taylor even more.

She grabbed his arm, forcing him to acknowledge her presence. "I just don't understand why she has to stay in the house, or why you can't . . ."

The sheet fell, exposing Taylor's naked body and Jerome pulled away with authority. "I worked hard to get that house and I'm not about to kick my kids' mother out on the street!" He grabbed his watch off the nightstand and walked out of the bedroom.

Taylor didn't want to believe he was leaving. She put on her robe that was hanging on the door and chased after him. He was standing in front of the mirror in the living room brushing the tight curls on his head when she caught up with him. Taylor threw her arms completely around his waist, hoping he would stop, but Jerome kept moving, dragging Taylor's tightly-toned, two hundred pound body along with him. "Jerome, baby, I'm trying to understand. But, how long do you expect me to accept this?"

Jerome reached for his leather jacket hanging from the dining room chair and placed his brush in the inside pocket. "Taylor, please! We go through this every time." He used his entire body to free Taylor from his waist. "I'm not going to keep explaining myself. If you can't wait for things to change . . ."

Taylor knew she couldn't stop what was coming, but tried anyway. She had already humiliated herself. What else was there to lose?

She moved in closer, believing a deep and passionate kiss would help Jerome see how much she needed him. Only Jerome was tired of this routine. He held his arms out, placing his hands in her chest. He looked Taylor in the eye, trying to mask any feeling he had for her. "If you can't handle this anymore, maybe we shouldn't be together."

Paralyzed by his words, Taylor realized she was defeated. She wiped the tears from her eyes and turned away. "Then lock the door behind you," she said, and walked back to her bedroom, slamming the door behind her.

3

Renee

Renee's eyes automatically opened when she heard the front door close. She quickly checked the time. Jerome had never come home this late before. *He must have been with a woman*, she thought. In a situation where most wives would be angry and find themselves ripping the house apart in search of evidence, Renee was relieved. She was tired of dealing with his drunken escapades and lies. It was time for someone else to take over.

Safely inside the house, Jerome crept up the stairs and down the long hallway into their bedroom. Renee remained still, ignoring the obvious creaks in the floor. Any slight movement on her part would trigger the start of a conversation. He would feel compelled to tell some outlandish story about his whereabouts, and they would end up arguing. Renee didn't feel like hearing his nonsense this early in the morning, especially when her alarm clock would be going off in less than two hours.

Jerome took off all his clothes and slid under the covers. He attempted to place his arm around Renee's waist. She cringed at his touch. Her womanly instincts told her that he had been with another woman. Jerome didn't smell like a brewery tonight. His scent was soft, almost sweet. The thought of Jerome being with another woman, then coming home to her at 3:17 in the morning wanting to make love, infuriated her. Why couldn't he just lie on his side of the bed and keep to himself? They had a king size bed. There was plenty of room for separation.

Jerome reached for her with more aggressiveness. "C'mon baby, I just want to hold you."

Go hold your late night strumpet, she wanted to yell, but that would indicate that she cared. And, she really didn't care. At least not tonight. Renee turned from her side and laid on her stomach. "I'm asleep, Jerome," she mumbled in a groggy voice. "Leave me alone." Jerome received her response as an invitation to move in closer. "You've got to be kidding," Renee said under her breath, feeling the hot air from his nose warming her neck. With every ounce of strength in her body, she wiggled her way from under his arm. "It's too early in the morning for this, Jerome. Just go to sleep."

"Aw, baby. It's been months since we've been together. I want to show you how much I love you," he moaned, tugging at her nightgown.

Renee wanted to throw up. She twisted and pushed her knee into Jerome's midsection. The hint that she didn't want to be bothered wasn't strong enough. He was still trying to cuddle. Renee tried again, this time using her entire foot to kick him. He flew off the bed, landing hard on his side and injuring his foot against the wheel of the bed frame.

"Ouch!" Jerome shouted, rubbing his arm. "Is this any way to treat your husband?" Renee was silent as he rose to his feet. "One day you'll be begging me to make love to you." He snatched a pillow from their bed and limped to the other side of the room. Muttering to himself, Jerome pulled out an old pair of sweats from his dresser. He turned abruptly and hit his funny bone on the edge of the dresser. Wincing in pain, he gave his wife a pitiful look. She tried to control her laughter as she buried her face deeper under the covers. In disbelief, Jerome stood still, rubbing his elbow in a circular motion. Slowly, he put on his sweatpants and walked out the room. As the sound of his footsteps faded into the distance, Renee smiled.

Despite her husband's early morning episode, Renee was dressed and cooking breakfast at her regular time of 7:15 am. Reggie and Jerome Jr. were sitting at the table, dressed but still half asleep.

"Mommy, I wanted some bacon," Jerome Jr. whined.

"We're not having bacon. Your father forgot to bring some home yesterday when he went to the store." Renee removed the turkey sausage from the pan and placed two links on each of their plates. "Reggie, pour some orange juice in the cups for me, please." She turned the fire that was warming the grits off then checked the biscuits in the oven. "Just a few more minutes." When she turned around, Reggie's eyes were glued to the television set. She lightly smacked the top of his head. "Didn't I ask you to pour the juice?"

"Ouch! That hurt," Reggie grumbled, then pried himself from the chair and did as he was told. He opened the refrigerator and took out a carton of orange juice. Without thinking, he removed the cap and tossed it on the counter. He poured juice into the first cup successfully, but when he went to pour the second cup, the carton got away from him and orange juice sailed across the kitchen floor. Renee hit the side of the stove and closed her eyes.

"Oooo! You're in trouble," teased Jerome Jr.

"Shut up!" Reggie replied.

"Don't talk to your brother like that! Now run and get the mop." Renee grabbed a roll of paper towels from the counter and rolled it along the trail of juice. "And, hurry up! You're going to make us late!"

Reggie hurried back, dragging the mop behind him and imme-diately started to wipe away the pool of liquid.

"Wait a minute, Reggie!" Renee said, holding her hand up to her son. "Let me get up the paper towels first. Junior, help us out. Bring the trash can over here. And watch your step!"

"You really made a big mess," Jerome Jr. said, tipping around the kitchen floor.

"If you weren't so busy watching TV, you wouldn't have missed the cup," Renee snapped, gathering the paper towels and rolling them into one huge ball. She threw the mound of soggy paper towels in the trash and stepped to the side.

"But I wasn't watching TV. The carton was too heavy."

"You were too watching TV. I saw your eyes on the screen," Jerome Jr. instigated.

"How could my eyes be *on* the screen?" Reggie asked, making his brother feel childish.

"Don't start you two! Reggie, wet the mop and wash the floor real good. I don't want sticky spots left anywhere." Renee placed Jerome Jr.'s plate on the table and leaned against the counter. "Start eating so we won't be late."

"Where's my biscuit?" asked Jerome Jr.

"Boy, eat what's on your plate. I'll get your biscuit in a minute," she said, taking a spoonful of lukewarm grits out the pot and stuffing it inside her mouth.

Renee watched Reggie as she ate her breakfast standing up, making sure he mopped the floor to her expectations. When he was finished, she served him breakfast. "Next time sweetheart, pay attention to what you're doing. Okay?"

"Yes," Reggie said quietly. "I'm sorry."

Mistakes happen. Renee knew that, but Reggie had been making too many mistakes lately. If she didn't assert some kind of authority, he would be a lot worse. Reggie was a teenager now and had to learn to be more attentive and responsible. Rubbing his shoulders, Renee sat in the chair next to him. "We have about five minutes before we have to leave, so eat up."

Muffled noises from the basement caught Renee's attention. She heard the footsteps coming up the stairs before the boys did and could feel her body tense up. When Jerome reached the top stair, he stopped in the doorway and yawned. Renee frowned at the sight of him. He looked a mess and in need of a good shave.

Losing fifty pounds wouldn't hurt him either. There was a time when she thought he was irresistible, but that was years ago. It's amazing how much people change after high school. In those years, Jerome was charismatic, super fine and tall. He was a great athlete and a little too popular. Renee thought she had found a pot of gold. Now, as his belly continued to grow, Renee wished she had prayed a little longer and listened to her mother.

It's hard to say when her feelings started to change. Jerome was the only man she had ever been with and the only man she had ever wanted to be with. Looking at him today, she wondered where the man that once promised her the world had gone.

"Hey, Dad," said Jerome Jr. "You slept in the basement last night?"

Jerome stared at his wife and squint his eyes. "Yes, son."

"Why'd you do that?"

Jerome walked to the counter and poured himself a cup of coffee. "You ask too many questions."

"Don't talk to him like that. He was just asking an innocent question," Renee blurted, then instantly wished she could take back her words. She wasn't in the mood for another argument, especially not in front of the kids.

"You would take up for him," Jerome replied, taking his favorite non-dairy creamer from the cabinet.

Renee watched as he poured half the container in his coffee. "Why don't you just drink a glass of milk?" she wanted to say. Instead, she lifted a glass of orange juice to her lips to keep from speaking. *Thank you, Lord, for keeping me silent when you don't want me to speak*, Renee prayed silently.

"Dad, you forgot to bring home some bacon," Jerome Jr. nagged.

Jerome looked at his son as if he wanted to tape his mouth shut. "I didn't go to that kind of store last night."

"What kind of store did you go to?" Jerome Jr. was persistent and Renee wasn't about to keep him quiet.

Ignoring the question, Jerome looked at his older son and asked, "Did you finish your science project?"

Reggie focused on the food on his plate as he spoke. "No, I was waiting for you to come back last night."

"When is it due?" Renee almost created another orange juice disaster. Her cup hit the glass table and wobbled a few times before settling.

"Friday," Reggie whispered.

"As in tomorrow?" Renee asked, puzzled.

Reggie didn't answer.

Renee looked at her husband with daggers in her eyes. "Jerome, you said you'd handle this one."

"We'll finish it tonight. We have plenty of time," her husband replied.

"He's going to fail science if this project isn't done on time," Renee stated.

Keeping his cool, Jerome took a long sip of coffee before addressing his wife. "I said we'll finish it tonight." He poured a little more coffee in his mug and headed out of the kitchen.

"Before you go, I need to talk to you." Renee jumped out her seat and followed him into the living room. "I need you to take the boys to the barber shop after school."

"Why can't you do that? I already made plans," Jerome asked.

"Something more important than helping your wife and children?" Renee crossed her arms, waiting for his response.

"Can they wait until Saturday? I'm off then," he pleaded.

"You've obviously forgotten about Kid Fest. Reggie is in the basketball tournament. There won't be any time for the barber then or tomorrow and he has practice after school."

"Look, I can't take them today. I promised Brandon I'd replace his brakes after work, and I don't know how long I'll be."

Renee resisted the urge to strangle him. If it weren't for the kids, she would have divorced him years ago. She knew Jerome was lying. And what hurt the most was the fact that he put someone else before his own family. "Fine," she said, dropping her arms. "I'll figure something out, like I always do. I can't depend on you for anything these days." She walked back to the kitchen;

her voice loud enough for Jerome to hear. "If it were up to you, our children would turn into wolves. I guess I'm the only one that can see they need a cut."

Sensing that his mother was upset, Jerome Jr. said, "Mommy, I don't have to get my hair cut. I like it long."

Renee was frustrated, but listening to her son calmed her. "No, pumpkin. I won't make you suffer." She looked at her watch. "All right, fellas. It's time to go."

Like many parents whose sons attended Chestnut Hill Academy for Boys, Renee parked along the side of the building and waited for the bell to ring. She watched her children join their friends in the schoolyard. Renee liked this school. She thought it would place her children in a better position for college and for life. But, as with most things in the past few years, Jerome disagreed. He didn't like that the boys attended a school that excluded girls. Afraid his sons would never learn to fully "appreciate" the opposite sex, he was lenient when it came to Reggie and his desire to have a girlfriend.

Despite his opinions, Renee knew she had made the right choice. Sure, she had to pay more than she wanted for their education, but then, was there a price too great for making sure your children are well educated? She wanted her children to focus on academics—not on girls, material things, or who was going to fight who after school. And, if interacting with girls was all Jerome was concerned about, the girls at the academy's sister school were not far away.

As she prepared to drive off, Renee could see Mother Wagner, one of the teacher's assistants, trying to get her attention. Renee rolled down her window and waited for Mother Wagner to reach the car.

"Good morning, Sister Thomas," Mother Wagner said. "I'm glad I finally caught up with you."

Since Mother Wagner was no longer an assistant in Jerome Jr.'s class, Renee knew this was a church-related visit, as Mother

Wagner also attended New Life Baptist. "Good morning. How are you?"

"Blessed and highly favored," Mother Wagner announced full of joy. "I've seen your boys, but I haven't seen you around church in months. We even missed you on Easter Sunday. Everything all right?"

"It's been really busy at the hotel," she said, fumbling with the keys hanging from the steering wheel. "We just ended our busiest season. March Madness took over our sports lounge."

"Too busy to take time out for God? He is the one that gave you that fancy job," she remarked, unaffected by the city's current basketball frenzy.

Not ready for battle against Mother Wagner, Renee carefully chose her words. If something inappropriate had escaped her lips, Mother Wagner would've pulled her out of the car and begin praying for her soul. "You're right. I shouldn't make excuses."

"Well, the hospitality ministry could sure use your expertise. You do know about Kid Fest, don't you?" Mother Wagner asked, looking deep into Renee's eyes.

Subconsciously, Renee started to tremble. "Yes, m'am. My kids will be there. Reggie is participating in the basketball tournament."

"Good," she said, releasing her eyes from Renee's. "I hope you and your husband will participate, too."

"We'll be there."

"Good. Well, I'll let you get to work." Mother Wagner reached for Renee's hand before she could roll up the window. "And remember, no matter what, God loves you."

Mother Wagner's words did something to Renee's spirit; like her soul had been awakened from a deep sleep. "I know, Mother Wagner," she replied. Renee pulled off and could feel needles pricking at her heart. "Does God really love me?" she asked herself.

Renee couldn't remember the last service she attended. It had to be months ago and maybe even a year since she, Jerome, and the boys had worshipped together as a family. Though she sent the boys with their Uncle Brandon's family, she hadn't set foot in one. She even distanced herself from her prayer partners. She thought about how those early phone calls with Elise and Kara always seemed to make the day flow a little better. But, Renee's life had changed. When Jerome started drinking heavily again, she stopped going to church and alienated her prayer team. It was too embarrassing for her to face everyone knowing what was taking place at home. She was sure some church members knew. Jerome didn't mask his pleasure of the local night club. He even had the nerve to come to church on occasion smelling of liquor. On those mornings, he would drown himself with Listerine, hoping no one would notice, but they did. Hard liquor is a difficult smell to cover up.

Though the battle to make Jerome quit drinking was over this time around, too much time had passed and guilt kept Renee away. Surely, her prayer partners had found someone else to replace her, someone more committed and not so angry with God.

Renee felt she had good reason to be angry. She had been a "good girl" in grade school and all the way through college, not missing the honor roll once. And, unlike her friends, she had remained abstinent. Why did God introduce her to Jerome? Didn't He know she wouldn't be able to resist his charm? Didn't He know she would be vulnerable to his wit and soft brown eyes? Wasn't there another man available, one that shared her same values and beliefs?

Renee sat in her car in complete silence before entering the hotel. She needed to erase the memories of Jerome's late night antics and Reggie's science project. When she stepped inside the hotel, she was no longer playing the role of wife and mother. She was the senior manager of event and guest services and had to be ready for business.

4

Taylor

Taylor sat in the back of the Cheesecake Factory half-listening to her friends. This lunch, which she had taken the day off for, was supposed to cheer her up and take her mind off Jerome's latest episode. Instead, her best friends were only adding more fuel to her emotional fire.

Sherry, Taylor's partner in crime since eighth grade, sat next to her nibbling on the last Buffalo Blast appetizer. Also in her early thirties, Sherry was still single. The struggle to find a sane male companion was borderline impossible, but Sherry was up for the challenge. She had a date every weekend. She was different from Taylor. She didn't cling to men, nor did she let her full-figure intimidate her self confidence. Although they had different views on men, Sherry understood Taylor's attachment to Jerome. No one likes to be alone. And, as Taylor's best friend, Sherry was by her side from the very beginning to celebrate the joys of the relationship and to dry the tears of frustration.

Kara, on the other hand, worked with Taylor at the Septa depot. For her, Taylor and Jerome's affair was unacceptable. She had learned firsthand the pain an affair could cause and in order to maintain peace in their friendship, details of Taylor's relationship were rarely discussed. Today was an exception. Taylor relied on Kara for motivation and encouragement, something she needed to get through the day.

"I told you this would happen," said Kara. "Married men who cheat will always go back to their wives. Promises can never be kept in those kinds of relationships."

"This is not the time for 'I told you so's,' Kara. Can't you see that our friend is hurt?" Sherry tried to defend Taylor. "Remember, *she's* the victim here."

"No, the real victim is his wife. She's the one who's been in the dark all this time. She's the one I feel sorry for," Kara explained.

"Not every man is happily married. Some men do leave their wives for the other woman," Sherry countered, bordering frustration.

"Just none of the ones we know about. Look, I'm not trying to bring Taylor down," Kara said, feeling a persistent tap on her seat from Taylor's leg. "Seriously though, there had to be some part of you that expected this. Loving a married man is a no-win situation for everyone involved." Kara pulled a cigarette from her purse and lit it. "You know, although Harold and I have made up, whenever I see him talking to or standing near another woman, I ask myself if she was the one. That's a terrible feeling to have in a marriage."

Kara was forty-two years old. She had the body and spirit of an eighteen year old, but an aged face, thanks to many years of smoking. She had been married to Harold for almost six years; the first marriage for him and second for her. Kara didn't talk much about her first marriage. Only that her teenage daughter, Sabrina, was the best thing to come out of it. Although she and Harold had only dated eight months before she got pregnant with the twins, they agreed to get married.

Harold wasn't ready for marriage. He was a considerable number of years younger than Kara and at some point became overwhelmed with the responsibilities associated with having a wife and kids. Before they could celebrate their first anniversary,

Harold had established a serious relationship with one of his colleagues.

Smoke from the cigarette permeated their space. Although Taylor and Sherry were used to Kara's habit, it still bothered them. Sherry slightly coughed and asked, "But if he's not happy, shouldn't he be free to move on?"

Kara placed the cigarette in the fancy glass holder on the table. "You don't really believe that, do you? Do you have *any* respect for marriage? You don't just pack up and run to the next hot thing when you're having problems with your wife."

"But Kara," Sherry interjected, "some people get married for the wrong reasons. In Jerome's case, he was too young. Just think about being eighteen. Can you honestly say that at eighteen you would've been thinking rationally and maturely enough for something as serious as marriage?"

Kara picked up her cigarette and inhaled deeply, then let out a circle of smoke that hovered around them before drifting away. "People make mistakes. I know that. But, Jerome isn't eighteen anymore. And, he's a father now. At some point he's got to start thinking like an adult."

For a moment, silence surrounded them. If there weren't so many people in the restaurant, Taylor would have burst into tears. In her heart she knew Kara was right, but she was torn. There was a part of her that really believed Jerome would leave his wife. She and Jerome had been together for two years. That had to mean something.

"You two act as if I'm not sitting at this table," Taylor finally chimed in. "Why don't we just get the check and go home?"

"I realize this is hard to swallow. Just pray about it," Kara offered, gently placing her hand on Taylor's. "God can help you through this."

Taylor and Sherry looked at each other and sighed. "Don't start with that church stuff," Sherry huffed.

Kara quickly countered, "Jesus is the best solution I have for this situation." She put out her cigarette.

"I see Jesus hasn't helped you kick that nasty smoking habit," Sherry said sarcastically. "What are you going to do when smoking is banned in restaurants next year?"

Sherry hit a nerve. Kara rolled her eyes and tried not to raise her voice as she spoke. "I'm not perfect. I have issues just like everyone else, but at least I'm working on them one at a time. And maybe next year, it won't be a problem because I'll be delivered."

"Well, preach to Taylor when *all* your issues are solved," Sherry remarked, slightly annoyed.

The girls gazed in different directions, not knowing what to say to one another next. Ever since Kara had started going to church a year ago, Taylor and Sherry were often subjected to mini sermons. Most of the time Taylor didn't mind, but sometimes, like today, Kara's messages were difficult to digest.

The waiter walked by and Taylor motioned for the check. She reached inside her Gucci bag and took out enough money to cover the bill. "Since I dragged you away from work, I'll take care of this."

"Nonsense," Kara said, sipping the last drops of her raspberry lemonade. "You shouldn't have to pay."

Sherry took a twenty dollar bill from her purse and tossed it to Kara. "Here's my contribution. You'll have to cover me until next week."

With one brow raised, Kara stared at Sherry. "You are a real trip."

"What? You know I love you. We're just not as saved as you."

The waiter returned with the check and Kara held out her hand. "There's no such thing, Sherry. Either you're saved or you're not," she replied, as she looked over the check.

"I still love you, too," Taylor smiled. "Keep praying for me."

"You still in that prayer group?" Sherry asked Kara.

Kara looked surprised that she remembered. "No, the girl that started the group moved to Florida. The other person stopped calling months before that. You and I can start a group though," Kara smiled.

Sherry looked at her watch. "I've got to get back to work. But ask me again in a couple years."

"A couple of years?" questioned Taylor.

Sherry winked. "Yeah, I'll be ready for a change by then."

"Well, if you change your mind before then, remember I'm available," Kara said, trying not to force the situation.

Taylor leaned back in her seat and rubbed her stomach. "Thanks for lunch. I really do appreciate you guys being here for me."

"That's what friends are for," Sherry sang to the classic tune made famous by Dionne Warrick, Gladys Knight, Stevie Wonder, and Elton John.

"It's really not a problem. You may not believe me, but I really do understand what you're going through." Kara placed a credit card in the thin leather folder. "Since we took the day off, you want to do some shopping? There aren't as many people in the mall on a Thursday afternoon."

Kara's idea sounded good. Taylor loved to shop, especially on days when it was easy to browse through the clothes without someone standing over her shoulder or constantly bumping into her. But she responded, "No, I just want to go home and take a nap. I didn't sleep well last night." Taylor took a quick sip of water. "I better go to the bathroom before we leave."

"Okay, we'll just meet you outside. The waiter should be here soon," Kara said, allowing enough room for Taylor to get by.

Maneuvering her way through the crowded tables, Taylor walked to the restroom tucked in the corner of the restaurant. She opened the door and acknowledged a woman brushing her hair with a meek smile. Other than the woman, who appeared to be a few years younger and several pounds lighter than Taylor, the bathroom was empty. She stepped into the handicap stall and locked the door. Taylor didn't really have to go to the bathroom. She just needed to escape for a few minutes. Although she loved Kara, she was beginning to wonder if inviting her to lunch was a good idea. Her conversation hadn't motivated or encouraged her.

Taylor leaned against the side of the stall and sighed. *This has got to stop,* she thought. *Jerome's not the only man on the planet. I'll find someone else,* she tried to convince herself. But the tears that started to fall told her otherwise. She lifted her hands to wipe away the tears. The more she thought about her life, the stronger the tears came.

"Are you okay?" a soft voice asked.

Startled, Taylor scrambled to her feet and stood closer to the toilet. She didn't realize the sound of her sobs could be heard. She sniffed a few times then said, "I-I'm fine. Just had a bad day, that's all."

"I understand," the woman replied. "I have bad days, too. Don't let it get the best of you. Life is too short."

Taylor unrolled some toilet tissue and dabbed at her eyes. "Thanks, I appreciate your concern."

"No problem. Whatever the situation is, it's not worth your tears," she said and left the restroom.

Taylor wondered what trials the woman had endured to make her so seemingly wise at such a young age. Taylor walked out the stall and stood in front of the mirror, fingering her long curls until they laid perfectly in place. She leaned in close to the mirror in search of any trace that she had been crying. She wiped her eyes once more and pulled herself together. The woman was right; life was too short.

Lagging slightly behind her friends, Taylor could think of nothing but Jerome and about what her next move should be. She knew he'd come crawling back, apologizing profusely for his behavior. And, as mush as she loved him, she knew something would have to change, especially if they were to continue with the relationship.

As Kara and Sherry conversed about unrelated topics, Taylor pretended to be interested. Every few sentences she would nod her head or give a quick "hmm."

Once they reached Taylor's car, Kara and Sherry finally stopped talking amongst themselves. "Now promise me you won't go home and call him," Kara demanded. "You'll find someone better than Jerome. He doesn't deserve you."

Sherry pushed Kara aside and tried to comfort her friend. "Do what you feel is right. You know him better than we do."

"Now, why would you tell her something like that? He isn't worth her time, or her tears," Kara argued.

"Please! Not again!" Taylor shouted. "I've heard enough for today."

Kara frowned, "You're right. I'm sorry. Sometimes I get carried away. But I am serious. You're much too good of a person to deal with a married man."

"You just can't leave well enough alone. She knows he's married. Stop repeating it," Sherry begged as she reached out to hug Taylor.

Listening to Kara and Sherry go back and forth, Taylor realized that her love life should have been kept a secret. Their conflicting opinions were too much for her to handle.

Taylor slammed her car door and turned on the ignition. No longer actively listening to her friends who were still engrossed in their debate, Taylor shook her head, beeped the horn twice and sped off, leaving her friends to inhale the fumes from the car.

Driving along route 202 was unusually hectic in the afternoon. Construction in front of the Hooters and Red Lobster restaurants interrupted the normal flow of traffic. Just as Taylor was about to clear the site, a worker held up a huge stop sign. The motion was so sudden that Taylor was forced to slam on the brakes. Her purse flew to the passenger side floor, spilling a few of its contents.

"Sorry," the man mouthed, noticing the disgusted look on Taylor's face.

Taylor tried to get the bag, but it was too far out of reach. As she patiently waited for further instructions, thoughts of the day Jerome gave her such an expensive gift surfaced.

About a month before her birthday, Taylor and Jerome were watching an *E! True Hollywood* special. Taylor had pointed out a bag that interested her on the arm of a well-known actress. After a few days of research, Taylor made several calls to Gucci stores across America and tracked down the location of a similar purse. All she needed to do was come up with fifteen hundred dollars and the bag was hers.

On the night before her birthday, Jerome entered her apartment carrying a Lane Bryant shopping bag. Taylor was filled with mixed emotions, afraid of what could possibly be inside the bag. Jerome's sense of style was not in line with her taste for clothes. Recognizing her hesitation, he presented the gift as if he knew Taylor would return the items the next day. Taught to always be polite, Taylor grabbed the shopping bag and said, "I'm sure I'll like it." She reached inside and removed the massive amount of gift wrapping tissue. "Besides, it's the thought …" Taylor's eyes widened when she looked inside. She lifted the Gucci purse she'd been saving for out the bag and immediately adjusted it on her arm. Screams of joy escaped her lips as she posed several different ways.

That night turned out to be very special. Not only had Jerome surprised her, he had also confessed his love. Thinking of the words he whispered in her ear that night, Taylor began to weep. She knew there was only one way she could eliminate the pain she was feeling inside. She had to speak to Jerome and give him one more chance.

The salsa tune on her cell phone broke her concentration. Since her bag had fallen to the floor, and her cell phone was inside it, she couldn't reach her phone. Hoping it was Jerome, Taylor pulled off the road and parked in a Wendy's lot. The message light on the cell phone was flashing when she was finally able to pick it up from the floor. Taylor quickly checked the caller ID and sighed. "Kara will have to wait," she mumbled, as she hit the speed dial for Jerome.

After three rings, Jerome answered. "Hey."

"Hey, I'm sorry about last night. Can we talk over dinner tonight? I'll make your favorite," she said, and smiled a Cheshire cat grin when he said yes.

5

Renee

Renee sat in her corner office of the Luxury Inn hotel in the Society Hill section of the city admiring the *Natural Elegance* painting by Charles Bibbs hanging above her desk. Although she had already spent the allowance to decorate her newly renovated office, she had convinced her boss, Mr. Kotlarczyk, that it would be a great investment.

"My office would look distinguished and dignified," she had suggested. "Besides, no other hotel in the city has one. *And,* it's a limited edition." Renee had mastered the art of getting what she wanted from Mr. Kotlarczyk. Using the right words was essential. As long as the situation promised to make him shine or place him in the role of a trendsetter, there was no way he could resist the temptation.

Starting as a front desk clerk, Renee quickly gained Mr. Kotlarczyk's respect. Although many of her colleagues were within the same age bracket, Renee was more mature and very serious about her position. Unlike her co-workers, many of whom were still in college and used their income to finance weekend road trips, Renee needed this job to supplement her husband's salary.

New to the Luxury Inn as well, Mr. Kotlarczyk, then a senior event manager, was determined to build up the reputation of the hotel. He would not rest until Luxury Inn was able to compete with the other big name hotels in the city.

In Renee's mind, Mr. Kotlarczyk held the key to her success. Whenever he had to organize an event, she made sure she was available to help. Her diligence and serious work ethic did not go unnoticed. It wasn't long before Mr. Kotlarczyk specifically requested her assistance full time.

The workers at the front desk were not happy about her change in position. Every time Renee passed through the lobby, she could hear their whispers and see the smirks on their faces.

"She must be sleeping with him," one would say.

And in response another would add, "Maybe I should sleep with him, too. Am I young enough?"

Rumors spread through the hotel like wildflowers. Employees felt that a twenty-two year old African-American female clerk socializing with a forty-five-year-old Polish male manager was a little suspicious. Yet they could not deny the fact that Renee deserved the promotion. She could do their jobs and hers easily and with both eyes closed.

Renee turned her chair away from the painting to face her computer. Before leaving for the day, she needed to check her email. She moved the computer mouse to get rid of the island screensaver. Only one new message. She clicked the inbox link and was pleasantly surprised when she recognized the name. In her thirteen years at Luxury Inn, Elise Bennett was her only true friend. Elise moved to Florida six months ago with her husband. Florida was more peaceful and a lot less stressful than Philly. They had been trying to have a baby and blamed the brazenness of the city for their many failed attempts.

Renee opened the email and a photo appeared. The picture was taken at the very first event she planned with little help from her boss. It was the event that spearheaded the boost in Luxury Inn's image. NBA player, Aaron McKee, stood in the middle of Elise and Renee, stretching his long arms around them. The picture caught a five-foot-three Elise staring up at the seven-foot player. Renee was on the other side of him grinning profusely. The photograph brought back many fond memories.

By default, Luxury Inn was given the opportunity to host a social event sponsored by the Sixers, Philadelphia's professional basketball team. The deal with the original hotel on City Line Avenue fell through and the team was desperate for a new location. Mr. Kotlarczyk was already swamped, coordinating several small corporation and local interest group meetings, so he had less than a week to organize everything and a very limited budget. He decided it was time to give his rising star a chance to fully exercise her creativity, and as he expected, Renee jumped at the offer.

"Instead of elaborate decorations, fancy silverware, and an exotic meal the players and fans won't remember or even notice, let's turn the restaurant into a lounge," Renee had suggested, hopping around the room as the adrenaline running through her body increased. "We could rent huge plasma TVs from Rent A Center, and we can run ESPN all night. I bet they even have cool sofas and chairs."

"But what about the food?" Mr. Kotlarczyk asked, although he knew Renee had already chosen a menu. At this point, asking was just a formality.

"People are not going to be thinking about food. All they really want to do is meet the players. I can get a ton of appetizers from Costco. The restaurant should already have the drinks covered. I'll just make sure they have enough on hand. I just know we'll have a full house that night."

Renee's enthusiasm and previous work performance convinced Mr. Kotlarczyk that she could handle this assignment on her own. And in the end, he was glad he had followed his instincts. Meet the Sixers night was spectacular! Not only had the Sixers become their biggest client, the lounge had also become the newest hot spot for sports fans and athletes. Executing that event placed Renee in a position to manage even larger projects. And, when Mr. Kotlarczyk accepted the offer to become the General Manager of the hotel, there was no question about who would take his place.

Looking at the photograph, Renee had no regrets when it came to the professional decisions she had made. She scrolled down the screen to read Elise's message.

> To: Renee Thomas
> From: Elise Bennett
> Subject: Blast from the Past
>
> I miss the good ole days.
> You and the boys must visit soon. I miss you.
> FYI . . .
> I'm three months pregnant! :)

Renee was thrilled just picturing how excited Elise and her husband must be. They had been trying to conceive for several years. And now, after two miscarriages, they were finally going to be parents. "I guess God is good," she said, and immediately felt a wave of guilt for not doing a better job at keeping in touch. She blamed her husband more than her career for that. The extra responsibilities made it difficult to touch base with her friends on a regular basis. In fact, Renee couldn't remember the last time she had hung out with anyone other than her children. She used to attend monthly book and movie club meetings. She used to travel with friends in those groups to New York to shop and watch the latest Broadway plays.

Church used to be the place where she was also able to mingle with Elise and other member of the congregation. She and Elise had even formed a prayer group with the wife of Jerome's childhood friend, but time and the embarrassment of Jerome's drunken acts ended her participation.

Initially, Jerome promised to help with the kids when Renee got her first promotion, but she quickly discovered that she was on her own. He continued to spend countless hours at the basketball court and in the neighborhood bars.

Jerome wasn't always so selfish with his time. Before Renee started making more money than him, everything was fine. They struggled to make ends meet while she was in college. Sometimes all they had to eat were canned vegetables and Ramen noodles. But, at least then they were happy. Renee going to college was supposed to help them financially, not tear them apart.

Renee responded to Elise's email and checked the time. As she reached for a folder by her computer, a family portrait taken three years ago fell to the floor. She picked up the picture and sighed. The boys' smiles looked genuine. She and Jerome stood behind the boys, a considerable amount of space between them. She hadn't realized until today how long she had been unhappily married. As Renee studied the photograph, she wondered if her marriage was over. She and Jerome had obviously grown apart and doubted if either of them really loved one another anymore.

At times, she wondered if her drive for success was the reason for their unhappiness. But, when she replayed all that she had accomplished and all that her children were able to do as a result, she dismissed the thought. Reggie and Jerome Jr. attended a good school, took music and sports lessons, and traveled to places she had dreamed of as a child. Her hard work was well worth the sacrifice. *Why couldn't Jerome see that?*

"Cause he's a selfish bum," she mumbled aloud, neatly positioning the picture back in its place.

A knock at the door halted thoughts of her failing marriage. "It's open," she called out, eyes still focused on the picture.

Bianca, Renee's college intern, entered the office. "I'm sorry to bother you, but there's a slight problem on the third floor."

"What kind of problem?" Renee asked, hoping it wasn't serious. It was almost time for her to go home, and she needed to pick up the boys. The after-care teachers didn't take kindly to parents who picked up their children after the agreed time.

Bianca closed the door behind her. "Marvin is in one of the rooms with a woman."

"Is he on the clock?" Renee asked, trying to figure out what the problem could be.

"Yes, and that's not the real problem." Bianca started to play with her fingers.

"Then what is it?"

"He was . . . he was having relations with a guest and her boyfriend showed up. Now there's a bit of an upheaval upstairs." Bianca moved out of the way, waiting for Renee's outburst.

Renee tapped her finger rapidly on the desk. She did this often when thinking of an immediate plan of action. And, as expected, Renee shot up from her desk and stormed out the door. Bianca followed closely behind. While en route, Bianca offered more information. "Mrs. Thomas, the boyfriend is threatening to kill him, and the other guests on the floor are frightened. He's sort of a big guy; football player big."

"What on earth was Marvin thinking? If the boyfriend doesn't kill him, I will." The two women raced up the stairs. "This is not good for the hotel. Is Mr. Kotlarczyk still here?"

"No, and Eric already called the police," Bianca said, out of breath, desperately trying to keep up with her boss.

"Good."

Renee could hear the boyfriend banging on the hotel room door as they drew closer to the third floor. When she turned the corner, Eric, the hotel's head security guard, was standing close by.

"He's calmed down a lot, but Marvin won't open the door," Eric said, as Renee approached him.

"Do you blame him? What's the man's name?"

"I think its Devon. He won't talk to me, but I heard the young lady inside call his name."

The guard stopped Renee from moving any closer. "Why don't you just wait for the police to get here? I don't want anything to happen to you," Eric stated.

Renee laughed. "Trust me, I've been through worse."

"All the same, I'd feel better if you stayed away," Eric pleaded. "I tried to get close and he nudged me pretty hard. I'll have to take him down if he tries anything with you."

Renee took a good look at Eric, then another look at the man at the door. She had a feeling Eric was more afraid than he cared to admit. The man could clearly take Eric's one hundred eighty pound body out with one arm tied behind his back. "Okay, okay. I'll let you be the boss this time." Renee stepped behind him, pulling Bianca along with her.

Renee watched the boyfriend pounding on the door and could feel the powerful thumps in her chest. Looking at the size of his arms, the hotel would probably need to replace that door. She was surprised it hadn't collapsed already. Occasionally, the boyfriend looked in Renee's direction. There was more than anger in his eyes. He looked sad, betrayed, and confused. Her heart went out to him. Renee wanted to tell him to move on and not to waste his time on someone who obviously didn't love him. These were all words Renee had heard from her mother each time she dragged Jerome home from a bar.

Renee checked her watch, remembering that she had to pick up her children. She let out a small sigh. It would take more than thirty minutes to get to the boys' school. In rush hour traffic, there was no way she could get there on time, even if she took the side streets. "Marvin's going to pay for that door," she yelled, becoming more and more annoyed as the time passed. She turned to Bianca. "Do you think you can handle this for about five minutes? The cops should be here soon."

"Sure . . . if you think I can, then I can," Bianca said nervously.

"You can. I'll only be gone a few minutes. I need to call my husband."

"Okay," Bianca said with more confidence.

Renee let Eric know that she needed to make a call and he reassured her that everything would be all right. "If Marvin comes out in one piece, will somebody please let him know he's fired," she said before leaving.

Eric laughed, "I think he knows that, Mrs. Thomas."

Renee walked back to her office and immediately dialed Jerome's cell phone. She knew he wasn't going to be happy, but at the moment his feelings didn't matter.

"Hello," he answered.

"Hey, there's a problem at work that I need to take care of before I can leave. I need you to get the boys and take them to the barber," she said, knowing he was going to put up a fight. But, she was ready and determined to win this one.

"I told you this morning that I had something to do," Jerome blasted into Renee's ear.

"And I'm telling you that I can't get the boys. I think Brandon will understand. Don't you?" Renee could hear his huffs through the phone. "Don't let the barber cut Reggie's hair too short. I like the afro."

"You know this isn't right. We agreed that I would get the boys on Mondays and Wednesdays. Today is Thursday."

At times Jerome was unbelievable. He knew Renee had to work late sometimes. She tried to limit the nights she worked late to the nights he picked up the boys. Wasn't that fair? Why couldn't he just help her out in emergency situations without complaining all the time?

"Whatever, Jerome," Renee said. "You act like these aren't your kids."

"Don't give me that," he retorted. "You know I take care of the boys. Just not to your standards."

"Well, my standards are the ones that count." From the window in her office, Renee could see the police entering the building. She wanted to send them to Septa to arrest Jerome. There had to be a law against irresponsibility. "Brandon helps his wife out all the time. And, they have three children! You could stand to learn a thing or two from him."

"His wife isn't always on his back, either. I'll take them, but don't expect me to hang around the house and wait on you all night."

"I don't know why everything has to be a battle with you."

"I promised Brandon I'd stop by and I don't want to go back on my word."

"No, you'd just let your kids suffer."

"Goodbye, Renee." Jerome hung up before she could say another word.

Renee plucked the family photograph she was looking at earlier and it fell to the floor. This time she left it there.

"God, why me?" she asked in a soft whisper.

6

Jerome

Jerome finished fueling his last bus for the day and clocked out. He strolled through the parking lot hoping no one had noticed him. He hadn't seen Taylor all day, which only meant that she was either intentionally avoiding him, or she had taken the day off. In either case, it wasn't a good sign, and all the more reason for him to stand clear of her friends, especially Kara.

Jerome and Kara's husband, Harold, were once good friends. But, Harold's confession to his own affair made Kara disapprove of Jerome's relationship with Taylor. Why Harold admitted to the affair was beyond Jerome's understanding. Kara never even had a clue. "I felt compelled to come clean," was Harold's response when Jerome questioned his actions. "Adultery is a sin. God won't continue to bless my life, much less my marriage, if I don't honor his commandments."

"And you feel blessed now that Kara has kicked you out?" Jerome had asked the day he helped Harold move into a studio apartment. He was tired of people using God as an excuse for their behavior. Didn't Harold know that adultery was a sin the night he decided to abuse his marriage vows? This was one of the reasons why Jerome stopped going to church. To him, church was full of hypocrites. As long as he was inside the church, everyone smiled and was encouraging, but the minute he stepped outside, those same people turned the other way and were judgmental. Church was supposed to make people better humans. Even Renee, the one person he looked to for spiritual advice, had turned away from the church; although she blamed him for not being able to show her face.

Jerome knew the members of New Life Baptist talked about his family. He could see it on their faces whenever he came around. Many of the members were so concerned about how his drinking was affecting his family, that they managed to overlook the problems within their own homes. And he knew they had problems. A few times he witnessed someone from New Life drinking more than a small taste of wine. Since Jerome could not tell the sincere worshippers from the fakes, he put them all in the same category. He knew it was unfair to judge them, but he was tired of people he did not know trying to tell him what was wrong with his life.

Harold, his childhood buddy and former partner in crime, was lumped in that category as well. Since Harold and his wife joined New Life, he started acting funny. He didn't want to share more than one drink, and if they went out, the strongest drink he had was a Root beer soda. Even though Harold changed, Jerome remained his friend until the day Harold scolded him about his relationship with Taylor. Harold quoted scripture after scripture about the sanctity of marriage.

> *What God has joined together, let man not separate. Mark 10:8-9.*
> *He who finds a wife finds what is good and receives favor from the LORD. Proverbs 18:22.*

Jerome couldn't take anymore. He needed Harold to express how he *really* felt, and not how the Bible said he *should* feel.

"Man, the bottom line is, a *real* man wouldn't disrespect his wife by sleeping with another woman." This was coming from the master of the game. Harold successfully maintained a five year extramarital long distance relationship, only confessing because of his guilty conscience. There was no way Renee would have bought excuses for repeated and lengthy absences. But then, he wasn't a lawyer. He was a mechanic and mechanics didn't travel much for business, so there was no way to test that theory.

"You of all people have no right to preach to me about being loyal," Jerome said highly offended. "You lied to your wife for five years!"

Harold stood to his feet. "I admit I made a mistake; a very bad mistake." Harold pointed to his meager living space. "And now I'm paying for it. But at least I'm trying to make it right." Harold looked Jerome in the eye. "You should, too. What you're doing isn't right."

"Don't tell me what to do," an enraged Jerome snapped as he put on his jacket. "And, where do you get off judging me? This act you're putting on may fool Kara, but in case you haven't noticed, I'm not her." Jerome walked to the door and opened it. "You cheated once, you'll cheat on her again. It's just a matter of time."

Jerome slammed the door behind him, ending their once solid friendship.

On the way home from work, after receiving Renee's phone call, Jerome considered having one of his relatives pick up the boys but knew his wife wouldn't approve. Of all his relatives, she only liked Brandon, his youngest brother. Having someone else pick up the kids needed to be approved well in advance. Since Brandon didn't get off work until seven, Jerome had to complete the task himself. Normally, he wouldn't mind spending time with his children. It was just that he had already made plans with Taylor. And, after the way they parted last night, Jerome needed to see her and apologize.

When he pulled up to Chestnut Hill Academy, the boys barely

had time to get in the car and fasten their seatbelts before he sped off. Jerome whizzed through the streets, cutting in front of cars with little warning, causing drivers to blow their horns and swear at him.

From time to time, Jerome Jr. would say, "Slow down, Daddy." But Jerome couldn't slow down. His relationship with Taylor was on the line.

Despite a few close calls, they made it to the barber shop safely. Jerome was disappointed at the number of men waiting. "How many heads in front of my boys, Dre?" he asked their barber of ten years.

Dre did a quick count. "Just three."

Jerome rolled his eyes. "And about how long do you . . ."

"Maybe an hour," Dre said. These questions were routine for most barbers.

Jerome leaned against the wall, gnawing at his bottom lip as the boys settled in available seats. He kept his eyes on Dre, who seemed to operate his clippers in slow motion, stopping frequently to dramatize his conversation. If Jerome had extra money to spare, he would have bet Dre was doing this on purpose.

For a second, Jerome considered leaving. But, when he looked at Jerome Jr.'s head, he knew that wasn't an option. Had he waited a day longer, his youngest son would have sported an old mile high seventies afro.

"Hey Reggie," Jerome said, "come get me when it's your turn. I'll be in the car."

Jerome headed out the shop and got into the car. Once inside, he leaned his seat back. This was the only way he could relax. He closed his eyes, pretending he wasn't in a time crunch. As he tried to calculate how long the boys would be, he remembered Reggie's science project and punched the steering wheel with his fists. He shuddered at the thought of canceling dinner plans again. How did he allow things to get this far?

When he met Taylor, she was only supposed to be a drinking partner and good friend. But the more he and Renee argued about money and other household responsibilities, the closer he let himself get to Taylor. Now, he was caught in the middle of two relationships—one with his wife, the woman he thought he'd love forever, and the mother of his children, and the other with his girlfriend, a woman who makes him feel like a real and whole man.

Renee used to make him feel like a man, but once she started working, things slowly changed. Jerome should have seen it coming. First, she didn't want to go to their favorite weekend night spot anymore. Then she stopped attending social functions with their high school classmates. "They're too immature," she'd often say. With the exception of Harold and Kara, whenever they went out with friends, Renee would bring a book along to read.

Renee eventually formed a new circle of friends, friends Jerome felt uncomfortable around. They talked about college, theatre, and traveling around the world. Jerome didn't go to college, had no interest in watching plays, and had never been anywhere further than the East coast.

Money started to become a major issue when Renee wanted to go to graduate school and their budget had to be readjusted to accommodate her educational goals. Jerome only agreed because he didn't want to upset her. As long as he had enough money to spend on the weekends and for Sixers season tickets, he was fine.

But then Renee got pregnant again. In the midst of all the stress associated with graduate school, working, and taking care of family, she forgot about her birth control pills. Jerome Jr. was conceived in a romantic weekend attempt to relieve stress. Additional adjustments to the budget were made, including giving up the Sixers season tickets, so they were still able to manage. Only not enough for his in-laws. Without either Renee or Jerome's permission, Renee's mother stepped in with a plan. In order to pay the mortgage on a house they couldn't afford, she pulled a few strings, as a former Septa supervisor, and got Jerome a job as the night mechanic. This way, Jerome could stay home during the day to watch the baby and avoid expensive day care costs.

As much as he loved Renee, he had to be honest with himself. One day, she would become tired of him. With all of her education and professional success, she really didn't need him anymore. Whatever Renee wanted, she could obtain without his assistance. Jerome hated to admit it, but Renee had grown, and he was out of her league.

Taylor made Jerome feel special. They enjoyed evenings at Sam and Pete's night spot, day trips to Atlantic City, lunches in the park, and shopping. Jerome became more conscious about the clothes he wore when Taylor was around—no more beat up sweats and rugged jeans. Khaki pants and colored button down shirts now filled his wardrobe.

Unlike Renee, Taylor freely displayed her appreciation for Jerome. The first time Jerome cooked her dinner. She came home from work and almost cried at the feast that was prepared especially for her. It was rare for Renee to even say a simple, "Thank you" for his home cooked meals. Jerome couldn't afford the gifts he purchased for Taylor, but he loved showering her with tokens of his affection. Perhaps it was the way in which she expressed her gratitude that made him go the extra mile. Her attentiveness and affection made Jerome swell with pride, pride in being able to take care of his woman.

By the time Jerome and the boys got home from the barber shop it was well after six o'clock, and Renee had yet to come home. He immediately plopped on the couch and dialed her office phone.

"Hello. You've reached the voicemail box for Renee . . ." her pre-recorded message stated. Jerome hung up the phone. He closed his eyes for a minute, trying to come up with a plan. He considered leaving, but knew that Renee would never let him live it down. Jerome was stuck. He had no choice but to stay put and help Reggie with his project.

"Don't get comfortable," Jerome told his oldest son. "Go get what you need so we can get started with your science project."

Reggie, who was propped in front of the television, turned to his father. "Aw, Dad. Can't we start it *after 106 and Park?* It's almost over."

"*106 and Park?* We don't have time for that." Jerome walked into the dining room and started clearing off the table.

"Okay, can I at least wait for a commercial to come on?" Reggie begged.

"You have five minutes, and I do mean *five* minutes," Jerome reiterated. He looked at his youngest son who was slouched on the couch playing with his Game Boy. "Go start your homework, Junior."

Jerome Jr. started to whine, fingers still rapidly hitting the keyboard of the game. "Mom let's us eat dinner first."

"Well, your mother isn't here yet. Until she comes, which I hope is very soon, you'll do things my way," Jerome scolded.

"But I'm hungry," Jerome Jr. said and dropped the electronic device.

"I don't have time for this, Junior. I said she'd be here soon. Now stop whining before I take off my belt."

Jerome picked up the phone by the kitchen door and dialed Renee's cell. "You've reached 215–555–3746. At the tone . . ." *Voice message again.* Jerome hung up the phone and looked at the clock on the microwave. 6:27 pm. "Reggie! What's taking you so long?"

"I bet he was watching videos on his television," Jerome Jr. said.

"He better not be!" Jerome headed for the stairs, but Reggie was on his way down with a hand full of unfamiliar equipment.

"Daddy, can you fix us something to eat, please? I'm starving," Jerome Jr. cried, now standing next to his father.

Jerome threw his hands in the air. There was just no end to Jerome Jr.'s complaining. "Go upstairs!" he yelled. "And don't come back down until I tell you to."

Jerome Jr. grabbed his bags and stomped up the stairs in tears.

Jerome made a mental note to talk to Renee about his behavior. He was getting too old to cry over unnecessary things.

While Reggie set up the materials on the table, Jerome could hear his youngest son crying as if he had just lost his best friend. The boy was way too dramatic. *Just like his mother,* Jerome thought as he checked his watch again. 6:33 pm. He walked to the kitchen and dialed Renee's cell again. "You have reached 215—" He slammed the phone down and walked to the window in the front of the house. *Where is she?*

"Dad, are you going to help me?" Reggie asked, eager to begin his assignment.

Jerome walked back to the dining room. "Yeah, I'm ready. I was just waiting for you to set up." Jerome surveyed the table and wanted to faint. There were parts and pieces all over! "What do we have to do?"

"I'm going to create a tsunami," Reggie said proudly.

Jerome looked confused. "A tsunami?"

"Yep. These simple directions explain how." Reggie handed Jerome an eight page booklet, which Jerome paged through quickly to scan the directions.

"We have to mold clay?" Jerome exclaimed. "This could take all night!"

"Not really, Dad. This whole thing should take about two hours."

"Can't we try something simpler?" Jerome suggested, desperate to change his mind.

"It's too late. I already told my teacher I was doing this."

Jerome leaned back in the chair and almost fell. Reggie laughed and Jerome cut his eyes in his direction. "Let's get started."

Before Jerome and Reggie could begin, Jerome Jr. crept in the room holding a pillow under his chin. "Didn't I tell you to stay upstairs?" Jerome sighed.

"I'm sorry, Dad. But I'm really hungry," Jerome Jr. griped.

Jerome looked at the front door, praying Renee would open it. After ten seconds, he realized that he was going to have to make dinner. He walked to the kitchen with Jerome Jr. close on his heels and opened the refrigerator in search of something quick and easy to microwave. No luck. Renee had cleaned the refrigerator a few days ago and had thrown away all leftovers. Jerome pulled a pack of hotdogs out and threw it in the sink.

Jerome Jr. frowned. "I don't want a hotdog."

"Too bad," Jerome said, filling a pot with water. "And if I see one tear, you'll go to bed hungry." Jerome Jr. sat silently at the table with his arms crossed in front of him.

"All right, let me know when the water boils," Jerome said and walked back to the dining room.

Once in the kitchen doorway, he stopped in his tracks. Reggie wasn't at the table. Jerome could feel his blood pressure rising. Music blasting from the family room gave away Reggie's whereabouts. Jerome raced through the house and found Reggie mimicking a rapper in the video he was watching. On any other day, Jerome would have joined him. He loved learning the latest dance grooves, but today, he was on a tight schedule.

"Reggie, what are you waiting for?" Jerome turned the television off and Reggie stopped dancing.

"Sorry, Dad. I was waiting for you to come back."

"Well, I'm ready now. Let's get started," Jerome urged.

Minutes into the project, Jerome Jr. hollered, "The dogs are ready!"

Jerome checked his watch before he got up. 7:09 pm. If Renee would just come home, he might still be able to get to Taylor's at a reasonable hour. Jerome turned down the flames and poured a can of baked beans into another pot.

Jerome's cell phone buzzed on the countertop and he rushed to answer it, nearly spilling the beans. The flashing light revealed Taylor's number and his heart pounded in his chest. Jerome wanted it to be Renee. He hit the silence button, afraid of what Taylor might say about his still being at home.

"You gonna answer that, Daddy? It might be Mommy," his youngest son inquired.

"It's not," he simply said and finished preparing dinner.

When Renee finally came home, Jerome was stirring the baked beans. Jerome Jr. left the table to greet his mother. "Daddy's making hotdogs on a Thursday," he moaned, after kissing her cheek.

"Hotdogs? Well, I guess we'll have to get some ice cream for dessert then," Renee said, smiling at her son. All Jerome could do was shake his head. How dare Renee come home late and be the savior! He opened the breadbox and placed a slice of Wonder bread on Jerome Jr.'s plate.

"Regular bread?" Jerome Jr. turned up his nose. "Aren't we supposed to eat hotdogs on a hotdog roll?"

"Don't start. We don't have anymore rolls," Jerome said, moving faster now that Renee was home. "I suppose you were at work all this time?" he asked.

"Where else would I be?" Renee responded, half-surprised at his accusation. She rubbed the back of Jerome Jr.'s head. "Thanks for taking the boys. They look much neater."

Jerome didn't have time for idle chit chat. "I called the office and your cell phone. Why didn't you answer?"

Renee took off her shoes. For a minute, Jerome thought she was going to throw them, but he repeated the question anyway. "Why didn't you answer?"

"Because I didn't want to," she said with a smirk on her face as she walked away.

Jerome ignored her response. He would deal with Renee later. For now, he was more concerned with sneaking out the door while she was upstairs changing her clothes.

"Reggie, how much longer do we have here?" Jerome asked, pretending to assemble the base of a makeshift ocean.

Reggie put down the tube that was in his hand. "Maybe an hour. Can we take a break so I can eat?"

Jerome looked at his watch. 7:36 pm. "You know," Jerome

began, flipping through the directions, "I think you can finish this on your own."

"But Mom said you had to help me."

"Do you really *need* my help?"

Reggie looked upset. "I guess not."

Jerome didn't want to disappoint his son, but he also didn't want to disappoint Taylor so soon after a disagreement. If he hurried, he could get there by 8:00. He looked at Reggie again. "Okay, son, let me run to Uncle Brandon's for a bit. When I get back, we'll knock this thing out."

Reggie was not enthused. "Sure," he mumbled under his breath. Reggie dropped the piece of clay he was holding on the table and walked into the kitchen. Disappointment was written all over his face. Jerome felt awful, but before he could feel the full effects of guilt, he grabbed his jacket and marched to the door.

"Where do you think you're going?" Renee questioned from the bottom of the stairs. Jerome rolled his eyes and turned around. Renee was watching him with the no-nonsense expression he hated.

"I'm going to fix Brandon's brakes," he lied. "I shouldn't be too long."

"Oh no you don't!" Renee yelled. "You promised Reggie you would help him. The project is due tomorrow. Your brother can wait."

"It only takes me ten minutes to fix brakes," he said, knowing Renee wasn't falling for his excuse this time.

"Then you plan to spend ten minutes fixing his brakes tomorrow. Tonight, you're going to help your son pass science."

Jerome was stumped. He remained at the door, holding the knob and considering his next move.

"Why are you still standing there?" Renee asked and fell on the couch. "You need me to call Brandon and ask for permission or something?" Jerome didn't move. Renee peeked over the arm of the sofa and gave him the "evil eye." "Don't make me get up and embarrass you in front of the kids," she tried to whisper through tight lips.

Jerome threw his jacket in Renee's lap. Instead of Taylor's homemade lasagna, he would have to settle for a hotdog on Wonder bread.

7

Taylor

At 9:00 Taylor knew Jerome wasn't going to show. Yet she sat on the couch by the window, hoping every set of headlights that pulled up belonged to Jerome's '98 Camry. Taylor remained in the same position for over an hour, moving only to sip the special champagne she had purchased for the evening.

The house phone rang at 10:34 and Taylor jumped to her feet. She stumbled across the room to check the caller ID before answering. When she recognized Jerome's number, she quickly hit the talk button on the cordless phone already in her hand.

"Where are you?" she asked, at this point more concerned than angry.

"I'm sorry," he began, "Renee had to work late, something about police coming to the hotel. Then I had to pick up the boys and take them to the barber. Then I had to make dinner and help them with their homework." Taylor was half listening, but Jerome continued anyway. "Do you know she made me help Reggie with a science project at the last minute? We actually had to build—"

Taylor cut him off. "So this means you're not coming over?"

Jerome hesitated before answering, "I want to, but . . . I know we have a lot to talk about and you made dinner and everything, but . . . Renee and I had a huge fight and I just don't think I should go out tonight."

Immediately, Taylor recalled everything Kara said at lunch. Loving a married man was a no-win situation. She could feel her heart slowly breaking in two and she knew what needed to be done. If only she had the strength to actually do it.

"Let's stop fooling ourselves, Jerome. This isn't going to work anymore. I want more than you can give me," Taylor said.

"What are you talking about? You know how much I need you. Things will be different soon. I promise."

"When, Jerome? Huh?" Jerome was silent. The pain in Taylor's voice was devastating.

"When will things be different, Jerome?" Taylor cried. "I can't believe I let you drag me along for two years. I can't do this anymore." Taylor recalled all of the money and hours spent preparing his favorite meal. "My friends are right, I deserve better."

"Your friends?" Jerome became angry. "You're not talking about Kara are you?"

"What difference does it make? I do deserve better."

"Don't let your friends ruin what we have."

"Tell me, Jerome, what exactly do we have?"

Jerome couldn't answer, so he shifted the focus back to her friends. "Since Kara and Harold got back together, she's been acting all self-righteous. Don't let her judge our situation."

"It's not just Kara."

"Please don't say Sherry is falling for Kara's sermons, too. She's just mad cause she doesn't have a man."

Taylor couldn't believe his insensitivity. *Was he always this way?* "Before you insult anyone else, I think I should go. Let's face it, if you really wanted this to work, things would be different."

"Taylor, I told you I wasn't going to leave her right away. It's just taking longer than I thought."

Taylor took a deep breath and closed her eyes. "I don't want to hear anymore. When you leave your wife *for real*, give me a call."

"Taylor . . . Taylor, please don't give up on me. I know it hasn't been easy, but I . . . I love—"

"But you what? Love me?" Taylor paused, wiping her eyes. "I'm not falling for that lie any longer. Goodbye, Jerome."

Taylor wiped the remaining few tears from her face and disconnected the call. She walked to the kitchen and took the seafood lasagna out of the oven. She pulled the foil off and admired her creation. Five shrimp were spiraled around the top of the dish. She pulled each one off one by one and ate them. Before she could change her mind, Taylor walked to the garbage disposal and dumped every ounce of the lasagna inside. The freshly steamed broccoli and garlic bread quickly followed. She then opened the refrigerator and grabbed the champagne bottle, already half empty. On the way to her bedroom, she passed the cookie bin filled with double chocolate brownies. She thought twice about disposing them. She opened the lid and took a bite of one. "Umm," she said aloud. They tasted too good to throw away. She repositioned the champagne bottle so that the entire cookie bin could fit under her right arm. Taylor started to walk toward her wine glass by the window but changed her mind. She didn't need a glass to polish off the champagne tonight.

To avoid bumping into Jerome at work, Taylor ate lunch earlier than usual. She sat at the table alone, not sure she could continue working at the bus depot. There would be no way to avoid running into Jerome. Before they got together, Taylor didn't remember seeing him hanging around the depot. It wasn't until Kara convinced her to join other co-workers at Septa's favorite after hours spot that Jerome crossed her path. He strolled in the bar alone that night, wearing a finely pressed Sixers t-shirt and jeans. He wasn't dressed in uniform like the other employees, so Taylor assumed he was part of the neighborhood crowd.

She couldn't explain it, but there was something magnetic about his presence. Her eyes followed him as he slowly circled the room. Their eyes met a few times, and each time, Taylor immediately turned away and took a sip of her mango Margarita.

After the last glance, Taylor looked up to find him leaning on the back of the booth where she and her friends were sitting. "Hello, ladies," he said, displaying a smile that melted Taylor's insides.

"Hey, Jerome. What's up?" Kara responded, noticing the apparent tension between Jerome and Taylor. "Left your wife at home tonight?"

Jerome grinned. "Yeah, she's studying for some class."

"Good for her. And how are the boys?" Kara further questioned, trying to erase any ideas Taylor may have had about Jerome.

"They're fine. Getting bigger every day. What about you? Harold back at home?"

"Nope," Kara simply stated, a little bothered that Jerome had brought up his name.

"He misses you."

Kara blew out a puff of smoke. "That's what happens when you cheat." Kara stared into Jerome's eyes, transmitting an unspoken message.

Jerome walked around to the front of the booth and folded his arms across his chest. He looked like he was posing for a men's magazine spread. Taylor sighed to herself. *The good ones are always taken.* She tried to shift her thoughts, but Jerome started flexing his muscular arms to the beat of the music. He wasn't diesel like the model Tyson Beckford, but his arms could definitely lift and handle a fair amount of weight.

"So, are you new to Septa?" Jerome asked Taylor.

Kara spoke before Taylor could. "She's been around for a few months. Why?"

"Just being friendly. That's all."

"Umm, a little too friendly if you ask me," Kara noted, pressing cigarette remains in an ashtray.

"Can a brotha at least sit here for a while and share a drink with you lovely ladies?" he asked, avoiding eye contact with Taylor.

"If you're buying another round you can. I'm drinking ginger ale and cranberry juice."

"You're a trip," he laughed. "Sure, I'll buy *one* round." Jerome searched for a waiter. When he couldn't find one, he excused himself and headed for the bar. Once he was out of hearing range, Taylor's curiosity took over.

"You seem to know a lot about him," Taylor said.

Kara gave Taylor a suspicious look. "He's a good friend of my ex-husband. Why do you care?"

Taylor stared in Jerome's direction. "Just making a statement. And, Harold isn't your ex-husband. You two will work things out."

"I wouldn't bank on that," she told Taylor. "But don't you get any ideas about Jerome. His *wife* seems like a nice woman."

Jerome returned with the waiter carrying drinks. He was about to ask Taylor to move over, but Kara had another plan. "There's plenty of room on this side," she said, patting the space on her side of the booth."

Jerome shook his head but obliged Kara's gesture.

For the rest of the night, Jerome wowed the ladies with stories about his childhood. Taylor took in every word. *Why did he have to be married?* she thought.

Shortly before the bar was about to close, Kara excused herself from the table. Taking this as the perfect opportunity, Jerome casually slipped an empty matchbook in Taylor's hand and said, "I service most of the buses coming out of the depot. If you need anything or have any problems or just want to talk, give me a call."

Against her better judgment, Taylor placed his number into her purse. If only she hadn't have taken Jerome's number that night, maybe she would be having lunch with a different man. One that was unattached and totally into her.

People started to fill the lunchroom, and Taylor gathered her belongings. She didn't want to take any chances. Rushing out of the room, she bumped into Kara.

"Hey, you're heading out early. You okay?" Kara asked.

"I'm fine. My route ended early," Taylor replied.

"Don't make this a habit. You know how the man upstairs feels about the bus schedules," joked Kara.

"I won't."

Kara could sense that something was wrong and pulled Taylor to the side, away from the heavy traffic of employees. "You sure you're okay?"

Taylor could feel tears forming but tried to keep herself together. "I'm sure."

"You don't look all right. Still upset about Jerome?"

Taylor paused, contemplating how to answer the question. She wasn't in the mood for a lecture today, especially after what happened last night. "You wouldn't understand, Kara. Why don't I just talk to you later?"

"Okay, this isn't the best time to talk, but I *will* call you later. We need to talk about this."

Taylor sucked her teeth and moaned like a child. Kara imitated her actions. "You can moan and pout all you want. I'm going to pray Jerome out of your life."

"What if I don't want him out of my life?" Taylor said sorrowfully.

"Then I have a lot of praying to do. Jerome belongs to someone else. You have to realize that."

To keep from letting Kara see her cry, Taylor walked away.

Going to the movies always lifted Taylor's spirits when she was down. Nothing beat watching a good film with a diet Coke, buttered popcorn and dollar store chocolates. She decided to drive out to the King of Prussia theatre. The screens there seemed larger than the ones she typically visited in Ardmore. She parked midway between the theatre and Nordstrom Rack. Since there was a considerable amount of time before the movie was scheduled to begin, Taylor decided to shop. A new pair of shoes always made her feel better.

She strolled through Nordstrom Rack, heading straight for the shoe section. It was much easier to shop for shoes. Shopping for clothes only depressed her. It was rare that she could find anything worth buying in her size. And she was certain after all the emotional stress Jerome had put her through that she had gone up at least one more size.

Although dozens of shoes were thrown on the shelves haphazardly and cramped on top of one another, Taylor loved the variety the store had to offer. The prices weren't bad either. Spending a little extra time and effort searching for shoes was well worth what some called, aggravation. In less than an hour, Taylor had not one, but three pairs of shoes in her hand. And she purchased each pair. She was having that kind of day.

She put the huge shopping bag in the trunk of her car and dumped the dollar store candy she bought earlier in her tote bag. As Taylor walked toward the theatre, she wished she'd purchased her tickets online. Even from outside she could see that the lines were long.

Taylor opened the doors to the theatre and considered turning around. Children were everywhere! Taylor loved kids, but she didn't want to hear their cheery voices today. She wondered why so many kids were in the theatre. It had been a while since she's been to a theatre on a Friday night, but she was almost certain Friday evenings were mostly for couples and girlfriend packs. There must have been a new Harry Potter movie out or something.

A few kids were running through the admission lines and Taylor wondered where their parents were. Annoyed, Taylor stepped to the left a little to get a better look at what was going on ahead of her, when one of the hyper kids stepped on her toe.

"I'm sorry, ma'm," the young boy said and quickly skipped away. The little girl he was playing with trailed closely behind, teasing him. Taylor looked at the scuff on her shoe. *Calm down. He's just a kid.*

"Uncle Brandon," she heard the child say, as he ran to the front of the line. "Ayanna's making fun of me." Taylor moved to the side, this time watching for any unexpected oncoming traffic. She wanted to give Uncle Brandon "the look" for his unruly kids. When the man turned around, Taylor was shocked. Uncle Brandon was actually Jerome's brother. She had met him a few times at Sam and Pete's. Upon further examination, Taylor realized that the little boy had to be Jerome Jr. She stepped back into place, hiding behind the couple in front of her. As the line began to shorten, Taylor followed Brandon's movements with her eyes. He walked to the corner of the lounging area where he joined his wife and children, as well as Jerome and Renee. She recognized Jerome's wife from a photo she took out of his wallet a while ago. Renee looked a lot shorter in person than she did in the picture. Taylor's heart started to race and she could feel herself begin to panic. *What should I do?*

Taylor had her eye on the two families the entire time she was standing in line. After Taylor purchased her ticket, Jerome was ordering snacks at the concession stand. Jerome's oldest son and nephew were standing next to him, holding tubs of popcorn and treats. Taylor positioned herself and waited. After finishing up at the concession stand, Jerome practically ran into Taylor. "Hello, Jerome," she said to him.

"Hey." Jerome coolly looked around the theatre.

Taylor cracked a smile and shifted her eyes to his son. "This must be Reggie. He looks just like you," Taylor said, "I would shake your hand, but I see that they're full of snacks for the movie."

"This is one of my colleagues," he nervously told the boys. "She drives the bus that goes to the Plymouth Meeting Hall."

"Nice meeting you," the boys said in unison.

"Well, enjoy your movie," Jerome said, ending the conversation prematurely. They started to leave and Taylor grabbed

Jerome's arm. "What are you doing?" he whispered. "My wife is here." He yanked his arm away and went to join his family.

Taylor felt as if someone had ripped out her heart. *How could he treat me that way?*

Jerome didn't look back once. And what started as a day to rejuvenate her spirit, was turning into a day of misery. The one woman that stood between Taylor and Jerome becoming an official couple was less than three yards away from her. She watched in pain as Renee walked ahead of Jerome, holding tight to their youngest son's hand. Taylor skipped the buttered popcorn and soda so she could spy on Jerome a little longer. She lingered behind them, hoping she wouldn't be discovered.

"Theatre number four," the attendant told Taylor after he ripped her ticket and handed her the stub. Taylor headed in that direction, glad to see that Jerome's theatre was only two doors away.

Renee and Brandon's wife made a detour to the women's room and before Taylor could think about what she was doing, she followed them inside.

"This better be a good movie," Renee shouted from her stall. "I could've been doing laundry."

Taylor ducked in the open stall close by and went through the motions even though she didn't have to urinate.

"I'm glad you decided to come out," Brandon's wife said. "We should really do the family thing more than once a month."

"I know girl. I hate to abandon you, but I get so busy at work," Renee commented.

"I know Jerome loves it when you're around," she replied after flushing. Renee didn't respond to that.

"Are you still coming to the game tomorrow?"

"Brandon and the kids are looking forward to it."

Once Taylor heard Renee leave the stall, she peeked through the space in between the door of her stall to get a better look. She waited patiently as the women washed and dried their hands. As soon as they left, Taylor flew out of the stall. Other patrons gawked at Taylor's behavior, but she didn't care. She stayed a few paces behind the women as they walked into the dimly lit theatre, praying the attendant that took her ticket didn't recognize her going into the wrong movie. Previews were playing and the kids had not yet settled. Light chatter and faint giggles filled the room. Brandon got up from his seat to let the ladies down the row. Jerome was on the other end, smacking on the popcorn he was sharing with his son. He turned slightly to look at his wife and his eyes widened when he saw Taylor sliding down the aisle two rows behind them.

When the movie started, Jerome couldn't concentrate. He hadn't eaten another kernel of popcorn, or munched on any of the treats going back and forth between his crew. Midway through the movie, he excused himself and Taylor didn't hesitate to follow. As soon as she stepped outside the doors, he pulled her around the corner. "What are you trying to do?" he yelled in a whisper.

"I was enjoying the movie. Why are you screaming at me?" Taylor asked.

Jerome leaned against the wall. "You're asking for trouble."

"I don't know what I'm doing, Jerome. Seeing you with your kids, I-I," Taylor tried to lean on him, but he jerked away. Taylor was stunned. "I miss you, Jerome," she pleaded.

"You told me it was over," Jerome reminded her, moving a few steps aside to widen the distance between them.

"I was upset, but I can't stand being without you," Taylor moaned. "When you get a chance, why don't we—"

"I have to go," Jerome interrupted. "I've already been gone too long."

When Jerome walked away, a nearby attendant sweeping the floor giggled. Taylor covered her face and slid down the wall. *I feel like such an idiot.*

Still angry and upset when she got home, Taylor pushed her door open and threw her keys in a bowl by the door. She couldn't believe Jerome treated her like a complete stranger, or that she followed his family around the theatre. There was no excuse for her behavior. She put a frozen pizza in the oven and hoped a warm shower would wash the humiliation she felt away.

As she stood in the shower, the warm water beating on her skin helped to clear Taylor's mind. Jerome didn't love her, he couldn't have. Taylor put her face under the steady stream of water, rinsing away her tears. She let the water massage her body until the tension that built up was gone. When Taylor turned the water off, the smell of burning pizza was in the air. She jumped out the shower and ran to the kitchen, dripping water along the way.

The pizza was crisped on the edges and a few pepperonis were black, but Taylor was hungry. She cut the pizza into four huge slices and carried two of them into her bedroom on a paper towel. She made room for the burnt pizza on her night stand and grabbed a towel to properly dry off. The cell phone rang and Taylor sat on the edge of her bed and rubbed lotion onto her arms, trying to ignore the noise of her phone. The tone she had assigned Jerome once soothed her heart, now it was annoying and stupid. The phone stopped ringing before the voicemail picked up, and Jerome would call right back. "Just leave a message!" she yelled at the phone. She was becoming more and more agitated.

Taylor finished with the lotion and put it back in the bathroom. Her cell was still ringing. She stood over the phone willing it to stop with her eyes. No luck. She turned the ringer off and busied herself with laundry she forgot to fold all week. Although she was across the room, she could still see the light flashing with each ring. Taylor threw her socks back in the laundry basket and finally answered the phone. It was the only way she was going to have any peace of mind. She lifted the flap with such force, it could've broke. "What is it, Jerome?"

"I know you're angry about today, but you—" he started.

"You don't have to explain. I had no right to approach you like that." Taylor could hear kids playing in the background. "So, you're still with your family?"

"Brandon and I got stuck with the kids. I'm in Burger King."

Taylor didn't know why she needed to know, but asked, "And Renee? Where is she?"

Jerome didn't answer her question. He pretended his youngest niece needed his attention. Taylor didn't push the obvious. Whether she was in Burger King or not, she was around, probably in the mall shopping with Brandon's wife. "How was the movie?" she asked.

"Not bad," he replied. "Did you still want to talk about us?"

"Not really." Taylor had had enough drama for the day.

"You up for some company? I think I can get away later. I picked you up something—"

Taylor snapped, "I'm tired of you trying to 'get away.' Admit it, Jerome. I don't really mean anything to you. You just keep me around because I do things Renee won't."

"Can we straighten this out tonight?" he asked, appearing more sincere than he was in the theatre.

"Don't bother. Let's just forget about trying to make this work. We both know it's too much for us to handle. See you around." Taylor slammed down the phone. *I need a new man in my life.*

8

Renee

Renee could feel the stares of the other families as she walked through the parking lot of New Life Baptist church. Jerome had not been there since Deacon Bernard pulled him into his office a year ago. Truth be told, if Reggie wasn't playing in the basketball tournament, Jerome would not have come today. At least today he was sober.

The parking lot, which had been turned into a huge carnival, was full of people of all ages. There were all kinds of games and activities for children to enjoy. The church had arranged for a local horse ranch to provide free pony rides. There was also a moon bounce, cotton candy machine, and mini amusement park-type rides.

Before they found a space on the bleachers in the section of the lot marked off for the tournament, Renee thought it would be wise to check in with Mother Wagner. Renee didn't want her to think she wasn't there. A no show would have given Mother Wagner a reason to ask too many uncomfortable questions when she dropped the boys off on Monday.

Renee had no trouble finding Mother Wagner. She could hear

the sultry coarseness of her voice leading the praise team in a song about victory.

In the name of Jesus, in the name of Jesus, we have the victory.

She followed the voices and stood among the crowd gathered around the small group of women singing. People were participating in their own way—singing, shouting, and dancing as if they had just won a battle. Jerome Jr. was so moved by the music that he pretended to be filled with the Holy Ghost. Jerome thought he was making light of the spirit and popped his arm. Jerome Jr. jumped from the unexpected hit and ran to his mother for comfort.

Renee whispered in her son's ear, "Some people don't like when you play like that, baby." Jerome Jr. poked out his lips and held on to her waist.

Jerome watched the two of them and leaned into Renee's ear. "You're turning him into a wimp." She ignored his comment. If Jerome was looking for a fight, he wasn't going to get one today. At least not while they were on church grounds.

"Why don't you go look for Brandon?" she said, swaying to the music. "They should be here by now."

"We'll see them at the court. I want to stay here for a while," replied Jerome.

"Okay," Renee said then began to sing along with the crowd.

They patiently waited for the end of the song, which must have taken fifteen minutes. People hearing the song for the very first time had the words memorized by the time it was over. Renee thought she was dreaming when Jerome clapped along with the other worshipers.

"She can saaang!" Jerome said when he realized Renee was observing him.

When the song finally ended, Jerome Jr. called Mother Wagner over to them. Her smile brightened at the sight of the family. "I'm so glad to see all of you," she said cheerfully.

"I like the way you sing," Jerome Jr. commented.

Mother Wagner blushed. "Thank you kindly, sweetie."

"I was about to cry," Jerome added. Renee looked at her husband. She couldn't believe her ears. She inconspicuously sniffed the air for traces of alcohol. Jerome had never expressed an interest in worship songs. "This is good weather for Kid Fest," Jerome mentioned.

"April can be funny, with the rain showers and all, but God has shown us favor again this year." Mother Wagner looked toward the sky. "Not a rain cloud in sight." Mother Wagner clapped her hands and then looked in Reggie's direction. "How are you today, handsome? Ready for the game?"

"I think I am," Reggie replied, bouncing the ball he was holding under his arm.

Mother Wagner gave him a hug and wished him luck. Since Reggie was a baby, Mother Wagner had taken a special interest in him. Renee knew Reggie was part of the reason she volunteered at his school. Reggie continued to maneuver the ball in different ways, trying to impress her with his skills. Jerome Jr. wanted some of his big brother's attention and tried to knock the ball out of his hands. But Reggie was too quick with his moves and Jerome Jr. grew more and more frustrated.

"Can I help with anything?" Renee asked, silently praying the boys wouldn't get out of control.

Mother Wagner looked around the parking lot. "Let's see," she said, "I think Sister Hawkins could use some help collecting raffle tickets. But that can wait until after Reggie's game." Mother Wagner winked at Reggie and he blushed.

Renee noticed a teenage fan club pointing in Reggie's direction. "Somehow I don't think he would miss my presence."

"I'm sure you're still his biggest cheerleader," Mother Wagner laughed.

"Are you coming to the game?" Reggie wanted to know.

Mother Wagner looked at him with gentle eyes. "I might miss the beginning, but I'll be there." She smiled and Reggie smiled back. "Well, let me go. I need to make sure everything is running smoothly." She turned to Jerome and hugged him. "It was great seeing you. Don't be a stranger."

Renee lured Reggie away from his admirers, whom he constantly entertained with his dribbling skills. The young ladies seemed thrilled by his athleticism. The attention was making Renee feel uneasy, so she asked about Zora, his current girlfriend.

"She'll be at the game," Reggie assured his mother.

Heading toward the tournament area, Renee spotted Kara and Harold holding hands a few steps ahead. Jerome Jr. tugged at Renee's arm. "Isn't that Uncle Harold?"

Renee looked at Jerome, but didn't say a word. The last time he had seen Harold, they had an argument in his studio apartment. Jerome stumbled home that night drunk, claiming Harold had disrespected his manhood. The last time Renee spoke to Kara, Elise was in town. They had gotten together to pray for one another, just as they used to in the past, but that night had felt different. Kara acted strangely and hardly spoke to Renee at all. They didn't speak to one another after that, so this was sure to be an awkward reunion.

Jerome Jr. ran next to them. "Hey, Uncle Harold," he yelled excitedly, grabbing his hand. Harold and Kara turned around, surprised to see their old friends.

"Hey," Renee said. Kara barely looked her in the eyes as she half-heartedly returned the salutation.

"Why don't you come over anymore?" Jerome Jr. asked, joyously jumping around them. "Are the twins and Sabrina here?"

Renee could tell Harold was searching for the right words to say. "I've been working a lot. Sabrina is with the twins at the face painting booth." Harold turned to look at Jerome. "How have you been?"

Renee spoke for her husband in fear that he might say something that would create a scene. "We're good. And you?"

"God has been good to us," he said, clinging tight to Kara's hand.

"I'm glad to hear that," Renee smiled.

There wasn't much more for them to say, and the stretch of silence that followed made that evident. Harold did ask about old acquaintances, to which Jerome bluntly said, "You should call them sometime."

The sound of families laughing and enjoying themselves surrounded them. It reminded Renee of the fun their two families used to share together. She wondered if Harold's infidelity was the reason Kara stopped communicating with her. Renee knew how painful it was to look people in the eye after something like that was exposed. Jerome had often made her feel that way with his drinking.

A young boy running through the crowd stopped in front of them. "Coach wants us to get ready," he yelled to Reggie, full of excitement.

"Go ahead, Reggie," Jerome said. "We'll get seated in a few minutes."

"It was good seeing you again, man," Jerome said. "Kara, I'll see you Monday."

"Same here," replied Harold. No other friendly gestures were exchanged. Not a hug or the grip men give one another to signify their connection as friends.

Renee, on the other hand, was alarmed when Kara hugged her. "God bless you," she whispered in her ear.

"God bless you, too," Renee said in return.

There was something strange about Kara's embrace and the words transferred between them. It left an unsettling reaction in the pit of Renee's stomach. She dismissed the feeling for the moment and focused on her son. He was standing at the check-in table playing around with some of his teammates. Reggie and the team practiced at the Community Center, often referred to as "the club," a few days after school every week, and had become very close. She was glad to see that he had developed friendships with a few kids at the church. A few years ago, he had complained that he was an outsider at school. He seemed to be bothered by peer pressure at a much younger age than she had. As an only child, Renee depended on friends to satisfy her loneliness. Since her classmates were often involved in things her religious parents would not approve of, it was Renee's friends at church that she bonded with the most. From the looks of things, Reggie seemed to be following in her footsteps.

Jerome tapped her on the shoulder, "Brandon's already here." He pointed toward the bleachers where Brandon and his family were sitting. "You ready to sit down?" Renee nodded and followed her husband.

Attending Reggie's basketball games was one of the few times Renee, Jerome, and the kids acted like a real family. Jerome wouldn't dare miss the opportunity to brag about his son's phenomenal skills on the court. "That's my boy!" he shouted every time Reggie scored a basket. She didn't mind Jerome's ownership of their son's athletic prowess. There was no question that Reggie got those genes from him. She sat in the bleachers next to Jerome and tried to live in the happiness of the moment. It wouldn't be long before the game was over and she went back to being a lonely wife and mother.

During the game, Renee noticed that Jerome wasn't Reggie's only cheerleader. On the other side of the court, cheers and chants for every basket, steal, and blocked shot Reggie made were executed and led by Zora. Renee remembered the days when she used to cheer for Jerome. Zora reminded her so much of herself at that age. Given a few pounds and a little less cleavage, Zora even resembled her physically.

When Reggie asked if he could have a girlfriend at the beginning of the school year, Renee adamantly said no. Jerome of course disagreed. "He goes to an all boys school for crying out loud. It's normal for him to want to be around a girl," he had said.

It may have been normal, but Renee still felt it was too soon for Reggie to date. At Reggie's age, Renee was not allowed to speak to boys, much less call one her boyfriend. But, she had to admit her views on dating before sixteen slightly changed when she met Zora. Zora seemed focused and much more mature than other girls her age. She was book smart, there was no question about that. Renee only prayed she was just as intelligent when it came to overactive hormones.

Renee sat through the entire game full of pride. Although Reggie was an aggressive player, just as his father had been, he wasn't disrespectful. Unlike his father and some professional ball players, Reggie did not show negative emotions on the court. Renee credited her genes for that. Reggie didn't argue with the referees, whether they made a good or bad call. He always accepted their decision and moved on with the game.

Near the end of the fourth quarter, Reggie made a basket from the middle of the court. Jerome almost leaped from his seat and onto the court. Renee had to remind him that he was at a church basketball game. He was so energized, she was afraid profanity would slip out of his mouth in any moment. As Reggie ran to the bench, Renee saw him blow Zora a kiss. Zora looked as if she was floating on air. She blushed and blew a kiss back to him and Renee's eyebrow arched. She couldn't tell if she was jealous or concerned. Although she trusted Reggie and Zora, she knew where a simple kiss could lead. She needed to have "the talk" with them soon.

Renee looked at her sons sleeping peacefully in the backseat of the car. It was only four o'clock in the afternoon, but everyone was exhausted. After the game, she had helped Mother Wagner with the raffle tickets while Jerome and the boys enjoyed the rest of the festival. Now, all she wanted to do was sit back and read a good book while sipping on a cool glass of iced tea. But, she had chores to finish. At least the boys were going to spend the night at Brandon's house. Other than going to church together on Sundays, it was rare, especially during basketball season, that the boys had quality time to spend with their cousins. Renee looked forward to spending some quiet time at home. With the boys gone, she could actually clean the house and wash clothes in peace.

Hopefully Jerome would find some other place, outside of their home, to entertain himself. That would make the perfect ending to such a busy day.

Jerome parked the car behind Brandon's. Reggie and Jerome Jr. immediately woke up. Both of them jumped out the car, racing one another to the front door.

"Get back here and get your bags!" Renee yelled, and the boys and their cousins all raced back to the car, pushing and shoving each other along the way. Renee got out of the car and handed Jerome Jr. his backpack, which he immediately inspected.

"Where's my Game Boy?" he asked.

"You need to leave that in the car. You wouldn't want something to happen to it, would you?" answered Renee.

Jerome Jr. looked to his father, hoping he'd counter Renee's words, but he didn't. Jerome Jr. poked out his lips. "Okay, I guess your right." He placed his backpack on his back. "I'm going to miss you, Mommy. Are you going to miss me?"

"Of course I'm going to miss you," she said, feeling her heart grow warm with love. She leaned down to kiss his forehead, "But you'll be back tomorrow. Uncle Brandon will bring you home after church. Have fun, and be nice to your baby cousin."

"I will," he said, and ran toward the house. Reggie took off behind him.

"Hey, big man! Come back here and give me a kiss," Renee demanded.

"Aw, mom! Uncle Brandon is looking," Reggie frowned.

Renee put her hands on her hips. "So what! You should never be ashamed to kiss your mother. I don't care who's looking."

Reggie dragged his body to Renee's side and tilted his head. She kissed his cheek and before she could speak another word, Reggie sped off, bouncing his basketball up the walkway. "I love you," she mouthed, not sure she could handle his new nonchalant attitude. Renee had a feeling Reggie's teen years were going to be rough on her emotionally.

"Tell your Aunt Jocelyn I'll call her later," she said. Reggie acknowledged his mother's request with one head nod.

Jerome mumbled something and then got out of the car. "I'll be right back," he said to Renee, jogging toward Brandon's house.

"Okay, but don't be too long." Renee hopped back into the car to wait for Jerome. He and Brandon were joking around about something. This was the most she had seen Jerome smile in one day. She actually liked his smile. It reminded her of the times they used to stay up late telling each other corny jokes. Jerome looked her way and she raised both hands, signaling that it was time to go. Jerome held up his index finger and Renee sat back, tempted to blow the horn. She sat in the seat with eyes stationed on the clock. She was ready to get home to enjoy every minute of her time. Jerome must have sensed that her eagerness to leave was growing. He shook Brandon's hand and walked to the car.

Renee realized he had on a new pair of jeans. They actually complimented his body. His stomach didn't look like he was concealing an eight pound bowling ball. "Nice jeans," she said when he sat in the driver's seat.

"Thanks," Jerome said, surprised.

"What? Just because I don't like you doesn't mean I can't give you a compliment," she smiled.

Jerome started the car and pulled off. "I guess I should be grateful that you noticed. I bought them with you in mind."

"Please, Jerome. They were probably on sale. You just got lucky, that's all."

"You know me so well."

"After all these years, I know you better than you know yourself."

Jerome turned on the radio. *Pretty Brown Eyes* by Mint Condition was playing.

"That's my song," Renee shouted, bobbing her head to the beat.

"Remember when I used to sing this to you?" Jerome asked, tapping his finger on the steering wheel.

"Yeah, we were in love then and you meant every word," replied Renee, still grooving to the music.

"But I still love you, Nay-Nay," Jerome said, trying to sound convincing.

Renee stopped moving and looked at him. "Nay-Nay? You haven't called me that in ages. You all right?" she questioned, and resumed singing the lyrics.

"Why does something have to be wrong? I love my wife. Is that a crime?"

"Actions speak louder than words. Now, be quiet so I can enjoy my song." Renee turned the radio up. "Start to make sense and quit playing these love games," she sang along.

"Actions, huh?" Jerome pulled the car into their driveway. "What if I do the grocery shopping today? I don't have to work this weekend."

Renee was shocked. What had gotten into him?

"How can I pass that up?" She hit the last note of the song and opened the car door. Jerome remained in the car. She leaned inside the open window. "You're going now?" Jerome nodded. "Okay. Don't forget bacon for my baby." Renee gently closed the door and skipped into the house.

When she opened the door, Renee was instantly reminded of her weekend ritual. The stench of sweaty socks and soiled underwear hit her nose before she reached the pile of clothes lying on the kitchen floor. She took off her shoes and decided to get the cleaning over with. No use in reading a book and drinking the iced tea she was craving. She might not get up and complete the much needed chores around the house. Renee gathered the boys' dirty clothes and thought about Jerome's sudden, but pleasant change in behavior.

Carefully, she walked down the tricky steps leading to the basement with an arm full of smelly clothes. She dropped them by the washing machine then walked to Jerome's hamper, hidden deep behind his exercise equipment and under a mound of dirty clothes. Renee had stopped washing his clothes a year ago. One day she came home tired from working an extra three hours and Jerome asked if she would mind washing his uniforms during the week to help him out. "Wash them yourself. When do I have extra time to wash clothes during the week?" she had responded. The argument ended with Jerome washing his own clothes all the time from that point on.

For a brief moment, Renee thought she had been too hard on Jerome. Maybe he really was trying his best to be a good husband and father. Although he had tried to escape helping Reggie last week, Jerome had managed to complete the science project, and Reggie received an A. Since they were both in fairly good moods today, Renee decided to do Jerome a favor and wash his clothes. She emptied the contents of his hamper and sorted them. There must have been at least three weeks of dirty laundry inside. She grouped the whites and combined them with Reggie and Jerome Jr's. She placed them in the washing machine and pressed the start button. While the clothes were in motion, Renee walked back to the exercise area and began to separate the remaining clothes. She hadn't realized Jerome had such a large wardrobe. There were garments she had never seen before, especially the bright red silk pants suit at the bottom of the basket.

"Where did Jerome go in this?" Renee laughed aloud. "I sure hope he didn't have a matching hat and belt." She figured he wore it to one of the clubs he frequented after work and most weekends. Jerome always liked to dance. Renee lifted the pants from the bench and a square-shaped greeting card that was folded in half fell to the floor. She picked it up before she had time to think about what she was doing. On the outside of the card was a huge purple heart. Renee's own heart pounded louder than the noise of the washing machine as she opened the card.

> *I never knew love could feel this good.*
> *I look forward to lovin' you in many different ways.*
>
> > *My heart belongs to you,*
> > *Taylor*

The card automatically dropped to the floor. Renee stomped over it and marched directly to the washing machine. She pulled out Jerome's clothes and threw them back into the hamper, still wet and full of bleach.

Jerome returned from the market carrying several bags of groceries. Renee was sitting on the couch in the living room reading *I Wish I Had a Red Dress* by Pearl Cleage.

"I guess I can't get any help with these bags," Jerome teased, but his words fell on deaf ears. Renee continued to read, patiently waiting for him to finish unloading the car. Each time Jerome returned with new bags, he struggled to get through the front door. "Oh no, sweetheart, don't get up." Renee turned the page of her book as if he wasn't speaking to her. "Okay, I guess I'll handle this on my own," he said, unaware of Renee's mood change. He went out to the car two more times. When he dropped the last bag in the kitchen he studied his wife. "That must be one good book." Renee only moved to turn a page in her book. "I guess I'll put the groceries away, too."

Jerome walked back to the kitchen shaking his head. When he was done, he walked back into the living room. "Nay-Nay, the book can't be *that* good."

Renee rolled her eyes and looked up at him, fighting the urge to bust him in his already thick lips.

"Excuse me, Mrs. Thomas," he said playfully, still clueless. "I'm sorry for interrupting you. I just thought . . ." Jerome leaned in close to Renee's face. "I thought we could spend some private time together."

Renee closed her book and sat up straight. "Why don't we start with a movie," she said, forcing a smile. She handed him the remote. "Turn the TV on."

Jerome cuddled beside her. "I thought we'd get right to it, but if you want to watch . . ." Jerome pointed the remote at the TV and stopped talking. "What's that on the screen?" he asked, puzzled.

"You have 20/20 vision. What does it look like?" Renee said, holding back her anger.

Jerome jumped from the couch and snatched the card from the television screen.

Renee couldn't think of a better way to question the card she had found. If she hadn't taped it to the television, she would have pressed it deep into his face. Jerome was speechless. This was truly a first. She walked over to her husband ready for whatever was about to happen.

"Renee, I know what you're thinking," he said, bracing himself for Renee's next move. He knew a swing would be coming at any moment.

"What am I thinking, Jerome? That you're a lying adulterer?"

"This doesn't belong to me. Where did you get this?"

"Who do you think you're talking to? I'm not one of those chicks you fool around with in the bar," Renee stated, her light skin now flushed.

"I'm serious. This doesn't belong to me. I don't know any . . ." Jerome opened the card and read the signature. "Taylor. Who is Taylor?"

"You know good and well who this woman, Taylor, is," Renee started, her arms moving wildly as she spoke. "I call myself doing you a favor by washing your stinkin' behind clothes. Imagine that, me actually trying to be nice to my low-down husband." Renee poked him in the chest. "The card was in your pile of nasty clothes, right under your bright red clown suit."

"Whoa, slow down, Renee. You're getting yourself all worked up over nothing." Jerome looked at the card again. "You know what? I bet this is from one of Brandon's friends."

With twisted lips, she folded her arms across her chest. "And just how would the card get in *our* house?"

"I bet he was trying to hide it here."

Renee snatched the card and smacked his cheek with it. "Don't blame this on your brother. You know you've been messing around with the tramp."

"C'mon, Renee," Jerome pleaded. "Let's not call anyone names."

"Oh, so now you're defending a woman you claim not to know?"

"Renee, you're overreacting."

"Overreacting? I'll show you overreacting!" Renee repeatedly punched him in the chest. "I want you out of here tonight!"

Jerome backed away just enough to stop the blows to his chest. Renee was breathing heavy and still ready for battle. She picked up a nearby vase and aimed it at his head. Jerome's eyes widened and he ducked just in time. Water and glass from the vase shattered against the wall and splashed on his back. He stepped to the side and headed for the stairs, but Renee blocked him. This time, Reggie's basketball trophy was in her hand.

"Renee!" he yelped. But, that didn't stop her. She swung at him, barely scratching his left arm. "Hold on, babe."

"Don't tell me to hold on. You save holding on for Taylor." She swung again, this time missing him altogether. Before Renee could swing once more, Jerome leaped over the table and ran behind the sofa to hide. "And I'm not your babe!" she screamed. "Does she even know you have a wife?"

"This is just a misunderstanding," Jerome pleaded, slowly standing to his feet.

"What is there to misunderstand?" Renee was breathing heavy, her chest heaving up and down faster than normal, but she was still raring to go. "Be a man for a change! Own up to what you've done."

"But, I haven't done anything!" Jerome argued. "If you just calm down, I can explain." Renee didn't move, but she held tight to the trophy. Jerome eased from behind the sofa. "I'm not lying. You've got to believe me."

Other than the card, Renee had no concrete evidence that he was cheating, but she knew he was. "We were having such a great day." Jerome slowly eased closer to her. "Every time I let my guard down, you do something stupid to mess things up between us," Renee said.

"But, it's Brandon who . . ."

Renee threw the trophy on the sofa and Jerome's reflexes jumped. "Are you serious? You're still blaming this on Brandon?" Renee closed her eyes and counted to ten to keep from damaging her home any further. She couldn't believe she was so angry. She suspected he was fooling around months ago, but hoped she was just being overdramatic. But now she had some proof to her suspicions, and the pain of that reality had finally set in. "Well, tell you what. Get your crap out of this house and go shack up with her. Let her deal with your nonsense. I'm through!"

Renee tried to walk away, but Jerome grabbed her. "Renee, I'm not seeing Taylor or anybody else."

Renee snatched away from his grip. "Touch me like that again, and you'll be laying up in a hospital. I'm serious, Jerome. I don't want to see your face around here anymore."

"You can't just tell me to leave my house, especially when I didn't do anything wrong," Jerome responded.

"The last time I checked, *my* name was on the deed."

Renee's words stung. Yes, her name was on the deed, but Jerome had helped to make several of the payments. "Oh, since you're the big money maker, you get to call the shots?"

"Just leave before I do something I'll regret."

"I'm not leaving. I have a right to be here. This house belongs to me just as much as it belonged to you. Besides, what would you tell the boys?"

Jerome had a lot of nerve. Renee paused, but only for a second. It wasn't fair for the children to come home and find their father suddenly gone. "I'm not going to tell them anything. I'll leave that up to you. In the meantime, you can make yourself comfortable in the basement indefinitely!"

9

Taylor

"I can not believe you hid in the bathroom," Sherry laughed, tailing a few small steps behind Taylor.

"I know. Pretty pathetic, huh?" Taylor said. Taylor could joke about what happened now, but last night after she left the theatre, her heart had been crushed.

"I don't even think I ever did anything that bizarre."

Taylor stopped in front of Bedazzled, a store she passed everyday on her bus route. Today, there were jeans pinned along a wire rope hanging in the window. They weren't just the regular stretch or low rise jeans. Each pair had special designs—colored rhinestones, flowered embroidery, and hand painted numbers and letters. Every week there was something different in the window. The owners had interesting items, but they didn't quite know how to display them. Taylor was sure she could do a better job.

She had gone inside one day to get a better look at their merchandise and was overwhelmed by the boxes of clothes and accessories thrown on four long tables. Taylor didn't mind searching for clothes; sometimes unique pieces are discovered that way. But Bedazzled's set up was just plain tacky and unorganized.

"You want to go inside?" Sherry asked, peeking through the

store window. "I might find something I can wear to my brother's party."

"I don't feel like sifting through clothes today," Taylor sighed and started walking down the street, silently praying she'd one day have a boutique that would join the other trendy shops along Germantown Avenue.

"You getting your hair done today?" Sherry asked Taylor.

"Yeah, but not until two o' clock," she answered. "You going today?"

"No, I'm getting micro braids in the morning." Sherry rubbed her hair lightly. "My hair can use the break."

Sherry and Taylor waited at the corner of the street for the light to change. Taylor turned to face Sherry. "Kara's right about Jerome, isn't she?"

"Kara always thinks she's right," Sherry said.

"Well, this time I think she might be. You should have seen the way he looked at me," Taylor replied. "He treated me like I was the scum of the earth."

Sherry bumped her friend lightly. "You exaggerate too much. But, in all fairness, you were wrong for confronting him when you knew his wife was around."

"I know, but it doesn't matter anymore. It's really over," Taylor said, trying to convince herself.

"Yeah, I'll believe that when I see it," Sherry said, briskly walking alongside Taylor to keep up when the light changed.

Monday afternoon, Taylor entered the lunchroom with a new energy of confidence. Over the weekend, she had convinced her hairdresser to give her a new look. Short and spunky curls now replaced her regular bobbed cut. To spice up her standard bus driver uniform, Taylor unfastened an extra button, exposing a small part of the rose tattoo on her chest. No more masking the natural fluffiness God had given her. She was determined to exercise her pride in her curvaceous shape. Jerome loved it, so to her that meant other men might like it, too.

"Look at you, hot mama. I love the new hairdo," exclaimed Kara when Taylor entered the lunchroom. She folded the newspaper she was reading to give Taylor a space to put her lunch. "It works for you. I couldn't get away with that on this big head of mine. What's the occasion?"

"Nothing, I just wanted to do something different."

"You wanted something different, or you wanted to make a certain someone sitting over in the corner jealous?" Kara tilted her head in Jerome's direction.

"I don't know what you're talking about," Taylor smirked, slowly easing into the seat across from Kara.

"Where have you been hiding anyway? I've been trying to call you. I know you got my messages."

"Yes, I did. All thirteen of them," Taylor laughed.

"You had me worried. Next time, I'm going to drive over there," Kara told her.

Taylor took her lunch out of the bag she had it packed in. "I just needed to get my head together. You were hard on me last week."

"So you punished me for being honest?"

"No, I appreciate it, but next time can you please be a little more gentle with your words?"

"There's no guarantee, but I'll try," Kara said, biting into an apple. "So, I take it you've decided to move on?"

"I'm getting there."

"Maybe now you can focus on the dream you abandoned." Taylor looked confused as Kara continued, "That man really had you hooked. You wanted to open a boutique and bring Hollywood to the ghetto, remember?"

Taylor had completely forgotten about that. She was too engrossed in her relationship with Jerome. "I did have goals at one time, didn't I?"

"A man shouldn't let you walk away from something you really want to do for yourself," Kara confirmed.

Taylor looked around the room trying not to be obvious.

Jerome was discussing the latest basketball stats with a few drivers. He looked as if he didn't have a care in the world. "Do you think he misses me?"

"It doesn't matter," Kara said, remembering her personal experience. "In the end, he'll always have his wife."

"You're right," she sighed. "I can't turn back now."

"I'm glad to hear you say that," Kara said, relieved. "You have a new look now, and Harold has a few nice single friends. I'm sure he'd be happy to hook you up."

Taylor laughed. "I don't think his church-going friends can handle a girl like me." Taylor reached for the salt shaker across the table and knocked her yogurt cup on the floor. When she reached down to pick it up, her hands met the comforting hands of an old friend. She sat back in her chair and looked up. "What's up, Lance?" she said, admiring the view. "Where have you been hiding?" Lance was an old friend, husky by nature and with a smile that could grace the cover of any toothpaste advertisement.

Lance placed the yogurt on the table. "I've been around. You've just been too busy to notice me."

Taylor batted her eyes. "I'm never too busy for a friend."

"Have a seat, Lance," Kara said as she got up, "I need to talk to my manager before heading back out." Kara tapped his broad shoulder lightly and winked at Taylor before leaving.

"I can sit for a few minutes," he said, and sat in a chair barely strong enough to hold him.

Lance and Taylor talked non-stop for twenty minutes, and from the corner of her eye, she could feel Jerome watching. It felt good to know that he was bothered. At one point, Jerome had walked by two trash cans to one near her table just to throw away an empty potato chip bag. Taylor had to smirk at his efforts to listen in on her conversation with Lance. His blatant jealousy encouraged her to turn on the charm.

Taylor got up from the table and gave Lance a big hug. "We've got to get together more often. I'd forgotten how much fun you are to be around." She rubbed his back for added effect.

Lance returned the embrace. "You still have my number?" he asked, holding Taylor's free hand.

Taylor lightly rubbed his arm. "You know, I don't think I do. Why don't you walk me to my bus. I have some paper in there."

"Lead the way," Lance responded, enjoying the attention.

Taylor couldn't wait to tell Sherry about her day. Although they were both in their thirties, they still gossiped like they were back in high school. Taylor walked in her front door and put her keys in the bowl by the door. She then checked the caller ID. Only the numbers from annoying telemarketers appeared. She hit the speed dial button for Sherry and put her on speaker.

"Is the hibernation over?" Sherry asked when she answered.

"I needed some me time," Taylor replied.

"Must be serious. I used to be a part of your *me time*. Hey, am I on that speakerphone?" Sherry didn't like the way the speaker made her sound.

"Be patient. I'm changing my clothes," Taylor informed her.

"Well, call me back when you're done. You know I hate that thing."

"Calm down, big baby. I'm almost done. I wanted to tell you about my day," Taylor bellowed from across the room as she pulled a pair of stretch jeans from the dresser.

"Let me guess. You and Jerome are back together."

"Wrong." Taylor paused. "I cut my hair and—"

"You did what? How short is it?"

"Old Toni Braxton short, but it's just hair, Sherry. And, that's not what I wanted to tell you."

Sherry sighed, "What could be bigger than cutting you hair? It took years for it to grow. I can't believe Arnez cut it."

Taylor put on an old Eagles football T-shirt. "Lance seems to like it. Remember him?"

"There's a name I haven't heard in a while."

"I gave him my number today and he asked if we could hang out sometime." She chuckled and put the cordless to her ear, re-

leasing Sherry from the speaker. "So, we're going out this weekend."

"I thought *we* were going out this weekend. Am I on the back
burner again?"

"Lance and I have a Saturday night date. You and I are still on
for Friday." Taylor searched through her shoe collection for comfortable tennis shoes. "And, don't front. When you get a man,
you won't remember my name."

"Well, from what I recall, Lance is charming *and* fine," Sherry
noted. "Don't enjoy the date too much."

"You're a mess. Remember, I'm not fast like you." Taylor's stomach growled, reminding her that she had not eaten since noon.
"Let me go," she said, rushing Sherry off the phone. "I'll call you
back after I eat."

Taylor hung up and walked to the kitchen to search for her
Popeye's coupons. She was in the mood for their mouth-watering
biscuits. She put two coupons in the inside pocket of her purse
and noticed Lance's number on a ripped piece of paper. Taylor
couldn't remember why they stopped dating years ago. It couldn't
have been anything too serious, otherwise she would have remembered. Although they had met at Home Depot several years
ago, it was ironic that they ended up working together. They had
gone out a few times, but lost touch when she moved out of her
mother's house and into her own place in Germantown. Taylor
should have been happy about the possibility of starting over, but
for some reason, her heart blocked the emotion to feel anything
for anyone other than Jerome.

10

Renee

"Good night, Eric. Try and keep it quiet tonight," Renee said as she locked her office door.

"You know I'll keep things under control," he responded.

"Oh, I don't know. You didn't have a good grip on Marvin, and now he's out of a job," Renee joked.

"That young man is hurting my reputation."

"Don't worry. I still trust you." Renee put on her jacket. "I'll see you tomorrow."

Renee threw her briefcase in the backseat of her Lexus jeep. Her cell phone vibrated on her leg and she reached into her jacket pocket. She looked at the caller ID and frowned.

"What is it, Jerome?" she asked as soon as she hit the talk button.

It had been four days since Jerome moved into the basement. He tried to talk to her on numerous occasions, but Renee refused to listen to anything he had to say. He even had Brandon come by and shamefully confess that Taylor was his secret woman, but Renee knew Brandon was lying.

"How was your day?" he asked joyfully.

Renee sucked her teeth and asked in a monotone, "What do you want? I'm on my way to get the boys and I don't want to be late."

"No need to rush. I'm in front of the school now. I'm getting the boys today."

Renee almost dropped the phone. "But, it's Tuesday. What are you up to?"

"Nothing, babe, I'm just trying to bring harmony back into our home."

"I think it's too late for that," she snapped.

"I'm still going to try. Go ahead home," Jerome insisted. "The boys and I will see you soon."

Renee ended the call curious about what Jerome had up his sleeve. She decided to take Jerome's sudden kindness as an opportunity to do some shopping, alone. Instead of going straight home, she drove to the DSW in Plymouth Meeting. There was a big meeting coming up at work and she wanted to look good for her presentation. She wanted the top executives to leave with a lasting impression of her as well as her accomplishments. Even though she didn't have a huge amount of money saved to spend on herself, she decided to splurge anyway. Renee had already used the Master Card Jerome was in control of to purchased a Donna Karan suit a week ago while Jerome Jr. was at drum practice. Jerome was going to flip when he saw how much she had spent.

Renee tried on several shoes and walked down the aisles as if she were a runway model. Her cell phone buzzed in the middle of her imaginary fashion show, and the smile she possessed quickly disappeared.

Slightly annoyed, she lifted the flap on the phone and answered, "Hello."

"Mommy, where are you?" Jerome Jr. cried. "We're worried about you."

Renee was relieved it wasn't her husband. "I'm fine, sweetie," she assured him. "I'll be home before you go to bed. Okay?"

"Okay, but hurry up! Reggie's being mean to me."

"No, I'm not!" Reggie wailed in the background.

"All right, baby. Let Mommy go so she can get home faster."

"Wait a minute! Daddy wants you."

Renee rolled her eyes and sat on the stool at the end of the aisle. "Hey, baby. You okay?" he asked, having the nerve to sound concerned.

She sucked her teeth and closely examined the shoes currently on her feet. "I'm fine," she sang. "I needed to make a quick stop." She looked down beside the stool and picked up a taupe pointy-toed sling back. *Conservative and classy*, she thought.

"No problem, babe, you're entitled."

"Okay, then. Bye," she said, rushing him off the phone.

"Renee, wait a minute. I hope you haven't eaten."

Renee wanted to smack him. Surely he didn't think he could erase what happened with a home-cooked meal. He wasn't *that* great of a cook.

"I grabbed something at McDonald's," she lied.

Jerome sounded disappointed. "Oh, okay."

"Okay, I'll be home soon." Renee hung up and held up a pair of chocolate pointy-toed shoes. These were a little different. The heel was much higher and the straps around the ankles were covered with dark brown fur. She slid off the shoes on her feet and put them back in their box. They were plain compared to the two in her hand. She then bent down to search for her size in the furry shoe, and when she found it, had to stuff her foot inside. *These must run small.* Renee wiggled her foot into the other shoe and made her way to a mirror. "Fierce," she said aloud. Renee turned her head from the shoes on her feet to the shoe in her hand. *Which one should I choose?* Unable to make a decision, she searched for the other shoe in her size and danced to the register.

The cashier checked the shoes, with her long acrylic nails getting in the way, to make sure they were the same size. "These are fly," the young girl said, and neatly tucked them back inside the boxes. Renee could tell she was still in school, though her tiny individual braids made her appear to be older. The girl flipped the hair that was hanging in her face with one quick head movement and checked the other box of shoes. "You got taste."

Renee pulled out her wallet. "Thank you. I have a big meeting in a couple of weeks. Both of these match the suit I want to wear." This was more information than the girl wanted to know. She was more interested in the chip in her finely designed nail.

"Heels like these would make me feel powerful," the cashier said, holding up the box with the furry-strapped shoe inside. "One fifty three ninety-eight is your total."

Hearing the amount made Renee gasp for air. She didn't intend on spending that much money. She thought about the cashier's words. It was time she took more control of her life. Jerome always did what he wanted to do. She too wanted to play by those rules. Renee thumbed past her personal credit card and pulled out the Master Card.

Renee thought she had entered the wrong house. When she left this morning, there was clutter everywhere. Now, it was almost spotless. The stairs were free of scuffed gym shoes and Timberlands. There was no evidence that the boys had ever been in the living room. Their video games and toys had been arranged neatly in the corner and Jerome's movie collection was finally on the shelves he built into the wall. The dining room table was completely vacant of last month's mail and graded school papers.

Renee laughed aloud when she turned on the light to the kitchen. The dishes were not only washed, but put away. Jerome had even covered a plate of food with plastic wrap and sat it on the stove. She looked at the contents and shook her head. Jerome had made turkey burgers and baked beans. Was *that* supposed to win her heart?

The polite thing would have been for her to tell Jerome thank you, but he didn't deserve it, and she didn't feel like being polite. The basement lights were low, indicating that Jerome was already asleep or very close to it. The television being off struck Renee as unusual. It was rare that the television was off when Jerome was home. He could never get enough of the ESPN channel. She shrugged it off, figuring he had the television on timer and it turned off by itself. She hit the light switch for the basement and waited for a response. *Good, he's asleep.* Next, Renee needed to check on the boys. With Jerome asleep, they could be doing anything.

When she reached the top of the stairs, Jerome Jr. flew from his room and jumped into her arms. "Mommy, I missed you! We had turkey burgers on real hamburger rolls for dinner," he told her. "I'm glad we didn't have anymore hotdogs."

"Did you have a good day at school?" she asked, kissing his cheek.

"Yes, I got an A on my spelling test," he rejoiced, dancing to his own beat.

Reggie stepped into the hallway. "You only had ten words on the test. You should've gotten an A."

"For the record," he snapped back, still moving around, "I had *twenty* words."

"For the record, I think he told you," Renee teased and joined Jerome Jr. in his victory dance.

Reggie stomped back into his room. "*Uggh*, you're both corny."

"I'm glad you had a good day. Keep up the good work. Maybe we'll do Chucky Cheese on Saturday after your music lesson," said Renee.

"Yipee!" he shouted, and sailed back into his room. Renee was surprised to see that both boys were already dressed for bed, although she wondered if Jerome made them take baths. She decided not to ask and ruin the evening. Jerome had done a good job for once. Even if it was only to get on her good side.

Renee peeked inside Reggie's room and found him reading a book and wiggling to the music coming from his headphones. Renee walked in and took the headphones from around his ears. "I don't know how you can concentrate," she said.

"I know what's going on," he told her, without looking up from his book.

"Is that homework or pleasure?"

"Homework of course," Reggie answered, still focused on the page he was reading.

"I should've known." She turned to leave and realized that he wasn't on the phone. "What's up with you and Zora? She hasn't called in a couple of days."

"That's old news."

"Old news? She's a nice girl. What happened?" Renee sat on the edge of his bed, trying to ignore the disorganization that surrounded her.

"I told her I didn't want to be tied down by one person," Reggie said. "I'm too young to have a girlfriend anyway."

Renee knew Jerome was the force behind her son's new philosophy on life and women. "Just be careful. You don't want a good thing to pass you by while you're out there playing the field." Renee was tempted to put away the loose clothes dangling from his desk chair, but figured now wasn't the time.

"I told Zora I'd still hang out with her sometimes."

"Don't abuse her feelings," Renee asserted, feeling her insides tense. "If you don't want to be with her anymore, tell her. Don't make her think she still has a chance to be with you. You know, for every heart you break, it's going to come back to you double time."

"All right, Mom," he said, swiftly turning the page.

Renee was concerned that his raging hormones were starting to kick in. She'd have to monitor his female relationships more closely. Jerome was a "ladies man" in his day, and wanted to do what she could to keep Reggie from following in those footsteps. "I'm sorry, sweetie. But I want you to be a good man. Not a dog . . . I mean player like these other knuckleheads out here. Don't be afraid to be different and sensitive." Through all of his toughness and macho exterior, Renee could tell Reggie was really listening to her words. "Well, I think I've said a mouthful for tonight."

"Yes, you have," he said without hesitation.

Renee lightly smacked his legs. "After practice this weekend we'll hang out at the mall."

Reggie looked at his mother, "I'll pass."

"C'mon, it'll be fun. We haven't spent much time together lately."

"As long as we go to the one in Delaware or Jersey."

Renee chuckled inside. She remembered how taboo it was to be seen in the mall with her own parents when she was Reggie's age. "I'm not hip enough for you?" she queried.

Reggie looked his mother up and down. Dressed in her navy double-breasted pantsuit, most adults her age would agree that she looked good. Even with the few extra pounds. But, to a teenager, she looked more like a nerd. Renee danced across the bedroom, mimicking moves she'd seen on BET. "I'm more hip than half the kids you know."

Reggie threw his covers over his head to hide and drown out his laughter. To him, Renee looked like a wild chicken. Renee danced back to the door, pulling the covers from over his head along the way. "Why don't you try and clean up a little before you go to sleep."

"Saturday is cleaning day, Mom," he reminded her, still giggling to himself.

"Okay," Renee said, "but no woman likes a sloppy man."

Renee left his room glad that they had ended on a positive note. She continued down the hallway to her bedroom. "Odd," she thought. The television was on and the light was dimmed low. When she reached the door, she could see Jerome sprawled across the bed, wearing only leopard-print silk boxers. If he didn't look so ridiculous she would have thrown a cup of ice on him. Renee couldn't help but laugh. The boxers were bought as a joke ten years ago for Valentine's Day. They looked funny on him then, and even funnier now that he was nearly three sizes heavier.

She slid out of her shoes and tipped into her walk-in closet to search for a nightgown. Renee placed the shoes she purchased on the shoe rack then poked her head out the door. Jerome was still in the same position. She went to the back of the closet and hid the DSW shopping bag under her set of suitcases. She looked through the opening once more. Jerome must have been tired. When he was sober, he was normally a light sleeper. Since there was no evidence that he had been drinking, he must have been exhausted from cleaning the house. She left the bedroom, quietly easing down the hallway and into her bathroom. She wanted to end the evening with a smooth and soothing mint bubble bath. Waking Jerome up prematurely would ruin her mood, though she did intend to kick him and his tight boxers out once she was done bathing. She started the water in the bathtub and changed into her robe. While the water was running, she ran downstairs to fix a cup of hot tea.

Renee placed a cup nearly full of water in the microwave for two minutes. Thoughts of the upcoming meeting put her in a daze, causing her to jump at the sound of the buzzer. *I hope Jerome didn't wake up.* She put a Chamomile teabag in the cup and crept up the stairs avoiding the known creaks, careful not to disturb her husband. Her bedroom was still dark and quiet. *Thank God.* Renee pushed the bathroom door open and almost dropped her cup. "What the . . ." A few drops of her tea landed on the floor. Jerome, naked and unashamed of his body, was soaking in the bathtub, obviously enjoying the mint sensation.

"Don't ruin the night, Renee. Get in," he commanded. "There used to be a time when we looked forward to these late night baths."

Renee couldn't believe the turn of events. "The boys are still awake and I don't want to give them the wrong idea," she said, wiping the stains with her feet.

"You don't want them to see that their parents are still in love?"

"Please! I think we stopped being *in love* years ago."

"It hurts me to hear you say that." Jerome was making small

puddles with his hands. Renee was getting angry watching him enjoy the bath that was meant for her. "No matter what happened, or what you think I've done, I've never stopped loving you."

Losing the desire to enjoy a late night bath, Renee grabbed her night garments and placed them under her arm. "Look, it's too late to discuss who still loves who. We'll have to talk about this another time."

"This water is cold without you," Jerome said seductively.

"Good." Renee walked back to the bedroom and threw her clothes on the floor, spilling half of the tea on the carpet. She locked the door and leaned against it. She stayed there, sipping her drink until it was gone. All the while wondering, *What has gotten into Jerome?*

Renee sat at her desk reviewing notes for the big meeting next week. Although Mr. Kotlarczyk hadn't mentioned that people's jobs were on the line, she knew better. Usually, Mr. Kotlarczyk was more involved in the quarterly meetings. But lately he'd been too preoccupied with other "top secret" business matters, and that concerned her. She flipped through her calendar to check the date and time of her next hair appointment. As she tried to decipher her scribbles, Renee's eyes gravitated to the balloons and smiley faces drawn around May 21st. She had almost forgotten about her birthday. In a matter of weeks, she would be thirty-five, although she felt much older.

Thinking of the gift Jerome gave her last year, she hoped he had a better idea this time. Renee closed her eyes and the image of Jerome lounging in leopard boxers tickled her. If Jerome wasn't good for anything else, he was certainly good for a hearty laugh. She wasn't sure what he was thinking, but one thing was for sure: Renee had not forgotten about the card from the "mystery woman" named Taylor. No matter how nice he tried to be, Jerome was not getting back into the bed with her. She wasn't foolish enough to believe that Taylor was Brandon's lover.

Renee wrote one last sentence on her note pad and placed it inside her briefcase. For some reason, her wedding ring was shining brighter than it had ever before. She helped Jerome upgrade her ring three years ago. Tired of looking at the ½-carat Jerome's parents helped him get when they first got married, Renee had convinced him to pay for part of the three-carat white gold ring currently on her finger.

With her birthday practically around the corner, Renee questioned whether or not she should end the marriage. Proof of his infidelity was a sign that it was time to move forward. She already felt as if she had wasted several years of her life with Jerome. If she got out now, there was still a chance that she would find her *true* soul mate.

"Mrs. Thomas," Bianca announced through the intercom. "Reggie's teacher is on line one."

Renee looked up from her ring. "Go ahead. You can put her through."

There were a few clicks followed by Bianca's cheerful voice. "You're connected."

"Hello, Mrs. Santos," Renee said into the phone receiver.

"Hi, Mrs. Thomas. I hate to bother you at work—"

"It's no problem. Is something wrong with Reggie?" Renee could feel her body temperature rise.

"Well," Mrs. Santos began, "Reginald's behavior has changed these last few weeks. I would have called sooner, but he's been such a good student, I guess I thought it was temporary."

Renee used her left hand to keep her head from hitting the desk. She immediately thought about Reggie's relationship with Zora and hoped the two weren't having sex. Sex could certainly change behavior. "What type of change in behavior?"

"Well, he doesn't talk back to me or anything. He just hasn't been performing as well as I know he could. He doesn't complete all of his assignments and . . . he's becoming the class clown."

Reggie a class clown? Renee hadn't expected to hear that. He was always so laid back. "Has he been hanging around any new friends that you can tell?"

"Well . . ."

"It's okay, Mrs. Santos. Please be honest with me. I'm one of those parents that really wants to know." Too much money was spent on his education to accept anything less than the truth.

"He's in the eighth grade now and I think he's trying to 'fit' in with a few of the more socially advanced boys. You know how it is when you're trying to be a part of the group."

Renee did know. As a child, she longed to be a part of the "in" group. But the stronghold of her parents wouldn't allow it. Though she never rebelled, she wanted to. But that wasn't something "good girls" do. "I apologize for his behavior," Renee said. "I'll talk to him tonight."

Renee wanted to call Jerome, but didn't. Like so many other problems, this was yet another situation she'd have to handle by herself. If Jerome's solution would resemble anything like the decision to leave Zora alone, she didn't want to know how he'd handle this.

She grabbed the silver cross dangling from the chain around her neck. *Maybe it's time to go back to church*, she thought. Renee needed some guidance and assurance that everything was going to be all right.

Suddenly, and without warning, Renee started to cry. First, only tears signaled the pain that was buried deep within her soul, but soon the tears were accompanied by moans of sadness. Everything that she held inside had finally built up and exploded. She placed her hands to her face and began to pray. "God, I need your help. I don't know where my life is headed, but something has got to change."

11

Jerome

Jerome couldn't believe he was practically living in the basement. How did things come to this? It had been a week since Renee found Taylor's card, and yet he still couldn't get it off his mind. He was sure he'd been extra careful not to bring any evidence of his affair home. Either he had too much to drink one night, or Taylor had slipped the card in his pocket when he wasn't looking. In any event, he had to let it go. There was no chance it would happen again. Taylor was now out of his life. The smile on her face in the lunchroom the other day was a clear indication that she had moved on. It was a little too soon for her to be flirting with another man, Jerome thought, but that wasn't his concern anymore.

Jerome turned the futon back into the sofa position. He bent over and tossed the comforter and sheets underneath. When he stood up, a pain shot through his back. "I don't know how much longer I can take this," he grumbled aloud. All week he tried to get on Renee's good side, but his deeds seemed to go unnoticed. Renee hadn't bought the story he gave her about Taylor. He couldn't believe the lie that escaped his lips himself. Blaming Brandon was a bad idea. Renee was too smart of a woman. Now the basement was more than Jerome's sports room—it was his new home.

He walked upstairs to fix his morning coffee and Renee was already up and washing dishes from the night before. He could tell something was wrong. She had been washing the same pan for the past two minutes. It couldn't have been that dirty. Whatever was bothering Renee had her up most of the night.

When Jerome had gone to take a shower before bed, the door to Reggie's room was closed. He waited by the door, carefully trying to spy on the conversation Renee was having with their son, but was unsuccessful.

When he was done with the shower, the door was still closed. Hours later, when he went upstairs for a roll of toilet paper, he could hear Renee pacing her bedroom floor, crying. *Did she talk to Reggie about their marriage? Was she planning to leave him for real this time?* Jerome had wanted to go in and hug her, tell her that everything, whatever the problem was, would be all right. But, he didn't. He was too afraid of what she might do or say to him.

Jerome crept up from behind and whispered in Renee's ear, "Morning."

"You need to brush your teeth," Renee said, turning her nose up.

Renee's eyes never left the pan, and a thought crossed his mind. *Could she still be upset about Taylor?* Honestly, he didn't think Renee cared. "Sorry I offended you," he laughed and started to brew his coffee. "Got any plans for today?" he asked, praying his thoughts weren't true.

"Reggie has practice and Jerome has drums. Same as every Saturday."

"Do you mind if I tag along?" Jerome asked. Spending time together might change her mood, he thought.

Renee looked at him suspiciously. "I thought you had to work."

"Not until four."

"I can take them. I've been doing it this long."

Ignoring her response, he sat his coffee mug by the coffee pot.

He wasn't about to encourage another argument. He opened the cabinet and moved a few canned foods and candy bars around. "There's no more creamer?"

"I guess not," she giggled softly.

"This isn't funny. You know I need cream for my coffee."

"WaWa is open."

Jerome opened the refrigerator and took out the milk. "Oh, no!" Renee tossed the rag in the dirty water. "The boys haven't had their cereal yet."

"I'll keep that in mind." Jerome stood by the coffee machine and waited for it to stop. "So, you have another birthday coming up. Want anything special?"

Renee answered quickly, "Really Jerome, you don't have to get me anything." She picked up a hand towel to dry the few dishes on the rack.

Expenses were tight since Renee upgraded her car at the beginning of the year, but Jerome knew he had better get her something nice. He felt that the full-length mirror he put in her bathroom last year was a big hit and that Renee loved it! He had to top that for her thirty-fifth birthday.

Jerome didn't have much money saved and of the money he had left from his check every week, he only had enough to pay off an old debt and to buy one beer. Since Renee made more money, she managed and controlled the budget. He was responsible for all the utilities and tried hard to pay them on time. But, dating Taylor made paying bills on time difficult. The partial payments he'd made on his share of the bills had accumulated a large amount of late fees and interest. Jerome could've kicked himself. If his portion of the bills stayed current, Renee agreed to adjust the budget so that he could upgrade his Camry. Last night, he was up well past midnight figuring out how to catch up. If he disciplined himself enough, he could get current by Christmas and still get the new car. All he needed to do was make sure Renee didn't get hold of the past due statements.

Jerome didn't mind Renee handling the budget, like she often implied. Between the two of them, she was better at handling the important matters. He was only bothered when she used how much she made as a weapon. Like the night she reminded him that his name was not on the deed to the house.

Jerome didn't want to buy the house in the first place. It was outside of the city and a great deal more than they had originally agreed to spend. They could barely afford the down payment, but Renee had to have it. Jerome had refused to give his share of the deposit, believing Renee would get the hint and change her mind. But, she was just as stubborn and eventually cried the blues to her mother. As part of the agreement for paying the deposit, Renee's mother had one stipulation: Jerome's name was not to appear on the deed.

The sound of the coffee machine alerted Jerome that the coffee was ready. He poured a full cup into his mug and filled it with milk. Not as much milk as he would have liked, but enough to lighten the dark coffee. He could tell Renee was watching him. "Will this be enough?" Jerome held the milk jug in the air.

"That should be fine."

"Good." He grabbed his coffee and left the kitchen, "I'll be ready in a half."

Everyone piled into Jerome's car and the family headed to the Community Center. When they dropped the boys off at practice, Renee kissed Jerome Jr. and smiled as he dashed out of the car. Her face changed when she looked at Reggie. She gave him a small peck on the cheek and he slowly sauntered into the building.

"What's that about?" Jerome asked.

"What do you mean?" she answered, securing her seatbelt.

"You and Reggie?" Renee shrugged and Jerome probed a little more. "C'mon There's obviously something going on between you two. I might be able to help."

"The same way you helped him break up with Zora?"

Jerome sighed and pulled off, not wanting to pick a fight. "If there's anything I can do, please let me know." He turned the radio on and rolled down the windows.

The air coming into the car unraveled Renee's French roll a little. She pressed the button to roll the window some and tried to smooth her hair back into place. "I'll handle his education. You handle the sports."

"So, he's messing up in school?"

"I've got it under control."

"I should talk to him."

Renee twisted a strand of hair with her finger. "No need. Reggie and I have an understanding."

Jerome decided to leave it alone. If Renee needed his help, it would come out in an argument later. He popped in an old Gap Band CD and cruised down Germantown Pike. He and Renee were silent until he parked the car in the Wal Mart lot.

They walked through the parking lot with enough space between them for four people. "All I need is sweat socks. Then we can go," he said.

"I'm in no hurry."

Jerome shook his head and turned to keep from smiling. Renee was a trip.

"Hey, Jerome!" someone called from the Pep Boys located next to the Wal Mart.

Jerome looked in that direction and waved. A friend from his old neighborhood was leaning against a pole with two dogs. "We should go say hello," he said to Renee.

The two men greeted one another with handshakes and caught up on neighborhood gossip. Renee focused on the two dogs. They looked like miniature German shepherds.

"I saw Taylor last night on Hunting Park," the friend whispered. "She looked good. You still messing with her?"

Jerome shot him an angry look. "Man, do you not see my wife?"

"My fault," he replied. "I don't think she heard us."

Lucky for him, Renee was too consumed with the dogs to care about their conversation. Jerome didn't stick around to finish talking to his friend. He gave him the universal brotherly hug and said goodbye.

The mailman delivered the mail later than usual on Monday. Jerome hadn't expected to receive any after five o'clock, especially not the letter he'd thrown on the floor after opening it. He sat on the futon in the basement holding the phone in one hand and a shut off notice in the other. Nervously, he waited for the representative to come back on the line. The gas company had sent several warnings to the house, but with all that was going on, he had forgotten about them.

"Mr. Thomas," the representative said.

"Yes, I'm still here," Jerome replied.

"We reviewed your records. Since you've been consistently late with payments, the best we can do is make arrangements after you pay the last three months in full."

Jerome mumbled a few profanities under his breath. "How much would that be?"

"Twelve hundred forty-three fifty."

Jerome flinched. "I understand your position, but I have small children living here."

The representative heard excuses from customers all day. Jerome's story didn't change her mind. "But sir, you've been late for several months. We can't extend this any longer. Can you ask a family member or friend to help you?"

"If I could, I wouldn't be in this situation." Jerome's frustration was growing. "I'll call you back when I come up with some kind of plan."

"Okay, but if we don't hear from you by five o' clock eastern standard time, someone will be sent out to shut the gas off in the morning."

Renee is going to kill me, Jerome thought. The sweat from his hand was making the phone difficult to grip. He walked to his uniform thrown across his exercise bench and searched through the pockets for his wallet. "Do you accept Master Card?"

*   *   *

Jerome stomped upstairs in need of a drink. A nice cool beer would help control the panic that was developing. He opened the refrigerator and moved things around. He reached way in the back, hoping Renee had missed a bottle. No such luck. Jerome checked his watch to see how long he had until Renee came home and sighed. If Renee came straight home, she would be there in less than twenty minutes. Jerome decided to drink a glass of lemonade instead.

He walked in the living room, already halfway through the glass of lemonade. Jerome Jr. was on the couch watching television. "Where's your brother?" Jerome asked, looking around the room.

"He and Zora went to the family room to finish their homework."

Apparently, Renee had arranged for Zora to tutor Reggie in Geometry twice a week. He was sure Renee was hoping the two kids would get back together. But, according to Reggie, he and Zora were "just friends," and that was the way Jerome liked it. Jerome sat back and closed his eyes, then immediately jumped up. He walked to the back of the house and froze in place when he saw Reggie rubbing on Zora's thighs. The two teenagers were aggressively kissing one another in the middle of the floor.

"Boy, are you out of your mind?" Jerome yelled. Reggie and Zora jumped, frantically adjusting their clothes. "Your mother would hurt you, Zora, and me! Pull yourself together and get back in the living room. Better yet, do your homework in the dining room. And sit at opposite ends of the table!"

Reggie quickly grabbed the books he was supposed to be reading and charged out of the room, Zora racing behind him. Jerome sat on the edge of the couch when they were gone. He took a huge gulp of lemonade and swished it around in his mouth. He felt like he was losing control of his life. He was certain other shut off notices were on their way. And if he wasn't careful, Reggie would be having sex before he was ready. Before Renee could get to him, it was time for Jerome to have another man to man talk with his son.

Jerome looked around the room and discovered an old storage cabinet he had built when he was drinking heavily. He walked over to it and opened the bottom drawer. He pushed past a few binders and old folders and found his secret stash. He pulled out the bottle of Bacardi and mixed it with the rest of his lemonade.

12

Taylor

After singing the last note of Bobby and Whitney's, "We've Got Something in Common," Taylor and Lance bowed to an applauding audience. It was the first time either of them had performed at Karaoke Night. Though they were both off key and fumbled through most of the lyrics, they enjoyed themselves and gave their captive audience a true Bobby and Whitney performance.

Taylor was surprised at how smooth the night had progressed. Lance was the perfect gentleman. They danced and talked about their interest in music, art, and fashion. He seemed impressed when Taylor shared her dreams about opening an urban boutique.

"So tell me," Taylor said once settled in their booth, "why did we stop dating?"

Lance put down the cranberry juice mixed with Ginger Ale that was in his hand. "That's easy. I can sum it up in two words. Casey Moore."

Taylor had to think about that for a minute. When the memories finally surfaced, her hand flew over her mouth. Casey Moore helped her move into her first apartment. They had an instant chemistry and dated for several months after they met. By the time they broke up, Lance was long forgotten.

"You remember now?"

"Wow, that was too bad. Casey was a jerk."

"You dumped me for a jerk?"

"I seem to have a habit of making bad decisions," Taylor said, recalling the men of her past.

"Like Jerome?" Lance questioned and Taylor's jaw dropped. "Close your mouth. I don't think anyone else knows. I overheard you and Kara talking in the hallway the other day," he assured her.

Taylor was afraid to ask, but needed to know. "How much did you hear?"

He reached across the table for her hand. "We don't have to talk about it. I don't want him to ruin the night." Lance stood up and pulled her up with him. "Besides, I'd rather dance."

Taylor willfully followed him to the dance floor, hoping her relationship with Jerome had not bruised Lance's perception of her.

Lance pulled up along side of Taylor's Ford Explorer and rolled down his passenger window. "You didn't have to follow me home," she said, happy that he did.

"I know, but you can never be too safe. I wouldn't have been able to live with myself if you had an accident."

Taylor blushed, "You're so sweet. Well . . . umm . . . I-I had a nice time." Her body wanted to invite him inside, but she knew it was too soon, nor did she want to mess up the evening.

"I did, too. You working tomorrow?"

Taylor tapped the edge of the window. "Yeah, but not until two. I'm doing Kara a favor."

"Oh." Lance looked around the neighborhood. "Nice street you live on."

"Yeah, it's pretty quiet around here." Taylor took a deep

breath. *Maybe we can just talk.* "Would you like to come in? I can make you some coffee or tea or . . ."

Lance laughed, "I can come up for a drink. I guess I should find a parking space."

Taylor nervously watched Lance squeeze his silver Maxima into a space across the street then got out of her own car. She walked to the door of her apartment building and waited for him to join her.

"I live on the third floor. I hope you're in shape."

"Good thing I don't have asthma," Lance replied.

By the time they reached Taylor's door, she was hot and out of breath. It had to be her nerves. She did this everyday and rarely with any problems breathing. Lance, on the other hand appeared relaxed; not one bead of sweat in sight.

Taylor unlocked the door and immediately opened the windows in the living room. "It's so stuffy in here. Aren't you hot?" she asked, trying to calm herself. "Make yourself comfortable. I'm going to get us something cool to drink."

In the kitchen, Taylor leaned against the refrigerator until her body stopped shaking. Once her nerves relaxed a little, she poured Ginger Ale in two tall glasses and returned to her guest. "This is the best I could do for now, unless you want some water."

"This is fine," Lance said, accepting the drink. "I see you're a Batman fan."

Taylor had the complete DVD collection of the original Batman series. She was in the process of completing the movie and cartoon collection. "Batman is mysterious," she said, as if she was defending her fascination with the superhero.

"So, you like mysterious men?"

"That depends on the situation," she replied, still a little nervous. "Feel like watching one?"

"Maybe another time. I don't want to keep you up too late."

"A real gentleman," Taylor smiled.

Lance blushed, "I have something to do early tomorrow morning."

"Let me guess," Taylor said with disappointment in her voice. "You and your *girlfriend* have plans."

"I'm going to church with my mother," he stated, sensing the change in Taylor's demeanor. "There is no *girlfriend*."

Lance hung around for another hour and they made plans to attend a movie the following weekend. At the door, Lance leaned in for a kiss just as the phone rang. "Jerome's checking in," he joked, pecking her cheek.

"Real funny," she said, secretly hoping he was right. "Drive home safely."

As soon as she shut the door, Taylor ran toward to the phone, bumping her knee on the coffee table. She winced a little, and dove on the sofa where the cordless phone was laying. "Hello," she huffed.

"Hey, girl. What you doing?" Taylor was somewhat disappointed that it was Sherry.

"Nothing, just about to go to bed." Taylor rubbed her knee.

"How was your date?"

"Great."

"Is that all you have to say?" Sherry asked. "You sound out of breath. Is he still there or something?"

"No, he just left. I had to run to the phone before the answering machine picked up."

"Then the date wasn't all that great." Sherry laughed at her own response.

"He has to get up early in the morning."

Sherry let out a puff of air, "That's just a line they use. It's reverse psychology. They think you'll be so charmed by them leaving early, that the next time you'll beg them to stay."

"I don't know. Lance doesn't seem like the type," she said, trying to pinpoint any suspicious behavior.

"You didn't think Jerome was the type either," Sherry reminded her.

"Ouch."

"You know I didn't mean anything by it," Sherry added, realizing she had hurt her feelings. "Oh, before I forget. I saw your boy at Wal Mart today with his arm around his wife. They must be on good terms now, huh?"

Taylor felt a pain shoot through her heart. "I hate to cut you off, but I need to get some sleep."

"Sure, I'm sorry. I see I've upset you again."

"No, it's not that," Taylor lied. "Lance and I danced all night. I'm really tired."

"Okay, but I'll be up for a while if you want to talk."

Taylor hung up and rolled on her back. The reality of Jerome's lies hit hard. He and his wife were not at odds, and communication was obviously not lacking. Jerome and Renee should not have been prancing around Wal Mart looking like lovebirds. According to Jerome, they were not in love.

Taylor reached for a small pillow and hugged it. She thought about Lance. How could she be sure he wasn't like Jerome or any of the others?

Taylor dragged her body into the bathroom. Troubled by her reflection in the mirror, she opened a bottle of extra-strength Tylenol. She shook two pills in her hand and looked in the mirror again. She had a headache from crying all night, and her eyes were puffy and looked as if several blood vessels had burst. She secured the pills in the palm of her hand, and took the entire bottle of Tylenol to the kitchen. If her eyes were still puffy in an hour, she would have to search for her shades. Taylor couldn't go to work looking like she had been in a boxing match.

Taylor noticed the flashing light on the answering machine. All of the crying she did last night must have sent her into a deep sleep. She hit the play button.

"You have three new messages," the automated voice on the answering machine bellowed. *Beep* . . .

"Tay, I know you're upset, but call me back, please." Sherry whined into the machine. *Beep* . . .

"Hey Taylor, are you *still* asleep?" Lance's deep voice resonated through the kitchen. Taylor sat her glass of water on the table as she listened to him speak. "I just wanted to say good morning. I'll try you back later." *Beep* . . .

"It's me, Taylor. Don't forget you're working today. I owe you big time." Kara dropped her phone and fumbled for a few seconds trying to put it back to her ear. "Sorry about that. I'm on my way to church. Love you. Oh yeah, how was the date? Call me, girl."

"End of new messages." *Beep Beep* . . .

Taylor gulped down two pain relievers and sat in the living room. It was 10:30. She was usually up by 8:00. She gently tapped her right eye and flinched. *This can't be healthy.* Taylor flipped on the television and finished her glass of water. A pastor from a mega church on the west coast was in the middle of a sermon.

"You can wear fancy clothes, change your hair and buy expensive things and still be a mess inside. You can't get around pain by covering it up. You've got to call it out, look it in the eye, and demand that it go away in Jesus's name," the pastor said as he walked to the end of the pulpit and looked directly into the monitor. "You want to know how to get out of the slump you're in? Don't let your issues control your life." He pointed to the screen and Taylor could almost feel his finger in her chest. "Instead, you beloved, have to take control over your issues."

Taylor quickly pressed the power button. *Is God trying to send me a message?* She stared at the blank TV screen, trembling. The sermon frightened Taylor. She didn't have a close relationship with God. Truth be told, the only time she set foot in a church was for funerals and weddings. She wasn't sure if her mother had a relationship with God either. She was too busy chasing her father around the city.

Her hand still shaking, Taylor placed her glass on the table and picked up a photo of her mother. She had died over six years ago. Doctors said her mother suffered from a heart attack, but Taylor knew the real reason for her untimely death. Her mother had passed away from a broken heart. Since she could remember, her parents were on again off again lovers. When her father was finally ready to settle down and commit to one woman, it was with someone else.

Taylor's mother tried everything she could to stop the wedding from taking place, but all her attempts had failed. Her father was determined to marry a woman he met during a four day trip to Canada. Taylor wasn't allowed to go to the wedding. Instead, her mother made her sit through reruns of *Mash*, while eating Little Debbie cakes and Twinkies.

Taylor's head started to throb again. She put the picture down and swallowed two more Tylenol. Closing her eyes, Taylor allowed herself to rest so the medicine could kick in. The phone rang, disturbing her peace, and she decided to let the answering machine pick up.

"Hi, this is Taylor," the recorded message sounded. "I can't come to the phone right now, but please leave a message."

After the beep there was a short stretch of silence. Faint winds of someone breathing could be heard, but the person on the other end didn't say anything. Taylor was about to lay flat on the sofa, believing it was a prank caller or wrong number, when she heard a man's voice. Her eyes popped open.

"Taylor, I-I just wanted to say hello. I guess I'll see you around," Jerome said and hung up.

Taylor's gut told her not to return his call, but she couldn't control herself. She jumped off the couch and snatched the cordless off its base. She dialed Jerome's number quickly and held her breath. His phone rang once . . . then twice . . . then three times, and after the fourth ring it went straight into voicemail. Taylor grunted and jammed the phone back in its base.

13

Renee

Renee waited nervously in the conference room for Mr. Kotlarczyk. He wanted to meet with her privately before the top executives arrived. Although sales had been great the past year, job security was not promised. They were both nervous. A sister company in New York, also in good standing, went through a reorganization two years ago. Several managers were replaced or moved to a different hotel. Renee understood the logic behind the changes, but prayed her building wouldn't be affected in that way.

Mr. Kotlarczyk walked into the conference room dressed in his best suit. "Good morning, Renee. You look lovely."

"Thank you. A little gift from my husband," Renee smirked. "You look nice, too. Pin stripes work well on you."

"So," he began, and sat in the chair at the head of the long table, "are we ready for this?"

"I've been over the budget a hundred times. I had Bianca check behind me three times. I think everyone will be impressed by what we've done."

"Not too impressed I hope. Marcel called this morning. He

wants to have a word with me before the meeting," Mr. Kotlar-czyk said. "That worries me."

Renee was worried too, but hid her concerns. "I'm sure it's not what you're thinking."

"I hope you're right, Renee. My wife will divorce me if we have to relocate. She put a lot of work into our house." Mr. Kotlarczyk looked at his Rolex. "Okay, my dear. I'm sure you've done an out-standing job with the report. I'll see you back here in less than an hour."

"I'll be ready."

While Renee waited for the guests to arrive, she inspected the hotel to make sure nothing was strange or out of place. Bianca had made sure the conference room was set to perfection. Since many of the executives were originally from other cities and countries, Bianca ordered Philadelphia-related refreshments— hot pretzels, water ice, Tasty Kake assortments, Herr's potato chips, mini cheese steaks and hoagies, and Frank's flavored sodas. En-larged photographs of Philadelphia monuments complimented the arrangement. Guests were sure to recognize the pride the staff had for the city.

Renee was startled by a light touch on her shoulder. "Our guests have arrived," Bianca said, full of excitement.

"Already," Renee replied, looking at the clock on the wall. "Everything looks wonderful, Bianca. Thanks so much for all of your hard work."

"I'm glad you like it." Bianca walked to the dessert table and lifted the linen cloth. She pulled out a cooler from under the table. "I hid some of your favorite waters down here."

Renee's eyes lit up. "You know me so well." She opened the Dasani bottle and swallowed a mouthful. "This is good stuff."

"Here they come," Bianca warned, taking the bottled water from Renee's grip. "You look great. Go get 'em!"

Renee buttoned the jacket to her suit and walked to the door to greet the guests as they entered. She counted fifteen people. More than what was expected. Before panic could set in, Renee said a quick prayer to help her relax. She could tell that her staff was a little uneasy as well. They were unusually quiet as they mingled with the guests.

While they waited for Mr. Kotlarczyk, Renee had Bianca run additional copies of the presentations. She didn't want anyone to be left without one. They waited for almost thirty minutes before Mr. Kotlarczyk stepped into the conference room. Marcel Engleton, founder and CEO of the Luxury Inn hotel chain, strolled in behind him with two other men. The look on Mr. Kotlarczyk's face spoke volumes. No one else may have noticed the strained look, but Renee knew him too well. She could almost always tell what he was thinking without asking. He walked straight to Renee. "We're ready when you are."

Renee walked to the front podium. By this time her feet were throbbing, thanks to her monthly water gain and swollen feet, but her confident stride said otherwise. Her chocolate double-breasted suit accentuated her curves and did wonders to hide the extra pounds hidden underneath. Pleased that everything was under control, she welcomed everyone and reviewed the agenda for the day.

Mr. Kotlarczyk was the first to speak to the group. He discussed the year at a glance, highlighting the accomplishments of the hotel. Renee was paying attention to his words, making sure to take notes in case someone asked her questions at the end of the day. She prided herself in being knowledgeable and prepared. As she jotted key points on her notepad, she could sense someone watching her from across the table. She casually looked up to find Everett Coleman, chief operating officer, staring in her direction. Renee wasn't sure, but he seemed to have more than business in his eyes. She smiled, just enough for him to understand that she was being polite; nothing more. She focused back on her boss, raising her left hand so that her wedding ring was in plain view, and scribbled unimportant words on her notepad. There was no time to entertain whatever thoughts were going through his head.

When Mr. Kotlarczyk finished, he re-introduced Renee. She could feel Everett's eyes piercing through her body and tried not to let him distract her. Going over the finances for her department was an important task. There was no room for error. She looked into the medium-sized audience and encouraged herself. *I can do this. This is a piece of cake.*

Renee sailed through the Power Point presentation like a true professional, asking and answering questions with confidence. When she was done, Everett initiated a round of applause. She looked at Mr. Kotlarczyk and he winked. "Terrific job," he mouthed from his seat.

"I'd like to thank everyone for being so attentive and patient with me. Now that we have taken up a couple of hours of your time, we have a small treat for you," Renee said as she walked toward the refreshment tables. "Our wonderful intern has organized a welcome-to-Philadelphia lunch. Please browse each table and enjoy the delights prepared especially for you."

The guests were surprised and eager to enjoy the treats. For some, it was the first time they had tasted the famous Philly cheesesteaks. Renee waited for everyone to make their plates before standing in line. When most of the guests were seated and eating, she strolled over to the hoagie table and placed her index finger over her lips.

"I hear the Italian hoagies are the best," Everett offered, standing next to Renee with a plate full of food.

"Have you tried almost everything here?" she laughed, examining his plate.

"I don't want to miss a thing this fine city has to offer. So far, I haven't been disappointed," he said, placing an Italian hoagie on his plate. Was this man flirting with her? It had been years since someone was this obvious.

"I'm glad everything is to your approval." Renee couldn't control her blushing, and didn't quite understand what she was feeling inside. "I think I'll get a cheese steak," she said. "Enjoy your lunch." As Renee walked away, she was careful not to stumble over her aching feet.

After lunch, the meeting was placed in the hands of the top executives. Marcel Engleton stood before his employees, knowing the news he had to share would upset them. The room was motionless as the Philadelphia staff awaited the news. Renee silently prayed that any changes, if some were to be made, were going to make her life better, and not just for her, but for her children as well.

"Thank you, Mr. Kotlarczyk, for all of your hospitality," Mr. Engleton stated. "What a wonderful way to welcome us to this city. The manner in which you and your employees have handled this meeting says a lot about the way you manage this hotel." Mr. Engleton tried to adjust the microphone on the podium. He was shorter than the average man and needed the mic positioned a little lower. "Before we make the announcement I'm sure you all have been waiting for, I'd like to ask Everett to come forward."

Renee tried not to stare at Everett, but his presence had a way of commanding attention. He looked like a king in his finely tailored suit. Renee wished Jerome was more polished. Funerals were the only occasion she could convince him to wear a suit. He didn't even want to wear them to church. Jerome took the "Come as you are," saying to heart.

"As you all know, Everett has been with this company for ten years. In this time, he has been credited with the management of all the hotels on the west coast and in the last three years, the east coast hotels were added. He has a unique gift for this business." Mr. Engleton fiddled with the microphone again. Renee thought that was a sign of nervousness. *Not a good thing.*

"I may not look like I'm getting older," he paused as the people in the room chuckled, "but I'm going to need someone to help me stay on top of things. I've selected Everett to be that person.

And, as his first order of business, he's going tell you all about the future of Luxury Inn." A round of applause filled the room as Everett approached the podium.

"I'll get right to the point, since I'm sure many of you are on the edge of your seats." Everett's voice was striking and exerted authority. "We've been thinking of ways to expand our business. After several months of research, we've decided to open a grand hotel in Chicago. This hotel will include such things as a deluxe spa, an upscale hair salon, retails shops, a restaurant, and rooms more spacious and elegant than the ones we have now. To make this successful, we'll need the help of our finest and best employees." Everett looked in Renee's direction and her body tingled. Renee wasn't sure where he was headed yet, so she took in every word carefully. "Now, we can clearly see that you have a great team here. We don't want to change that, but the Chicago project is huge. We need to be wise when thinking about the long term revenue."

"So, people are going to lose their jobs?" the accounting manager blurted.

Unaffected by the outburst, Everett looked the manager straight in the eye and addressed his concern. "I realize that this may be a difficult pill to swallow, but we're really trying to find ways to save everyone's job."

"Basically, what you're saying is, there are no guarantees," the front desk manager interrupted.

"Unfortunately, very few things in life are," Everett responded, still with no sign of fear.

Unlike her colleagues, Renee raised her hand to acknowledge that she had something to say. Everett smiled with his eyes, "Mrs. Thomas."

"I want to point out the high staff morale in this hotel. That's what makes us special and successful. If you cut positions, you would increase the workload of the remaining employees. Morale will definitely suffer. I hope you take that into consideration."

Applause from her colleagues let Renee know that she was on point. She leaned back in her seat focusing on nothing in particular. *God, what next?*

Renee pulled into the driveway, still thinking about what happened at the meeting. With her high-powered shoes in one hand and a briefcase in the other, she walked into the house barefoot. She could hear Jerome's power tools, which only meant that he was working on something. Renee followed the noise into the kitchen, praying things were still in tact. Jerome was sitting atop the stove fixing a hanging light.

"Hey, babe," he said, adjusting the fixture. "How was your day?"

"Fine," Renee said, leaning against the door. She looked at him, wanting a hug or soft kisses to reassure her that everything would turn out fine. More than anything, at this moment, Renee needed her husband, but she didn't know how to verbalize it. And after seventeen years of marriage, she felt she shouldn't have to. He should know what she needed just by one glance. *If he didn't spend so much time getting to know Taylor . . .* Renee stopped herself before she became even more aggravated. "Where are the boys?"

A wrench fell on Jerome's bare foot and he mumbled in pain. "Reggie wanted to go to practice a little early. Junior tagged along," she said in agony.

"He's been doing a lot of socializing lately."

"He's growing up. Friends are important to him now." Jerome struggled to hold the light in place and Renee jumped to his aid without thinking.

"He's growing up too fast if you ask me. He still hasn't made up with Zora?"

"Is that a bad thing?" he asked, tightening a screw.

"Zora's a nice girl."

Jerome looked at her sideways. "She was here the other day. They were studying."

"I meant to mention that to you," she said, knowing Jerome was upset that she had not communicated that earlier. "Reggie needs some extra help in math."

"I guess you think they're gonna get back together, huh?" he questioned.

"Please," she began, "I never wanted him to date in the first place, remember? I just want him to get good grades."

"Yeah, well, I told Reggie that he has plenty of time for girls. He doesn't need anything to distract him from the NBA."

Renee shot Jerome a piercing look. "So now you agree that he should wait to have a girlfriend? Or are you saying that he should play the field?"

Finished with the project, Jerome sat at the table and rubbed his left foot with the right one. "I'm saying he needs to focus on basketball. Is something wrong with that?"

"Just be sure basketball is what Reggie wants to focus on. He should follow *his* dreams, not yours," Renee retorted. "And, I don't want him to have twisted views of women, or life for that matter."

Jerome seemed a little startled. "Is everything okay at the office? You seem a little uptight."

Renee didn't want to share the details of the meeting. She doubted he'd really understand anyway. "I guess you forgot about the meeting I had today."

Jerome was silent, which meant he had forgotten. Renee walked around him and grabbed a bottle of water from under the sink. Her blood was boiling and she knew it wasn't entirely Jerome's fault. Renee thought it was best that she leave before she said things she didn't really mean. "Can you pick up the boys after practice?"

"Only if you agree to go upstairs and take a long bath."

Is that the best he could do to calm me? she thought, drinking half the water in just three gulps. *I bet if my name was Tay . . .* She grabbed her briefcase and left before her impulses made her hit him with it.

* * *

Renee blew on the suds that covered her. Being submerged in warm water did wonders to her tired body. The mellow tunes of Maxwell's "Fortunate" could have done wonders to her soul if she and Jerome were a happy couple.

Living under the same roof was becoming harder as each day passed. But Renee knew she had to stick it out for the boys. Though sometimes, she wondered if the current situation was doing more harm than good. Somehow the bickering between Renee and Jerome didn't seem fair to the children. The boys didn't need to hear or see how unhappy their parents really were. As husband and wife, they weren't even sleeping in the same room. What kind of example was that for Reggie and Jerome Jr. to follow? Renee wanted them to grow up with a better image of what marriage should be like.

I should have pushed him to go to college. Maybe then he would've been a different man. Jerome was never enthusiastic about education. Basketball was his only motivation for staying in high school. When his basketball career didn't take off as planned, Jerome never thought twice about attending college. College without basketball would have been torture for him. Renee agreed with his decision, but only because he had alternate goals. He was going to run a basketball league for the kids in the city. He was off to a good start until Renee got pregnant her senior year of college. With a baby on the way, he was forced to use the free time he had to juggle between a second full-time job; a job her mother helped him get.

Reggie was born two months after Renee graduated from Temple University with honors. They were excited about their son, but even Jerome's second income didn't improve their finances by much. They had another mouth to feed and desperately needed to find a place bigger than their three-room apartment. Something had to change.

Neither of them wanted to turn to their parents. Renee's mother would've helped, but not without reminding her of the mistake she made marrying Jerome. Jerome's parents would not have been as supportive. His parents traveled at least twice a year, yet whenever Renee and Jerome needed help, they claimed they were broke.

Renee believed his parents did this to punish her. They blamed Renee for Jerome's career-ending injury. "If he wasn't so blinded by love, he would've been more concerned about playing in the NBA," his mother jokingly reminded everyone at every family gathering. They acted as if she had damaged Jerome's knee with her bare hands.

On most occasions, Jerome came to her defense. And for a time, Renee actually thought he was genuinely proud of her. In the beginning, he enjoyed the fruits of her labor. "Baby, we're in this together for life!" he'd say after an expensive gift or extravagant meal. But that all changed the day he couldn't cover the cost of a grocery bill.

That afternoon Renee stood at the end of the counter putting bags in the cart. Loud growls, harsh moans and a few clicking teeth caused her to stop what she was doing. Renee could tell Jerome was short on their bill by the way he was fumbling around in his jacket pockets. The growing line behind them was becoming antsy, and in an effort to avoid embarrassment, Renee went into her purse and handed the cashier fifty dollars. "This should cover it." Renee smiled at her husband. But, instead of a thank you or heart-felt embrace, Jerome gave her the cold shoulder. "I thought we were in this together for life?" she asked him later that night.

Jerome looked at her with a blank stare. "I guess you're the head of the house now."

Forgetting about when her marriage took a turn for the worse, Renee closed her eyes and let Maxwell's voice send her into a tranquil state. She only had fifteen minutes until the boys came home. She'd have to think about her marriage later.

14

Jerome

Jerome looked at the clock and counted the hours until he could go home. He signed up to work double shifts until he was caught up on his share of the household bills. He also needed the extra hours to buy Renee a present for her birthday. Though Jerome didn't understand why he was considering buying her a gift at all. She'd been getting on his nerves all week with her sarcastic comments and foul mood, not to mention the fact that he was still living in the basement.

The scent of a familiar perfume shifted Jerome's thoughts. He turned from the engine he was working on and saw Taylor walk by. Lance was by her side. Watching them, Jerome's temples jumped.

Taylor looked great, even sexier than before, just as his friend at Pep Boys had said. Images of the nights they shared together surfaced and he fought back the urge to confront them. He wiped his oily hands on his pants then hit his forehead with his hands repeatedly. "Taylor is no longer my woman," he said to himself until the images disappeared. He reached into his pocket for his cell phone and called the only woman he should be giving his attention to. Even if she didn't want it. The phone rang two times. "Hey, beautiful."

"Hey, Jerome. What's up?" Renee said, rushing her words, which meant that she was in the middle of something important.

"Just thinking about you. You've had some rough nights."

"I guess I should apologize."

"No need to. I understand that you're stressed right now."

Taylor's laugh across the depot distracted Jerome's conversation, causing him to look in her direction. Taylor was leaning against her bus and glaring into Lance's eyes. Jerome wondered if Lance was enjoying her in the same way that he had.

"You up for some seafood tonight?" Jerome asked Renee, still studying Taylor.

"Get some Alaskan crab legs from Sam and Pete's. And don't forget . . ."

"The extra butter sauce, right?"

"Can't forget the butter sauce. I guess my hips will survive the extra calories. I'll have to start working out."

"I like you just the way you are," he affirmed.

A brief pause followed his compliment. "I have to go. Mr. Kotlarczyk just walked in."

Jerome hung up the phone and went back to work. Maybe tonight would be a good night to ignite the spark they once had.

15

Renee

Lying to Jerome used to be easy, but for some reason, Renee felt guilty about it today. Mr. Kotlarczyk wasn't in her office and she hadn't expected to see him for at least another hour.

Jerome's call made her nervous. His recent attitude change made her nervous. He was being too nice, which raised many questions. What had happened to Taylor? Was she still around? Where did they meet? Was she older? Younger? Whatever the answers, at this point it really didn't matter. Taylor could have him because Renee was positive she wanted a divorce. She was just waiting for the right time.

Knowing that Jerome wouldn't be part of her future made living under the same roof a little easier. No more sleeping under the goose down pillows to drown out his loud snores or playing tug of war with the sheets. As far as Renee was concerned, Jerome would never sleep in her room again. She slept much better without him.

Before the meeting with her boss, Renee browsed through her proposal. Renee had memorized every detail. The Luxury Inn had already gained a great reputation in Philly, now it was time to take it to a higher level. The sports lounge she and Mr. Kotlar-czyk developed many years ago was still a thriving portion of the hotel. It was now time to enhance the experience of the guests by adding a fitness center. Before the threat of lay offs, she had asked her boss about adding a space for guests to exercise. She was surprised to learn that he was still interested and wanted to hear her ideas.

As she approached his office, several voices echoed from the room. She thought this was supposed to be a private meeting. Renee pressed her ear to the door but could not make out whom the voices belonged to. Nervously, she knocked on the door.

"It's open," called Mr. Kotlarczyk.

Renee turned the knob and the first person she saw made her heart flutter. Everett was seated across from Mr. Kotlarczyk dressed in another expensive suit. Mr. Engleton sat in the corner of the room, holding several files in his hands. *Why would they want me to be a part of this meeting?*

"Renee, have a seat. Marcel and Everett are going to join our discussion."

Beads of sweat formed across Renee's forehead as she sat in the chair next to Everett. She crossed her legs and folded her hands neatly in her lap. She looked at Mr. Kotlarczyk for a sign that this might be her farewell meeting. His wrinkle-free brow let Renee know that he was not stressed. Still, she was anxious.

"Glad to see you again, Renee. We're looking forward to hearing your proposal," Everett said, displaying his pearly whites.

Renee tried not to look his way too long, but this was the first time she had a chance to examine him at close range. The richness of his deep, cocoa brown skin held her attention. She had seen his picture dozens of times in the company newsletter, but the photos chosen for that didn't do the man any justice. He was fine! His perfectly manicured hands rested on the arms of the chair; his left hand void of any jewelry, in particular a wedding band. Only a bracelet full of enough diamonds to brighten a room hung from his wrist. Renee's eyes roamed to the floor, where she noticed his size thirteen shoe, made of good leather, and with a Gucci engraved metal bar across the top. The man had a great sense of style.

Surprisingly, Mr. Engleton's presence didn't bother her as much. It was Everett that caused her thoughts to become jumbled and out of place. After all, he was the future HNIC, Head Negro in Charge. Renee opened her binder to the outline she had prepared as a study guide. "I'm sorry gentleman," she said, with a mild tremor. "I didn't make enough copies of the proposal." She handed Mr. Kotlarczyk a copy.

Mr. Engelton sat back in the chair. "No, problem. I have a great memory."

"And whatever he forgets," interjected Everett with amusement, "I'll remember."

Renee nervously responded, "Okay," and began her presentation. Using her outline as a guide, she stressed the value of adding a fitness center to the hotel.

As she spoke, Everett's eyes never wavered from her face. And to her surprise, Renee didn't feel uncomfortable or nervous. Everett clearly oozed power from his pours, but the vibe that she was feeling was gentle, and it propelled her to continue with ease. By the time she finished, she knew she had captivated all three men.

"As we move into this new era, gentlemen," Renee spoke, "we want to strive for excellence." She turned to face Mr. Engleton. "It may not be the grand hotel that you're planning in Chicago, but with this and a few other ideas I have, this Philadelphia hotel will not be far behind."

"Mr. Kotlarczyk," Mr. Engelton said, in a friendly manner; "you have a very smart and motivated young lady on your team."

"She is the best there is," Mr. Kotlarczyk agreed.

"You've really done your research," Everett said, seriously. "And, that's why we're here." His warm eyes locked with Renee's.

"We could really use your talents in Chicago." A strange energy passed through her body as he continued to speak. "We'd like to offer you the general manager position in Chicago."

Stunned by the offer, Renee was speechless. A million thoughts raced through her mind.

"There is a significant increase in salary and benefits," Everett added. "Of course, we'd pay for you and your family's relocation as well."

"Everett will be there for about seven months, maybe longer to help you get adjusted," Mr. Engleton added. "But after that, he'll return to the main office in California and the hotel will be in your hands."

Renee looked at Mr. Kotlarczyk. "It's really a great opportunity, Renee," he said. "You'd be foolish to pass this up."

"I-I- I don't know what to say," she managed to say.

"Say yes," Mr. Engleton said. "We know you have children, so we're thinking you could fly out to Chicago for a few days next month to meet everyone. Then, let's say the second week of July, you could start there full-time. How does that sound?"

Everett cleared his throat and spoke, "This should give you enough time to make the transition."

"Will anyone here lose their job?" she asked, concerned.

"It'll be a stretch, but if we can convince a few people to relocate, I don't think we'll need to cut positions," Everett said bluntly. "So, what do you think?"

Everett stood up and walked to the corner of the room. He picked up a folder from a small table and walked back to Renee, stopping less than a foot in front of her. Renee held her breath as his six-foot frame hovered over her. The thought of working so closely with Everett intrigued her and she wanted to accept the offer on the spot. But, instead she said, "Can you give me a few days?"

"Of course, Renee," Everett smiled, exposing his stunningly white and perfectly straight teeth. "Take this with you. We've put together an overview. You might find it helpful when making your decision."

Back in her office, Renee kicked off her shoes and leaped in the air. She tipped over a lamp by the door and it crashed to the floor. Bianca heard the noise and rushed in the office. "You okay?"

Renee picked up the lamp and noticed a crack in the base. "I'm fine," she said and jumped in the air again, this time careful not to touch the lamp. "I can't believe what just happened."

Bianca jumped, too. "Did he approve your ideas?" Renee shook her head. "Then what is it?" she asked, confused.

"They asked *me* to be the General Manager of the new Chicago hotel," she whispered.

Bianca screamed and hugged Renee. "I'm so happy for you!"

"Shhh, I didn't accept the offer yet," she replied softly and closed the door.

"But you are, aren't you?"

"It sounds like the perfect job, but I really need to think about it first. I wouldn't actually start until July."

"It's already May and June will fly by." Bianca was excited. "You have to say yes," she pleaded, "so I can come with you. I hear Mr. Coleman is overseeing the project. And, he's single."

"Everett is too old for you," Renee smirked, as the image of Everett popped into her head. Like Bianca and dozens of other women, she was drawn to his strength and character.

"He probably has a girlfriend anyway," Bianca sighed. "So, what's there to think about?"

Renee walked to the window of her office. *What is there to think about? This could be my ticket out of my marriage.*

Jerome was vacuuming the inside of his car when Renee pulled up to the house. Jerome Jr. jumped out as soon as Renee shut off the engine. "Dad, we're going to Rita's after dinner."

Jerome looked surprised. Renee rarely allowed sweets during the week. "What's the occasion?"

Renee wasn't ready to tell them about the job offer, so she told a half-truth, "I had a stress-free day."

"I'll eat to that! Why don't I pick up the water ices on my way back from Sam and Pete's?" he offered.

"Get some mussels and shrimp, too," Renee added, reaching inside her purse for money.

Jerome covered her hands. "I told you . . . I'm treating tonight. Put your money away."

Renee closed her purse and walked into the house before Jerome could change his mind.

While Jerome was out getting dinner, Renee helped the boys with their homework. "Repeat the steps one more time," Renee said. Reggie had a test on photosynthesis in the morning and she wanted to make sure he passed.

Reggie huffed a few times, but did as he was told. "First, the sun . . ." The phone rang and Reggie cheered, anxious to answer it.

"I'll get that," Renee said, signaling for Reggie to stay put. "And, if it's for you, I'm gonna tell them to call back tomorrow."

"Mom," he moaned.

Renee leaned back in her chair just enough to grab the cordless laying on the table. "Hello," she said and tossed Reggie his study guide to review.

"Sister Thomas, this is Mother Wagner," the voice said from the other end of the phone.

"Hi," Renee said, sitting up straight in her chair. "How are you?"

"Blessed," she said. "Listen, I thought I should bring something to your attention."

Mother Wagner didn't always call with bad news, but tonight the lull in her voice indicated that there was a problem. The happiness Renee felt all day fell a few notches. She prepared herself to hear something about Jerome. Perhaps Mother Wagner had seen him with Taylor. She motioned for Reggie to go in the other room. "What's wrong?"

"You know how much I love Reggie, and I'm only mentioning this because I don't want to see him go down the wrong road." Renee's heart started to beat a little faster. "I talked to him last week about this, but I caught him cutting school again today and . . ."

"What do you mean?" Renee was stunned. "Jerome and I drop him off and pick him up everyday."

"I know, that's why I wanted to make you aware of what was taking place at school. He's been sneaking out of the building after homeroom and coming back before the last bell rings."

Renee couldn't believe her ears. "How long has this been going on?"

"I caught him once last week, so I'm not sure."

"Thanks, Mother Wagner. I'll take care of this tonight."

"Renee, I know you're upset. If Reggie were my child I'd want to knock his head off, too," she said. "Please, pray first."

Renee hung up the phone and prayed she wouldn't draw blood. "Reggie! Reggie, get in here!" she screeched.

Reggie ran to his mother and his little brother followed. "Mommy, what's wrong?" Jerome Jr. asked.

"Go to your room right now," she told Jerome Jr. He was frightened by the tone in her voice and started to cry.

"Why? What happened?" asked Jerome Jr.

"Get upstairs, Junior!"

"You better go," Reggie told him, and Jerome Jr. ran upstairs quickly and in tears. Reggie stood in the middle of the floor, afraid to move.

"Before you can come up with a lie, that was your school on the phone. You've been cutting school?" Renee remained in her seat for fear of what she might do to him. "Where have you been going?" Reggie began to shake. "Boy, you better start talking and I mean you better start right now!"

"Manny's house!" he blurted and took a step back.

"Who the heck is Manny, and what are you doing at his house?"

"My teammate," Reggie answered, tears now rolling down his cheek. "We play video games and stuff."

"Are girls there?" Renee asked, afraid of what he might say.

Jerome walked in with dinner and immediately felt the tension. "What's going on?" he asked.

"I thought we had an agreement," Renee continued talking to Reggie, her leg bouncing rapidly. "I don't need to remind you that you're off the team. You can thank the new clowns you've been hanging around for that."

"But, Mom, I don't do it all the time. It's only been three times." Reggie looked at his father for help, his eyes begging for a counter to the punishment Renee just gave him.

"I don't care if it was only one time, Reggie. You know better than that. I warned you this would happen." Renee stopped talking long enough to look at Jerome standing in the middle of the floor holding dinner. "And quit looking at your father! This is between me and you. Now, answer me!" she demanded. "Any girls at his house?" Reggie stared at a coffee stain in the carpet. "Don't play with me, boy! Answer my question," she voiced and jumped to her feet. Reggie fell back into the wall, not sure if he should run. "Are girls there? And, don't lie!"

"Just once," he mumbled.

"If I find out that you've been smoking and drinking, or that you've been having sex, I'm gonna light your teenage behind up."

"Does someone want to tell me what's going on?" Jerome asked, laying the bags on the table.

Renee responded, "You're son has been skipping school." If Renee had had a belt in her hand, she would have used it.

Jerome dropped his head and slowly turned around. He was also upset, but at this moment he had to be the calm parent. Renee had enough emotion for the two of them. "Renee, let me talk to him."

"The same way you talked to him about Zora?"

"Are you bringing that up *again?*" he asked, throwing his hands in the air. "That's enough, Renee. You're going to have high blood pressure if you keep this up."

"Don't act like you're concerned about me. You need to get a little more emotional. Your son is cutting school to party with people we don't know and compromising his education. Isn't that important to you?"

"Reggie, go upstairs. I'll be up in a minute." Jerome sternly told his son.

"And I meant it," Renee hollered as he was leaving, "you're off the team until I see some changes!"

"Don't you think that's a bit extreme?" Jerome asked.

"This is not the time to contradict me."

"Why don't we find out what's going on with him before making any rational decisions." Renee tried to leave the room but Jerome blocked her path. She wasn't in the mood for him. "We need to talk about this."

"My mind's made up. Besides, you're only worried about making him a basketball star. You're trying to turn him into you, and I sure won't let that happen."

"Well, you're turning Junior into a mini you, but you don't see me jumping on you about that," Jerome lashed out.

"Please, every time he cries you blame it on me. He's only seven. He's going to cry!"

"You're turning him into a wimp." Jerome snatched the melting water ices off the table and took them to the freezer. Renee walked behind him carrying the celebration dinner they were supposed to eat as a family.

"If you weren't so busy with Taylor you'd have more time to *toughen up* your son," she said, pulling one shrimp out of a container.

"Now you're just down right out of control. I told you I don't know any Taylor," he said with confidence. "Though its times like this that make me wish I did. We should talk about this together. He is my son, too."

"You haven't been around to *discipline* your son for quite some time."

"Is this how it's gonna be from now on? You gonna bring her up every time something goes wrong?"

Renee looked the other way. The sad truth was that Jerome was right. This was how things were going to be, giving her undeniable proof that their marriage was over.

Jerome made himself a plate of food and went to the basement. Renee sat at the kitchen table alone, picking at the seafood in front of her. Maybe she did overreact, but her household was going in a negative direction, and she couldn't figure out how to turn things around. Moving to Chicago seemed even more appealing. They could all get a fresh start at life, everyone that is, but Jerome. He could stay right there in that basement for all she cared.

Renee made two plates of food for the boys and called them to dinner. Only Jerome Jr. came downstairs. She could tell he had been crying. "Go ahead and eat, baby. Your brother will be down in a minute." Renee walked upstairs and knocked on Reggie's door with her knuckles. No response. She knocked a little louder, this time with her fist. Still nothing. She opened the door slightly to see Reggie sitting at his desk, rolling his basketball back and forth with his foot. "Dinner's ready," she said.

"I'm not hungry," he replied, his head hung low.

"You've got to eat, Reggie." She walked over to him and stopped the basketball with her foot. "Your father and I are still very upset, and we will talk more about this change in your behavior, but just so you know, I'm going to type up my own progress report for your teachers to sign everyday. I hate treating you like a baby, but until I see progress, that's what I'm going to have to do." Renee tried to resist the urge to burst into tears and continued, "As your mother, I can't just stand by and watch you ruin your life." Renee turned away for fear that Reggie might see her eyes filling with tears. She saw his cell phone on the desk and grabbed it. "I'm taking this, too. Now, go eat. We'll deal with this some more tomorrow."

"Mom," Reggie called as she was leaving. "I'm sorry."

Renee felt like crying but she had to be strong. "We'll talk tomorrow," she said and left his room. She walked down the hall and straight into her bathroom. Once she was sure Reggie had gone downstairs, she fell to the floor and began to weep.

Three days after the job offer was made, Renee sat at her desk tapping a pen on a stack of papers. As with most of her career decisions, she didn't consult anyone for advice. If she made a decision, she only wanted herself to blame.

Mr. Kotlarczyk didn't pressure her. From experience, he knew Renee didn't like to be pushed or persuaded into anything. He respected her space. Still, Renee wasn't going to take advantage of the situation. Mr. Engleton and the executive board were running a business, and they needed to fill the position with a qualified person.

Renee put her hands together and prayed. *God, please help me make the right decision.* Getting up from her swivel chair, Renee smoothed out the wrinkles in her rayon blouse as best she could. Small steps toward the door were quickly replaced with large ones. *It's time to get this over with,* she said to herself, hurrying out of her office.

"I'll be down the hall if anybody needs me," she told Bianca as she passed her desk. Renee continued walking down the long hall; her heart beating faster with each step. What she was about to tell her boss would change her life forever.

Mr. Kotlarczyk's door was open when she arrived. Busy reading a document in a binder, he didn't see Renee walk up. She went to speak, but nothing came out so she coughed lightly. Mr. Kotlarczyk looked up and smiled, closing the binder quickly. "Hey, Renee. What can I do for you?"

"Do you have a minute," she queried, her voice still a bit weak.

He pushed his chair away from his desk and stood to his feet. "Of course I do. Come in and have a seat," he said, pointing to a chair in front of his desk.

He waited for Renee to be seated and sat back down. "What's on your mind?"

Renee took a deep breath before speaking. "When I first started at the front desk in college, I was pretty confident that I'd move up the ranks. But, I honestly thought my current position was the best I would do. I never dreamed I'd go any further than this." Renee folded her hands in her lap to keep from shaking. "So, I sit here with an offer to become the general manager of a large hotel chain. What a blessing. And for you, Mr. Engleton, and Mr. Coleman to think that I could handle such a challenge means a lot to me. It really does."

Renee paused, feeling her emotions getting the best of her. Mr. Kotlarczyk was becoming emotional, too. Only Renee could bring out this side of him in the workplace. To keep from shedding tears, he spoke. "So, my dear, what's the verdict?"

Taking both of her hands, Renee wiped her eyes and sighed. Then, in one breath she blurted, "I'm officially accepting the offer." Her face beamed as she looked at the smile on her boss's face. But, behind her own smile, she wondered how Jerome was going to take this news. Although in her mind their marriage was over, it wasn't official, yet.

16

Jerome

Jerome stood in front of the Kenneth Cole store staring at the mannequin on display. After Renee's outburst last week, he contemplated whether or not he should treat himself to something new. Renee's birthday was coming up and he didn't have a whole lot of money to spend on a gift for her. Although the mannequin was chiseled differently, Jerome knew the outfit would look just as good on him. Maybe even better. The sea green shirt would compliment his complexion perfectly, and the dark brown square-toed shoes would blend nicely with the brown khakis Taylor bought him last year.

Jerome did a mental count of the money he had in his wallet. If he purchased the shoes, he could get Renee a cheaper gift with the money left over. She didn't deserve the jewelry he originally planned to buy anyway. They weren't even on speaking terms and he was still living in the basement, sleeping on a rigid and cold futon. Jerome stared back at the mannequin, this time picturing his own feet in the shoes.

He walked inside the store and headed straight for the shoe section and picked up the shoe like the one he saw in the window. "Can I see these in an eleven, please?" he asked the nearest sales associate. The associate nodded and disappeared in the back of the store. As he waited, Jerome thought twice about what he was doing. He covered his face with his hands and blew out a puff of air. All week, Renee complained about every little thing—he didn't fasten the tie on the garbage bag tight enough, he left three hairs from shaving in the bathroom sink, he put the toilet paper on the roll backwards. Nothing he said or did seemed to be right. It took them three days to agree on an acceptable punishment for Reggie. Jerome decided that he deserved the shoes.

The associate appeared from behind the store carrying more than one box of shoes. Though he was eager to try on the shoes, the woman standing behind the associate was more appealing. "I bought two other types for you to try. They're on sale," the associate said, placing the boxes on an empty chair next to Jerome. "Do you have everything you need?"

Jerome couldn't respond. He was distracted by the way Taylor's denim mini caressed her shapely hips. The associate looked back and forth at the two of them somewhat confused, then smirked the way men do when they're in the presence of a pretty woman. "Let me know if you need any help," the associate said.

"How are you?" Taylor asked, and removed the lid of the shoe-box. She took one out of the box and examined it. "Nice shoe. I see you're taste has improved."

"I had a good teacher," Jerome answered and took the shoe from her hands. He couldn't look into her face. Her eyes would draw him in and he would be trapped figuring out ways to creep to her place again.

Taylor stood in front him, making it hard for Jerome to concentrate. "Shopping for your new boyfriend?" he asked at the sight of the Macy's bag on her arm.

Taylor smiled. "If you mean Lance, he's not my new boyfriend."

Jerome probed further. "Then you're just getting him a gift?"

"If you must know, I'm buying Sherry's *brother* something for his birthday. He turns twenty-one tomorrow."

With both shoes on his feet, Jerome walked to the full-length mirror by the cash register. Taylor followed. "They look good," she said, standing less than an inch behind him. "They will look great with the tan slacks and Claiborne shirt you got from Macy's."

The scent of her perfume was taking his mind to places he fought hard to forget. This was too close for comfort. Jerome stepped away from Taylor and reclaimed his position in the chair.

"So, how are Renee and the boys?" asked Taylor.

"We're all doing well," he felt compelled to say, though it was not the complete truth. "Renee's birthday is coming up, so me and the boys are planning something special." Jerome wasn't sure, but he thought he could sense a tinge of jealousy. "We've been trying to get our family back on the right track. She's a different person now." He paused. "We're happy," he forced himself to say.

Jerome checked the sticker on the bottom of one shoe. *Two hundred ten dollars*. He put the box down and glanced at the other pairs of shoes. They were on sale, but they didn't appeal to him as much as the ones on his feet. Taylor seemed to approve of them, too. Her lips had curled up when he opened the other boxes. Before he could change his mind, Jerome stuffed the shoes back in the box and took them to the register.

"Well, I'm really glad to hear that you and the family are doing well," Taylor responded. "I better let you go."

"I'll see you at work," Jerome replied, carefully recounting the bills in his hands.

"Right," she said and turned away, "I'll see you at work."

It was May 21st—Renee's birthday. Jerome woke up two hours earlier than his normal time. Despite their disagreements, Jerome loved his wife. He just wasn't sure if she still loved him. He poured the last of the non-dairy creamer into his cup of coffee, and looked at the breakfast he prepared. Belgian waffles, turkey sausage, and hash browns filled with onions, peppers, and cheese were placed in the middle of the table on their best dishes. As he sipped his coffee, Jerome could hear Renee making her way to the kitchen. She paused in the doorway and Jerome smiled. "Happy birthday," he smiled.

"There's a lot of food here. Expecting company?" Renee asked.

"No, this is for you. You only turn thirty-five once."

"Don't remind me," she said, taking a seat at the table.

Jerome sat in the chair across from her. "I hope you like it. Everything should still be warm."

Renee took in the savory aroma. "You're trying to put some pounds on me," she sighed. "You know it's hard to loose weight after thirty."

"Don't be silly. You better enjoy this before the boys come down here." Jerome handed Renee the syrup and they ate breakfast—together.

Later on, Jerome and the boys couldn't wait to give Renee her gift.

"Happy birthday, Mommy!" Jerome Jr. shouted as he ran through the house to find her. Renee was sitting in the kitchen watching Oprah, still dressed in her work clothes and nibbling on a leftover cheese danish. He wrapped his arm around her neck and gave her a big juicy kiss.

"Happy birthday, Mom," Reggie said, kissing her left cheek and handing her a huge card.

Renee was about to open the card when she noticed two balloons bobbing from the collar of a dog. He was a small pug with a face that should have had cigar or something stronger hanging from his lips. His short and stubby legs were moving nonstop.

"What's that?" she asked, and at the sound of her voice, the dog grunted and wagged its tail wildly. It looked as if he wanted to jump in her lap, and he might have if his middle wasn't so large.

"It's for you. It's a pug. Isn't he cute?" Jerome said, entering the room and then rubbing the dog's head.

Jerome walked up behind Reggie and gave Renee a bouquet of

flowers. He leaned in to kiss her on the cheek, and was relieved she didn't try to turn away. "Happy birthday, babe," he whispered in her ear.

"Is this pug for *me*?" she asked Jerome.

"We were going to get you a tennis bracelet, but Daddy said you really wanted a dog," Jerome Jr. noted.

Jerome placed his hand around his son's mouth before he could disclose anymore information. Renee did not need to know how much he paid for the dog or where he got it from. "I was only joking, Junior," he said, trying to play it off. Renee was silent.

"Well, are we still going to Olive Garden?" Jerome Jr. asked when his father removed his hands.

"We'll go wherever your mother wants to go." Jerome watched the dog circle Reggie, getting more excited each time he started a new lap, his beady eyes steadily following his son.

"Don't you just love him, Mom?" Jerome Jr. asked.

"We'll all have to chip in and help Mom take care of her dog, okay guys?" Jerome stated as if he knew what Renee was thinking.

Renee left the room and against his better judgment, Jerome followed. "You don't like the gift?" he asked.

Renee looked at the dog. "Where did you get a pug? Aren't they expensive?"

"From a buddy of mine." Jerome hoped she didn't ask anything more. He didn't want to mention the questionable terms in which his friend had come across the animal.

"Jerome, we can't afford a pet. We can barely afford this house." Renee looked as if she was about to cry.

"I can't do anything to make you happy, can I?" Jerome had hoped the dog would help mend what was broken between them.

"You just don't get it, do you?" Renee threw her hands in the air and sat on the sofa, placing her hands over her temples. "Who's going to wake up in the middle of the night to let him out to use the bathroom? Who's going to make sure he eats? Who's going to walk him?" She moved her hands to get a good look at her husband. "Who's going to take the time to train him?" Renee looked Jerome in the eye. "Let's be realistic. A pet is just another mouth to feed, and from the looks of him, he eats a lot. You can't even pay the bills on time."

Jerome was shocked. *How does she know about that?*

"Yeah, I saw the gas bill last month. You left it on the table," she continued. "Where is the extra money going, Jerome? Are you drinking again?"

"I resent that accusation," Jerome responded, wondering if Renee had gone through his things. He had a few bottles hidden in the cabinet in the basement.

"What am I supposed to think? It's not like we haven't been down this road before."

"Lower your voice," Jerome urged. The boys had stopped playing with the dog and were staring at their parents.

Renee stood up and Jerome jumped, and for good reason. When they first began arguing over his drinking, Renee's temper would take over her body. She would lash out and become physical without warning. "The kids aren't paying us any attention," she said unaware of their stares from where she sat. "They're too happy with that puppy."

Jerome puffed out his chest, "So, you've been going through my things?"

"No, you left the gas and electric bill statements on the kitchen table," she replied. "What are you spending the money on?" She moved into his personal space, but pride wouldn't let him move. Jerome held his stance. "Is Taylor getting your money?"

"Oh, boy! Here we go, again."

Renee studied him. "Nice shoes," she said sarcastically.

"This is crazy!" Jerome moved away, regretting his purchase. "It's your birthday. Look, I'll find a good home for the dog in the morning," he said sorrowfully.

"You can't do that now. It would devastate the kids."

Jerome threw his hands up in frustration. "Well, what do you want me to do?"

"So that I don't seem like the bad guy, I want you to make it perfectly clear that if the dog is not cared for by *everyone* in this house, he has got to leave." Renee walked to the hall closet to get her coat. "I'm going to find something to eat."

"What about Olive Garden?"

"We can't leave a dog alone on the first night, and I need some alone time." Renee walked out the door. "And, he's male! The last thing I need is another male in this house!" Jerome heard Renee yell as she got into the car and pulled out the driveway.

17

Renee

Renee drove down Germantown Avenue in silence. It wasn't often that she had a chance to casually look around at the stores on the downtown strip in Chestnut Hill. She used to shop there all the time when the boys were younger. Her car jerked a little to the left and Renee held tight to the steering wheel. Riding along the cobblestone road and old trolley car tracks often made that happen. If drivers weren't paying attention, they could easily end up in an accident.

She continued down Germantown Avenue, out of Chestnut Hill and into Philly's Mount Airy section, the place where she grew up. The pull of the wheels across the tracks started to annoy her, so she made a left turn on Mount Airy Ave. She made a few more turns, reliving the days of her youth in her mind, and ended up on Phil Elena in front of the house she used to live in with her parents. The house looked the same. She guessed the people now living there were taking good care of it. Her mother would've approved. The new owners even kept the wooden bench her mother found in a flea market. She'd had many tea parties with her dolls on that bench. It was old and a bit wobbly, but it gave the house character.

Renee reminisced on happier times and started to cry. This was supposed to be a happy time in her life. She had an offer to become the general manager of what would be the biggest Luxury Inn hotel. All of the years she dedicated to her career had finally paid off, and after being married to Jerome for thirteen years, she had lived to see another birthday. With such a turbulent marriage, she was surprised she hadn't suffered a heart attack by now.

It wasn't that she didn't like the gift Jerome chose. The scrunchy-faced dog was adorable in its own way, but they were just making ends meet as it was. Having a pet was not in their plans. Renee's salary was competitive, but she and Jerome's past was full of credit card debt and school loans. Along with those bills, they had a high mortgage, the boys attended an expensive private school and Jerome wanted a new car. It would be years before all of that was cleared.

Renee cried until the blouse she was wearing was drenched from her tears. She didn't know who to call that would understand what she was going through. Her mother was definitely out of the question. She would have reiterated her favorite line, "I told you he was a loser," and Renee didn't feel like hearing that tonight. Renee picked up her cell phone and scrolled through her address book. If something didn't change soon, she was sure to have a nervous break down. *God, please help me.*

Renee dialed the only person she knew would listen. When Elise picked up the phone, she tried to mask her true emotions. "Hey, Momma to be," she said, feeling a sudden wave of peace.

"Hello?" Elise said again, not sure who the voice belonged to.

"I know it's been a long time, but you should remember . . ."

Elise screamed, "Oh my God! Renee, is that you?"

"Yes, it is. How are you, mommy?"

"Very pregnant."

"I know. I'm so happy for you. When are you due?"

"I have three months to go. You should see me. I look like a whale."

Renee immediately felt guilty about not being there for her

friend, but this was not the time to pout over the past. She could only do right from this point forward. The two women wasted no time catching up on the past year. Elise talked about her husband as if they were still newlyweds. There was no sarcasm or tension detected in her tone when she mentioned his name. She was obviously still very much in love.

As Elise shared her joy, Renee didn't realize she was crying. But, her continuous and soft sniffles alarmed Elise. "What's going on, Renee?"

"Don't mind me," she sniffed for affect, "my allergies are acting up."

"Are you sure that's all it is?" questioned Elise, not believing a word Renee said. Renee burst into tears and Elise insisted, "spill the beans."

"I can't pour all my troubles in your lap. You might go into labor," she said, trying to make light of the situation.

"Then start pouring. I'm ready to deliver."

Renee told Elise about Jerome's alleged affair, Reggie's school behavior, the birthday gift and the job offer.

"I know this is hard, Renee. But, every marriage goes through a rough patch. Yours includes infidelity," Elise said when Renee was finished.

"What am I supposed to do?"

"I could tell you to go and beat the woman down, but that's done, the pain of what she and Jerome did wouldn't be erased. You may feel better for the moment, but that pain would still be in your heart."

Renee chuckled to herself; not because what she said was funny, but because she knew Elise was right.

"We used to tear girls up when we were in school. You're a professional and very successful woman now. You have to do the mature adult thing and pray," Elise continued. "I know it's been a while, but have you been back to church?"

"No, and I know that's why my life is crazy."

"Don't think that way. Everyone has problems, whether their

in church or not. Although having a relationship with Jesus is what helps us handle our problems."

"I do have a relationship with Him," Renee said. "I just have a lot of questions."

"It's okay to have questions. You just can't let them tear you away from God," Elise stressed. "I know this is hard. Life is hard and sometimes seems unfair, but you have to keep praying. God will take care of you."

"You think me and Jerome should've waited to get married?"

"Who knows? You and Jerome did get married at a young age. People don't *really* know what they want when they graduate high school, and the ones that do often change their minds as they mature and experience more of life. Your career took off before Jerome had a chance to figure out what he wanted his career to be. That's hard for a man, especially one with a family."

Renee listened with an open mind, but wasn't sure Elise's words could help change her mind about Jerome. She wasn't even attracted to him anymore. "I don't know what to do. All we do is argue."

"I know this is a cliché, but prayer really does change things," Elise said with sincerity. "Jerome loves you. Why don't you ask him to go to church with you on Sunday? Tell him its part of your birthday celebration."

"I don't know. The last time we went to an actual service he was drunk and talked to everyone and anyone that would listen. I was so embarrassed."

Renee took a deep breath. She appreciated Elise's advise, but wasn't sure if going to church could solve the problems that had accumulated between them over the years. "Plus, I think I'm afraid of what might happen. Have you ever felt like God was mad at you?"

"Look how long it took me to get married. Then I get married and miscarry twice. I felt like I was being punished. But, God knows. He knew I couldn't marry young," she laughed. "I would have been divorced by now, with the mouth I had." Renee had to agree. When they met, Elise had a vocabulary that could put a sailor to shame. "We get upset with God when we don't understand what He's trying to do, but we have to try and keep the faith. He knows what's best for us. But we can't hear what he's trying to tell us if we don't stay in a relationship with him. And, that includes going to church."

"Maybe I should try another church."

"You like New Life. I don't think you're the only woman there that has an alcoholic husband. Don't let people stop you from going to church. You go and hear what God has for you."

Renee looked at her old house one last time and started the ignition. "Thank you for talking to me. I feel better."

"Well, I hope you and Jerome work things out. Consult God before you walk away from your marriage. Hey," Elise changed the subject, "have you spoken to Kara at all?"

"I saw her and Harold at Kid Fest. She didn't really say much."

"I should probably give her a call. You go back home and enjoy the rest of your birthday. Kiss the pug for me," Elise teased. "And take a picture of Jerome's new shoes."

Renee stopped at ACME before going home. If the new addition to the family was staying, he was going to need a few things. The boys were playing with the dog when Renee returned home. The sight of their smiles warmed her heart. They were getting older, something Renee wasn't ready for. Jerome Jr.'s weight seemed to settle a bit, making him favor Renee more and more each day. Reggie's muscles were starting to bulge, making him appear older than he actually was. Renee hated to interrupt their fun, but she was getting hungry.

"Okay, guys. Go get the rest of the bags from the car," she ordered them.

The boys ran off and the dog chased after them, hesitating when he reached the front door. He looked out the door then back at Renee several times.

"You are a cute fella," she said. She rubbed his head and he rolled over on his back. Renee laughed at the sight of his huge belly and tickled him. He grunted and snorted loudly. "I don't know if I can get use to that. You need to work on that if you're going to stay here," she joked.

Jerome appeared by the stairs and Renee stood up. She put her coat in the hall closet and suddenly felt something cool around her ankles. The dog was licking her legs. "That tickles," she giggled. She turned to say something to Jerome, but he had already walked away; he probably went down to the basement.

The boys ran in with the extra bags filled with dog food, treats, and toys. The dog must have known a treat was near because his tail wagged rapidly and he sniffed the bags. "Be patient," Jerome Jr. told him as he placed the bags on the table.

"Did you think of a name for him?" Reggie asked his mother.

"Not yet. You guys can probably come up with something better than I could," Renee replied.

"I'm going to think of something *really* cool," Jerome Jr. stressed.

Renee put a bucket of chicken on the table. "Go get your father. We're going to celebrate my birthday together," she told Jerome Jr. "Reggie, put the dog stuff away and the plastic bags under the sink."

Instead of walking down the stairs to the basement, Jerome Jr. stood on the top step and yelled, "Daddy, Mommy wants you to come up here and eat!"

Renee shook her head. "Next time go all the way down the stairs."

"Sorry," Jerome Jr. said.

Jerome slowly walked up the stairs, looking only at the food on the table. Renee had fixed his plate. He eased into the only seat available at the table and lifted his fork.

"Before you start eating, can you say grace?" Renee asked and bowed her head before he could say no.

Renee could tell that he was still angry, but she had cooled off. It was her birthday. They'd have to have a serious conversation on a different day. Jerome lowered his head and sped through the grace. Renee had to bite her bottom lip to keep from saying anything sarcastic. "Let's eat," is all she said.

As everyone enjoyed their fast food meal, the dog nipped at Reggie's pants, grunting nonstop. "We forgot to feed him," Reggie said, stuffing a chicken leg into his mouth. The dog moved his short legs back and forth, staring at the table with his wrinkled mouth wide open. Reggie gave him a potato wedge and everyone laughed at how quickly he devoured it.

"I'll get him some dog food," Jerome said more relaxed. "I don't want him hooked on KFC."

"I know what we can call him!" Jerome Jr. exclaimed. "His name should be Oscar."

"Why would you name him that?" Reggie inquired, obviously in disagreement.

"He looks like Oscar the Grouch," Jerome Jr. replied with confidence and Renee had to agree.

"My parents will be here in a half hour," Renee said to Jerome. "Try and be on your best behavior, please." She didn't need to look up to know that Jerome had a scowl on his face.

"Special occasion?" he asked.

She took an orange from the fruit bowl that was sitting on the kitchen table and started to peel it. "One of their friends is retiring tomorrow," she said. Although it was only partially true. Renee had called them when she accepted the job offer and they wanted to see her before the move to Chicago. Her parents had no intentions of going to the retirement party before Renee called. She spit an orange seed in a paper towel and then looked up at the small television on top of the refrigerator.

Jerome took off his uniform jacket. "Are they staying here?"

"No, I reserved a room at the hotel." Jerome looked relieved and headed for the basement. "Before you get comfortable," Renee started and Jerome froze in place. "Oscar needs to go for a walk." Jerome continued downstairs, muttering under his breath. "Don't get upset with me. You promised to walk him at night."

Renee watched a rerun of *Living Single* as she ate her orange. She could hear Jerome kicking and tossing things around in the basement. He stomped up the steps, clearly aggravated about something. She sucked on an orange slice, trying to ignore his tantrum. She didn't care that he was mad. This was one agreement he was going to adhere to.

Jerome came back upstairs in the same dirty uniform and Renee looked at him strangely. "I don't have any clean clothes," he said.

"You know I'm not washing your clothes again. I can't handle any more surprises."

"I was just making a statement, Renee. I didn't ask for all that commentary."

"What you need is a regular schedule. That way you won't have to wear dirty clothes."

Jerome sucked his teeth and opened the refrigerator. "Did you make anything for dinner?"

"I did, but your sons ate it all."

Jerome closed the door with enough force for it to shake. "Where's the dog?"

"Probably in Junior's room."

"Are there any more oranges?"

"This is the last one," Renee said, exaggerating each bite, letting strands of juice trickle down her chin. "There is a banana left." Renee knew he didn't like bananas.

Jerome hovered over Renee. "Can I at least have a slice?" Renee hesitated, but gave in and handed him the smallest of the remaining slices. He nearly swallowed it whole. Renee covered the rest of the orange with a napkin and tilted slightly to the side.

Jerome groaned, "I'll be back."

* * *

When the Lincoln Continental pulled into the driveway, Jerome Jr. started hopping around the living room singing, "Grandmom and Pop-pop are here!"

Renee stood at the door waiting for them to get out of the car. Too anxious to wait inside, Jerome Jr. ran outside. "Hi, Grandmom!" he said before she could get one foot out of the door. Renee watched from the doorway.

"There's my number one seven-year-old," she said, with bright eyes. Her mother got out of the car and spotted something on the front lawn right away. She hugged her grandson then picked up a candy wrapper from under the oak tree, and searched the grounds for anything else that didn't belong. At sixty-three, her mother hadn't changed much. She was still the slender cheerleader-type with hair as thick as a lion's mane. Though fully gray, her hair was full and bouncy and there wasn't one curl out of place. Renee hoped she'd look that good when she reached her sixties.

"Hey, baby," she called and waved to Renee. She put the wrapper in the garbage on the side of the driveway and waited for her husband.

Renee's father stepped out of the car, and as usual, was dressed like he was going to church. He put on his hat and waved. "Hi, Daddy!" Renee said loud enough for him to hear. Though he didn't admit that his hearing was failing, Renee knew it was. She had found herself repeating everything whenever they talked. Her father walked to the trunk of the car and retrieved two huge bags of professionally wrapped gifts.

"Reggie! Come and help Pop-pop!" Renee hollered up the stairs then walked outside and met her mother on the porch. She kissed her lightly on the cheek and said, "Hello, Mother." If it wasn't for the gray hair, she could've easily passed for forty. Her size ten frame hadn't changed since Renee was a little girl. Renee clearly took after her father's side of the family. Hefty thighs were a dominate trait for both the men and women.

"My darling daughter, happy birthday," she said, giving Renee the once over, and pinching her waist. "I see you all are eating well. Junior's getting a little plump there, too."

"This is just baby fat, Grandmom," Jerome Jr. said, shaking his stomach wildly.

Reggie ran out the door and whizzed by the two women. "Hey, Grandmom. I'll be right back."

"Whoa, that boy is going to be a giant!" she remarked. "So Junior, what'd you guys do for your mother's birthday?"

"We got her a dog!" he exclaimed proudly.

Renee's mother almost broke her neck. "A dog? I don't have to guess whose idea that was."

"He's cute, mom," Renee responded.

"Well, where is the furry wonder dog?"

"Daddy, look at you!" Renee said to avoid answering her mother. She relieved his arms of the huge bag he was carrying. "Is there anything left in the store?"

"You know you're father and I get carried away when it comes to our babies." She turned to Reggie. "Come here, boy. I hear you have a girlfriend. Is she as pretty as your grandmother?" Renee was surprised at her approval of Reggie's girlfriend. She had fought tooth and nail in high school just to have a boy call the house.

Reggie blushed. "Naw, Grandma, you're much prettier."

"Well, let's go inside," Renee said and the boys charged passed everyone, eager to open their presents.

Renee's parents had outdone themselves. They had showered the boys with clothes, music CDs, and new Game Boy cartridges. They bought Renee a leather engraved Coach briefcase. Jerome walked in with Oscar as the boys were stuffing wrapping paper in garbage bags. Renee could tell that he was uncomfortable. With all of the paper and boxes lying around, Oscar was excited, too excited for Renee's mother. She kept jumping and moving around the room every time he barked or snorted. Jerome finally had to shut Oscar in the basement.

When Jerome returned to the living room, Renee's mother handed him a small box. "You didn't think I'd forget you, did you?"

"Thanks, Mom," he said humbly, and opened the present. Renee was nervous. Her mother didn't always put as much care into choosing his gifts. Jerome's eyes became wide when he opened the box. "Thanks."

"Ben and I thought it would be nice if you had your own court. This way you can train our future star," she said, rubbing Reggie's shoulders.

"What is it?" Renee asked.

Jerome was all smiles. "We're getting a basketball court built in the back," he said to Renee.

Renee did her best to show her gratitude. Her mother had given him a great gift, but Renee knew that no one would be able to enjoy it. She was making plans to move.

"You want to tell us why Jerome is in the basement?" Renee's mother asked once everyone had gone to bed.

"We're having some problems, but that's nothing new," Renee answered, dreading the conversation about to happen. "I'd rather talk about why you and Daddy insist on driving here every time instead of flying. Atlanta is too long of a car ride."

"Don't change the subject, young lady."

Renee looked to her father for help, but he was in the corner fast asleep. Well, he actually pretended to be asleep in order to avoid her mother's debates. And, this time Renee spared him. There was no need for him to get involved. "It's the same old thing."

"I think it's something more than that. A mother knows her only child. You shouldn't keep things from me. I worry about you, you know. And I'm getting older. It would be a shame if something happened to me because my only daughter . . ."

"All right, Mom." Renee lowered her voice. "Jerome had an affair, or he's still having an affair. I don't really know."

"Well, I can't say that I didn't see that coming," she responded.

Renee shifted in her seat, resting her head on the arm of the sofa. "Have you talked to your pastor?"

What? Renee sat up. She expected the same, "Your husband is a loser" sermon. "We haven't been going to church together."

"You're still going aren't you?"

"I can't lie to you, Mom. I haven't been to church in a while. The boys still go though."

"At least you have enough sense to send them. But Renee, that's what's wrong with your marriage. This marriage is only going to work if you worship and hear the word *together.*" Her mother was getting upset. "And I can't believe you haven't talked to the pastor. Or at least one of the deacons. What about Deacon Bernard? He helped Jerome through his drinking problem."

"He didn't get on him good enough. Besides, Mom, there's no point in talking to anyone about this anymore. I'm sure Jerome feels the same way I do."

"Then why haven't you told him about the job yet?

"Lower your voice," Renee begged. She didn't want to risk Jerome listening in on any part of their conversation. "I don't want him to come to Chicago with us. The kids and I need to start over," she whispered.

"You can't just take off without telling him."

"Why are you concerned about Jerome all of a sudden? I thought you'd be happy about this."

"This is wrong. You have to at least give him a chance to get better."

"How many years have I already wasted trying to give him that chance? What's gotten into you?"

"I can't believe I'm saying this, but I was wrong to judge your husband so harshly." She smoothed the wrinkles out of her pants to avoid looking at her daughter.

Renee made sure Jerome was in the basement and not walking around in the kitchen. "I asked him to go to church with me yesterday and he came up with some excuse." Her voice was escalating, but she couldn't help it. She was upset. "I don't think we have a marriage worth saving any longer." Renee sniffed a few times and blinked her eyes to fight away tears. "I want a divorce."

"You can't divorce him, Renee," her mother began, "You know, the older I get, the more I understand that marriage was not meant to be broken. I know I've been hard on Jerome, but you're my child. I can't help but be overprotective." She fiddled with a toy between the couch cushions. "You married Jerome because you loved him, and you have two children with him. Figure out how to make it work."

"I can't believe that God would want me to stay unhappily married. I'm not happy, Mom," Renee stressed. "You know that I've been unhappy for years. I can't keep living like this."

"I told you when you wanted to marry him that it wasn't going to be easy. You can't just give up. You know how to pray. Pray a little harder about this. And get your behind back in church!"

Talking to her mother was always a draining experience for Renee. She was glad they were staying in a hotel this time. There was so much she needed to digest. She watched as the car backed down the driveway and stopped when it hit the street. Renee's father got out and walked back to the house.

"You forgot something, Daddy?" Renee asked.

"Your mother means well. Whatever you decide to do, you know we're behind you one hundred percent." He kissed her on the cheek. "I'm very proud of you. We both are." He tipped his hat and headed back to the car.

Renee waited for the car to disappear before going back inside. She walked up the stairs carefully, so she wouldn't wake the boys and crept into Jerome Jr.'s room. She closed his blinds and covered him with the *Shrek* comforter her parents had given him. He was sleeping peacefully, with Oscar snoring loudly at his feet. He wasn't much of a guard dog she thought. Oscar hadn't so much as moved an earlobe when she entered the room.

Renee slid down the side of his bed and buried her hands beneath her legs. *I just want to be happy.*

18

Taylor

"This is nice. We have to come here more often," Taylor said, soaking up the imitation island atmosphere. Taylor, Kara and Sherry sat under the huge outdoor veranda at the Bahama Breeze in King of Prussia, enjoying the warm May weather.

"The food's not bad either. Wait 'til you taste my jerk chicken," chimed in Sherry, sipping on her tropical fruit drink.

Kara put a special sauce on the last half of her appetizer and took a bite. "This Jamaican patty is good, but too small," she said, chewing slowly. "I guess I have to go to the Jamaican store in West Philly for a bigger portion."

The girls laughed and continued to enjoy the afternoon breeze that sailed through the open spaces of the restaurant. In order for all three women to enjoy lunch together during the week, usually one of them had to take the day off. Today, it was Sherry's turn to use a "sick" day.

A tall waiter, dressed in beige slacks and a colorful top, came to the table. "Is everything okay?" he asked the women.

"Can I have some more water, please?" Kara asked as she placed a pack of Virginia Slims on the table.

"Sure. Anything else?" The girls were too busy watching five men walk to the tiny stage in front of them to respond. He laughed to himself, "We have live music during lunch hour all summer now. I hope you enjoy it."

The five men quickly set up their equipment and began playing happy calypso tunes. Customers seemed pleased with the music. Fingers were snapping, feet were tapping, and heads were swaying from side to side. "What a way to spend a Friday afternoon," stated Taylor, leaning back in her seat, bobbing her head slowly.

Sherry turned her chair around to face the stage. She crossed her legs and moved her upper body to the mellow rhythm. "I should take the rest of the afternoon off."

"It is nice out." Kara pulled a cigarette out of the carton. "Let's go see a movie."

"That's not fair. You two have the day off work, but I don't. You can't go until I get off work," Sherry pouted. "I have a root canal to help with at two, but after that I can leave."

"I don't think I have time for a movie," Taylor said, "I'm meeting Lance at 3:00."

"Still going strong I see," Kara mentioned, searching for her lighter.

Taylor blushed, "Yeah, he's a cool guy."

"Y'all do it yet?" Sherry asked matter of factly.

"No speed racer, we haven't been intimate, yet." Taylor replied, rolling her eyes.

"What are you waiting for?" Sherry questioned.

Kara found a book of matches in her purse and lit her cigarette. "Don't listen to her. You have plenty of time. Get to know him a little more."

Sherry rolled her eyes. "You're against sex before marriage now?"

"You certainly didn't expect me to encourage her, did you?" Kara put down the cigarette. "I'm just telling her to be wiser this time around. She needs to protect her heart. I'm tired of the pity parties."

"I'm not saying that I'm going to jump his bones tonight or anything, but what would be wrong if I did? You and Harold had twins before you got married," Taylor said, feeling the need to prove a point. She often felt as if Kara judged her behavior.

Kara picked her cigarette up and placed it between her lips. "And look at the mess we had to go through."

"I thought Christ covered your sins," Sherry mocked. "I'll be glad when that no smoking rule starts."

Kara looked away annoyed at her comment. "I'm still alive, aren't I?" she said and put the cigarette back in the ashtray. "Look, I don't have all the answers, but Harold's infidelity could be a result of us having sex before marriage. Who knows?"

"Umm. And, what about smoking?" Sherry said sarcastically.

"I've been trying to cut back," Kara said, realizing that she would have to change her habits if she wanted her friends to witness how God can change a person.

Sherry twisted her lips. "Well, if you ask me, it doesn't seem like God should operate that way."

"You can't look at it like that. See," Kara said, "people don't really understand God. When things are going great, we shout about how wonderful God is, but the minute something turns sour, we question His power." Kara took a deep breath. "Sometimes, God has to teach us a lesson. Think about it, when you were younger and did something wrong, your parents either whipped your tail or put you on punishment. The pain of the spanking was immediate, but the more powerful effects of the punishment, in many cases, wasn't felt until there was a party you wanted to go to but couldn't. All your friends were there, but you weren't. That punishment was a lesson to remind you not to do wrong again. Do you get my point?"

"Some kids, like myself, got on punishment for the same thing a hundred times before learning a lesson," Taylor snickered.

"That was your choice," Kara said seriously. "You knew the consequences of your actions after the first time."

"You need to be a deacon, Bible teacher, or something," Sherry added, paying more attention to the music.

"I'm not quite ready for that. I still have that bad habit to break, right?" Kara said to lighten the mood. "I'm just telling you what I experienced."

Sherry chucked. "I hear you, but sex is a hard thing to give up."

"Well, like Taylor said, she got in trouble for the same thing a hundred times as a child, this won't be any different. And, in your case," Kara pointed to both girls, "punishment may be in the form of repeated heartache."

Taylor sat her drink on the table. Kara's sermons always had a way of shifting the tone of their outings. She wanted to share the news of seeing Jerome in the mall last month, but figured it wasn't a good time. Swirling the ice in her drink with her finger, Taylor hummed along with the song now currently playing. She missed Jerome—hearing the sound of his voice, massaging his shoulders, discussing current affairs, laughing at his jokes. Her connection to him was deeper than intimacy. They were soul mates, connected on levels she had never experienced before with other boyfriends. Lance was a nice guy, but he could not in any way compete with Jerome. Subconsciously, she hoped he would come to his senses. Even though Jerome said he and his wife were back together, she sensed that it was just a matter of time before things turned sour and he was back in her bed.

Sherry turned her chair around. "I hope the food comes soon. I have to get back to the office." Sherry searched the room for their waiter and stopped when her eyes rested on a familiar face. A face from a picture Taylor kept hidden in her nightstand. "Hey," she said, squinting her eyes for a better view. She would hate to be wrong. "Isn't that Renee?"

Kara and Taylor looked in that direction. Taylor had to blink a few times, but yes, it was Renee. And, the gentleman sitting across from her was not Jerome. Taylor watched as Renee giggled and touched the fine man sitting across from the table. The man had to be a little over six feet tall, and clean cut. *She has good taste*, Taylor thought, straining to get a better glimpse of Renee and her date. She was a lot shorter than Taylor, but cute. Her

high-powered business attire let Taylor know that she was a serious woman. She had to be someone important at the hotel. Taylor thought about her Septa uniform and instantly felt envious.
In order for her to dress in fancy suits, she would have to get pro-
moted to a higher-level position at headquarters. But working for
Septa on any level didn't interest her, and within the next few
years, Taylor hoped to own a business of her own.

Renee's companion was just as professional and dressed in a
suit that had to be at least a thousand dollars. *What is she doing
here? Is she on a date?* The way Renee looked into his inviting
eyes he couldn't have been a relative. Before Taylor knew what
was happening, she was out of her seat and on her way to their
table. She could hear Kara and Sherry calling her, but ignored
them.

"Hi, Renee," Taylor said, not sure what she would say next.

Renee looked away from her company and smiled. "Hi," she
said, trying to place her face.

"I don't mean to interrupt you and your boyfriend's lunch, but
I just wanted to say hello." Sherry was now standing by Taylor's
side, trying to pull her away.

Renee looked confused. "I'm sorry. Do I know you from the
hotel?"

"Let's go, Taylor," Sherry begged.

The smile on Renee's face changed, as did her gentleman
friend, proving to Taylor that she had been caught. "You should
be ashamed of yourself," Taylor told Renee.

Renee stood to her feet and Sherry pulled Taylor back a couple
feet. Customers were starting to look their way. "Let's go, Tay,"
Sherry said with more aggressiveness.

"Excuse me, Everett." Renee stood up and moved away from
his hearing range. "How dare you approach me in a public place
and accuse me of something you have no knowledge of. I suggest
you walk away before this turns into a situation we'll both end up
regretting," she belted through clinched teeth.

Taylor couldn't control herself. "Jerome loves you! He told me things were working out between the two of you." Taylor started to cry, "He's trying to make things work. How could you do this to him now?"

Kara approached the girls and a startled look set across Renee's face. "Come on, ladies. Let's try to be mature adults." Kara grabbed Taylor's hand, avoiding eye contact with Renee.

"He bought you that fancy house in Chestnut Hill. He let you buy the Lexus. He takes care of you and the boys. If you don't love him anymore, tell him." Taylor was flapping her arms as she expressed herself. Customers, who were once enjoying the music, were now tuned into the drama taking place.

Their waiter was summoned to the floor and carefully stepped behind Kara. "Do I need to call the cops?" the waiter asked.

Kara was embarrassed. "No, that won't be necessary." The waiter slowly backed away, but Kara knew she would have to end the situation soon. "We're about to leave," she assured the lunch crowd, but not before Renee got in the last words.

The red blotches on her face let Taylor know that Renee was furious, but then so was Taylor. She held her stance as Renee moved closer into her personal space. "Listen, sweetie," Renee started, "let's set the facts straight. My name is on the deed. *I* pay the mortgage. *I* bought *my* fancy car with the money *I* earned at work. So, again, before this turns any uglier, I suggest you walk away."

Taylor was about to lift her hands to push Renee, but Kara jumped in between them. "She's right, Taylor. Let's go. I already paid the bill."

Renee was fuming. "Kara, this is a friend of yours?"

"You know her, Kara?" questioned Sherry, looking at the expression on both Renee and Kara's faces.

"People are watching us. Can we please leave before we get kicked out?" Kara pulled Taylor by the arm and pushed her out the door.

* * *

Sherry held her tongue until they reached the parking lot. "Why didn't you tell us you knew Renee?"

Kara sighed. "Harold and Jerome were very good friends at one point. Of course I know her."

Taylor felt betrayed. "Why didn't you tell me?"

"What difference would it make? Would you have stopped sleeping with her husband?" Kara asked.

Taylor thought about all that she had shared with Kara about Jerome. "Oh my, God! Did you two talk about me?"

"You're being ridiculous." Kara pulled car keys out of her purse.

"I don't think she is. We're supposed to be your girls," Sherry interjected.

Annoyed by the entire situation, Kara tried to remain calm. "I told you from the very beginning that I didn't want to be a part of this. I knew it would come to this one day, that's why I stayed out of it. I never asked for details from you and I never talked to Renee about you." She yanked her car door open. "Jerome managed to destroy the friendship I could have had with Renee, and from the attitudes you two are giving me, he's doing the same thing here. He's the bad guy here. Not me!"

"You may not have known details, but you knew enough. I cried on your shoulder many nights. This definitely changes our friendship. I don't know if I can trust you anymore." Taylor looked at Sherry for confirmation.

"I have nothing to say right now. I'm still in shock." Sherry tapped her watch to signify the time. "I have to go. I guess I'll grab a hotdog on the way back to the office. What are you going to do, Taylor?"

"I'll have Lance pick me up from here. You can go ahead without me," Taylor told Kara.

Sherry gave Taylor a hug. "I'll call you later then."

Kara threw her purse in the backseat. "Don't be irrational, Taylor. I drive by your apartment. I can drop you off."

"You can go ahead. I'm sure Lance will come get me," Taylor replied.

Kara tapped her car window with her keys. "You're being silly. You had to know that Renee and I knew each other."

Taylor wasn't in the mood to argue. "Knowing Renee and being friends with Renee are two different things. You were her prayer buddy," Taylor stressed.

"I wouldn't say that we were friends. We used to spend time together because of Jerome and Harold," Kara tried to explain her case. "As far as the prayer group, I quit when you started dating Jerome. I couldn't look her in the eye knowing what was going on between you and Jerome."

"It just doesn't seem right." Taylor frowned. "The hurt in Renee's eyes when she saw you says that you were more than just acquaintances."

"The hurt in her eyes is from meeting her husband's lover today," Kara retorted.

Taylor stood still for a few seconds. "I guess you would know that feeling."

"God bless you, Taylor," Kara said before slamming the door of her car.

Taylor walked across the street and into the King of Prussia mall. The last time Taylor drove up to the mall, Jerome was with his family at the movies. The mall was beginning to be a place for bad experiences. *Could my life get any worse? How long had Kara been keeping this a secret?* Taylor walked through the food court and ordered the mandarin chicken special. She sat at a table tucked in the corner contemplating her next move. This could be the way back into Jerome's life.

19

Renee

Renee watched the women leave the restaurant before taking her seat. As soon as she got home, she was going to make Jerome leave. This was definitely the last straw.

She walked back to the table and folded her hands when she sat down. Renee had to say something to Everett, but what? *What must he think about my character?*

Everett spoke, seeing that Renee was at a lost for words. "It's okay, Renee. Things like this happen."

This business lunch had changed Renee's opinion of Everett. He was much more than the hard-nosed tough guy he portrayed at the hotel. He was warm, considerate and funny. She didn't want to tell him about her troubled marriage. It would not only be unprofessional, but it also wasn't any of his concern. "This in no way reflects my behavior in or out of work. It's just that—"

"No need to explain. Husbands and wives have problems. I'm not going to change my mind about you. Many women in your shoes would have scratched her eyes out." Everett placed his manicured hands over hers. "You handled it very well. That's why we chose you for this position."

Renee knew he was trying to comfort her, but there was still no excuse for her actions. She didn't mean to stoop to Taylor's level, but the thought of Jerome sharing details of their life with another woman bothered her. She knew where she lived, what she looked like and what kind of car she drove. If Taylor was bold enough to approach her in a public place, then who knows what else she was capable of doing.

"I am really sorry," she said, fighting back tears.

"You don't have to apologize anymore, okay?" Everett said. "But considering what just happened, I do feel the need to ask you an important question."

Renee's stomach churned, but she kept a straight face as he continued. "Sure, ask me anything."

"How does your husband feel about the relocation?"

"Honestly, he doesn't know, yet. Without going into the details," Renee said, "the boys and I may go to Chicago alone."

"You're a smart and reasonable woman," he said, "I'm sure you'll do what's best."

After lunch, Renee went home and Everett headed back downtown. Since she lived closer to the restaurant, Everett insisted Renee work from home for the rest of the day, rather than battle traffic trying to get back to the office. Renee didn't put up a fuss. She could probably get more work done at home than in the office anyway. And, she needed some time alone after her encounter with Taylor and her crew.

After work, Renee was going to pick the boys up and drop them off at Brandon's house. In case the argument she and Jerome were sure to have escalated into a physical match, she didn't want the boys to be witnesses. She was going to try her best to keep her hands to herself, but just in case, she was ready for the battle.

It was times like these that Renee wished she had a friend to call—someone to help her pack his bags and put his belongings on the front lawn. Since Elise was in Florida, Kara would have been that friend. But she was friends with the enemy. Kara's strange behavior had finally been explained. *How long had she known about Jerome and Taylor? How could she of all people be friends with a woman like that?*

Oscar whimpered loudly from the basement when Renee opened the door. He was scratching at his cage, ready to be set free when she walked downstairs. Renee felt bad that he was cooped up all day, but she had spent way too much money on her hardwood floors to take a chance on him having an accident. It would be at least another week before Renee could trust leaving him out of the cage during the day. Oscar raced out of the cage as soon as Renee removed the latch. She quickly checked for any traces of excrements. "Good boy," she said, when it was clear that he had not gone to the bathroom. Oscar clawed at Renee's feet anxiously, letting her know that he was about to explode. "Okay, little buddy. I'm ready."

Renee opened the front door and Oscar forcefully pulled her to the tree in the middle of her lawn. Before Renee could yank him away, he lifted his leg and christened the tree. Renee thought he was done, but Oscar sniffed around the tree, searching for a good spot to squat. "Oh no," Renee yelled, and pulled him away. "You've got to do that number somewhere else."

Walking around the neighborhood gave her a chance to think. Coming face to face with Taylor had shattered her soul. No matter how many times she said the marriage was over, Renee was really hurt that her husband would run to another woman. With the exception of her attraction to actors, Idris Elba and Morris Chestnut, she never once considered sleeping with another man.

"He must like big-boned women," Renee said as her thighs lightly rubbed together. Like her, Taylor had healthy hips. Her sassy hairstyle said that she was fun and upbeat. Renee combed through her own hair with her fingers. She longed for something that would offset her conservative nature.

Rumblings from the sky made Renee look up. The clouds were thinning and spreading quickly toward the east. Within seconds, the sky turned gray. Renee tugged at Oscar's leash lightly. "Hurry up, Oscar." She could hear thunder approaching her neighborhood and tapped her foot, hoping Oscar would do his business a little faster. A roll of thunder sounded again and this time a flash of lightening decorated the sky. Oscar quickly squirted onto a patch of grass then pulled Renee down the street.

Flashes of lightening filled the sky again and Oscar tried to find refuge between Renee's feet. "Come on, boy. I can't walk if you keep that up." Thunder got louder the closer Renee got to the house. A few drops of rain pricked her skin and Renee took off her shoes and started to run. She was only a block away. A steady rain finally poured from the sky just as she reached the edge of her walkway. She let Oscar go and he ran under the porch to safety.

Renee stood on her porch, wet and sticky, allowing the sound of rain to soothe her. The mist that blew on her arm from the mild wind felt good. She could see her neighbors across the street rushing around inside the house to close their windows. This reminded Renee that she needed to do the same. She checked her pocket for her keys and noticed a black utility vehicle coming down the street. Although it was raining, the person behind the wheel was driving unusually slow. Renee thought the driver might be looking for a specific address. Since she was certain the driver wasn't looking for her, she started to go inside the house. Oscar growled toward the street, his paws moving nonstop. "C'mon, boy," she said, now anxious to get inside.

The truck stopped directly in front of her house and Renee backed up a little. She tried to get a good look at the driver, but the rain was coming down too hard. Her vision was blurry, but Renee was almost positive that the driver was Taylor. *What the . . .* Her heart was pumping even more rapidly; partly out of fear and partly out of fury.

Before Renee could come up with a plan of action, the car suddenly sped away, its wheels spinning a few times. Renee picked up Oscar, went into the house and slammed the door behind her.

* * *

Renee showered and fed the dog. Although she was no longer in attack mode, Renee was ready for Jerome to come home. She used a clip to twist her hair into a ponytail and put on her *Waiting to Exhale* CD. Next, she went into her closet and pulled out her old Ralph Lauren luggage set and started throwing his things inside. If Jerome never returned the luggage she didn't care, she just wanted him gone.

Renee sang each song that played as she tossed his clothes inside the suitcases. Mary's, *I'm Not Gonna Cry* came on and she had to stop. This was the scorned woman's anthem. Renee picked up a brush and pretended she was Mary J herself, rehearsing for an upcoming tour. The phone rang and she instinctively dropped the brush. Renee hoped it wasn't Jerome. She turned the music down real low and answered. "Hello."

"Hey, girl. What you up to?" Elise asked.

"Hey," Renee sat on the bed and leaned against the headboard. "You wouldn't believe me if I told you." She didn't want to tell her about the drive by. She wasn't absolutely sure it was Taylor and didn't want to appear paranoid.

"Uh-oh, you and Jerome okay?"

Renee sighed, "Well, I was packing his things before you called."

Elise was shocked. Renee told her about the incident in Bahama Breeze. "If she would have caught me ten years ago, I would have clocked her," Renee laughed.

"Lord, and I would've egged you on. Thank God for change."

Renee looked at her watch. Jerome should be home in an hour. "I just can't continue to pretend anymore. I know so many people trapped in loveless marriages. I don't want that to be me."

"I hear you, but you know I can't encourage divorce or separation. I'm telling you, if God can change water into wine, he can surely turn your marriage around."

Elise tried to talk Renee into saving the marriage, but it was too late. Renee was ready to move on. "Well, I think you and I need to start praying together again," Elise suggested. "I could use some extra strength during this pregnancy."

"Is everything okay? I've been so busy rambling about my life, I forgot to ask how you were doing."

"I was placed on bed rest last week, so I'm trying to hold on to my faith."

Although it was not evident in her voice, Renee knew that Elise was worried. "You're going to deliver a healthy baby. And of course we can pray in the morning. I think my life has been empty and suffering without it."

"Good, then it's settled." Elise confirmed the time for their prayer sessions, then asked, "So, is she cuter than you or what?"

Oscar was nestled on the end of the couch by Renee's feet when Jerome finally made it home. "Going somewhere?" he asked at the sight of luggage by the steps.

"It's over, Jerome. And, this time I mean it. You have to leave tonight."

"What are you talking about now?" he sighed, and took his Eagles cap off his head.

"I met your girlfriend today."

Jerome fumbled with the newspaper that was in his hand. "What?"

"The charade is over. She and Kara interrupted my business lunch with one of the top guys from California. She could have jeopardized my job."

"What are you talking about?" Jerome asked in an aggravated tone.

Renee snapped, "Your woman."

"I don't have time for this," Jerome huffed. "What woman are you talking about?"

"Taylor. Does that name ring a bell?"

"Renee, how many times do I have to tell you that she is not—"

"No," Renee cut him off. "Then tell me how Taylor knew about the kind of car I drive. How does she know where we live?"

Jerome was searching for an answer. "I do work with her. Maybe I mentioned it one day in the lunchroom or something."

Not believing his story, Renee rolled her eyes and Jerome continued with his explanation. "Maybe Kara told her. You two were good friends once."

"We weren't that close," she blurted. "But that's beside the point." She pointed to her husband. "You've got to stop blaming everybody for your own stupidity." Renee wanted to slap him upside his head, but had promised God earlier in prayer that she'd remain in control of her fury. That's why she remained stationed on the couch. And as long as Jerome kept his distance, she could keep her promise.

"And how on Earth did she get the idea that *you* paid for this house? And that *you let* me buy the Lexus? I guess that was Kara, too, huh?" she demanded to know.

This time, Jerome was speechless.

"Need I remind you that the house is in *my* name?" Renee knew that was a low blow, but she was mad and tired of his deceit.

Jerome rolled his eyes, "That line is getting old, Renee."

"But it's the truth." Renee stared Jerome down. "How could you share my personal business with her? You are supposed to be *my* husband." Tears started to well up in her eyes and she wiped them away before they could fall. "It isn't enough that you sleep with her, but you have to humiliate and belittle me, too?"

"Renee, I-I don't know what to say. I haven't entertained her craziness since before you found the card." Jerome fell into the chair closest to the door. "She's just upset because I won't be with her."

"You need to fess up, Jerome. This game is over," replied Renee. "Look me in the eyes and tell me that you never slept with Taylor. And if you really love me . . . I mean *really* love me, Jerome, you'll tell me the truth."

Jerome glanced around the room and pulled at a loose thread on his work jacket. He couldn't look at his wife, so he responded with a weak, "You wouldn't understand the circumstances. She . . ."

"But, you told me you didn't even know her," she said sadly. Renee didn't expect his confession to sting, but it did. "How could you, Jerome? Taylor knew more about me than most of the people I've worked with for years."

"I made a mistake. She's just someone I work with. It wasn't serious," he confessed. "But I promise you . . . this won't happen again. Just give me another chance, baby. I'll see to it that she stays away from us from now on."

"You don't have any chances left. I can't live like this any longer. You've embarrassed me and this family one too many times."

"I have nowhere to go." There was a crack in her voice and she was on the verge of tears.

"That's not my concern," she said, ignoring his emotional state.

"Where are the boys?" he asked, fighting back tears and noticing the quiet of the house.

Renee moved to the other end of the couch and accidentally sat on Oscar's paw. He moaned and Renee picked him up. "I took them to Brandon's. I plan on telling them in the morning."

"Renee, you're obviously upset and I understand why, but there's nothing between me and Taylor," he pleaded.

"Save it. It's too late, Jerome. I want you to leave," Renee affirmed. She didn't want to hear anymore. The damage was already done.

"Whatever you and this woman have isn't over and won't be as long as you both still work for Septa," Renee said.

Realizing he wasn't going get anywhere tonight, Jerome conceded. "I'll leave tonight, but I'll be back in the morning."

"Give it up, Jerome." To make him understand, Renee decided to break the news. "The boys and I are moving to Chicago."

"What? What are you talking about?" Jerome leaped out the chair and a nervous Oscar scrambled out of Renee's arms.

"I got a promotion. I'm going to Chicago next week to look for a place to live and then the boys and I are gone."

Jerome's eyes drooped. "What about me?"

"If you can pay the mortgage you can stay here, if not, you need to find a place to live. Taylor sounded like she'd take you back."

Jerome paced the floor a few times. "Is this really what you want?"

"Stop wasting time. The world can see that we don't love each other anymore."

Clearly distraught, and with his bags in his hands, Jerome looked at her. "I'll call you in the morning. Maybe you'll change your mind."

"I doubt it."

Renee and the boys sat in the pews of New Life Baptist in silence. As expected, Reggie and Jerome Jr. were upset about their father moving out of the house. While everyone around them was worshipping, they sat unmoved by the spirit that was flowing through the building. The sermon didn't do much for the boys either. Jerome Jr. fell asleep and Reggie scribbled on the church bulletin the entire time. Silent tears escaped Renee's eyes as she listened carefully to the message. Reverend Robinson was teaching about desire. As he preached, Renee looked at her children and realized what she wanted most was not material. She needed peace, love and joy back in her life.

When the sermon was over, Reverend Robinson welcomed people to the altar. "The one thing that I ask of the Lord, the one thing that I seek most, is to live in the house of the Lord all the days of my life."

Renee could feel something pulling her out of her seat, but she fought against it. The pastor closed his eyes and continued, "Listen to my pleading, O Lord. Be merciful and answer me! My heart has heard you say, 'Come and talk with me.' And my heart responds, 'Lord, I am coming.' Do not hide yourself from me."

A warm current moved through Renee's body and she started to twitch in her seat. Reverend Robinson stepped away from the podium and walked down the steps. He moved closer to the people hovering around the pulpit. "If this Psalm is speaking to you, don't hesitate. Come forward." He stretched his arms wide. "If you've never accepted Jesus, come forward. If you need to rededicate your life, come forward. Show God that you desire Him. No matter who you are, come and give your life to Christ."

Renee felt someone grab her hands, and without a thought, she willingly followed. "Don't fight it, baby. Let it all go," Mother Wagner cried as she led Renee to the pulpit. Renee fell to her knees and began to cry uncontrollably as Mother Wagner prayed in her ear.

Renee stayed on her knees until she was done releasing her worries to God. When she was done, she was expecting to feel restored and renewed.

Back at her seat, Jerome Jr. hugged her. "Everything's going to be all right, Mommy."

Though she didn't feel any different, Renee rubbed his head and reached for her other son, "I know baby. I know."

After the service, lines were forming in the lobby at various tables. Members were signing up for Vacation Bible School, retreats and other fun summer events. Renee weaved through the crowd hoping to sneak past any old acquaintances. She wasn't yet ready to answer questions about her whereabouts and absence. She was almost clear when Mother Wagner touched her shoulder. "Take a walk with me," she told Renee.

Renee couldn't say no to Mother Wagner. No one could. She tossed Reggie the keys to her car and told them to wait inside. "Roll down the windows, but don't blast the music." They ran off and Renee forgot to tell them to only play Christian music while they waited. She sent up a quick prayer and followed Mother Wagner to a quiet spot on the side of the church.

"Jerome stayed home?" Mother Wagner asked.

Renee couldn't lie to her. "We've separated."

"I had a feeling that was coming. Tired of his drinking?"

"That, and the fact that he cheated on me," Renee confessed.

"I see." She waved to people who recognized her and turned to face the trees instead of the mounds of people. "You thinking about divorce?"

"It's on my mind. It's more than the affair." Renee faced the trees, too. "We're two different people, and I don't think I'll ever be able to trust him again."

"For the first few years of my marriage, I threatened to leave my husband at least once a year. And every time God made him do something to show me why I married him in the first place. Pray about this. God will tell you what to do."

Renee placed her head on Mother Wagner's shoulder. "I just want to do what's right."

"You will. Some people, like me, may not agree with divorce, but you do what God tells you to do."

"I'm not sure I know what He wants me to do."

"That's why it's important to have a personal relationship with Christ. He speaks to us all, and in many different ways."

"You're the second person that's said that to me."

"That's because it's true," she smiled. "Now, get going before the boys take off without you." Mother Wagner gave Renee a hug. "I will see you next week, right?"

Renee walked briskly to the car. She was ready to go home and start dinner. She wasn't hungry, but the boys had to eat. As she approached her car, she saw a woman standing by the window talking to Reggie.

"Hi, Renee," Kara said when Renee was within range. "Reggie's been telling me about school. It's been a long time. I can't believe he'll be in high school next year."

Renee didn't know what to say, especially in front of her son.

"I guess you figured out why I drifted away," Kara whispered.

Renee checked inside the car. Jerome Jr. was almost asleep and

Reggie had headphones around his ears. "Why didn't you say anything? You've been in my shoes before." Renee pressed her hands in her chest. "You know what this feels like."

"In the beginning I felt like it wasn't any of my business. Then, I wasn't sure what to do. And if it means anything, I didn't approve of the relationship."

Renee could tell that Kara was really troubled by what happened, but it didn't change the way she felt. "I'm not sure I would've known what to do either, but I don't think I could've been around someone involved in an affair with someone married to a woman I was close to. We're not best friends, but we were prayer partners. We prayed about you and Harold together. We prayed about our children."

"But Taylor is my friend. I was in a tough position. I hope you're able to understand that one day." Kara left before Renee could see her cry.

As much as the situation troubled Renee, she knew this was not Kara's fault. Jerome was the person that dug this hole, but somehow Renee felt like she was being buried alive in it. Would she ever be able to climb her way out?

20

Taylor

It had been three days since the incident in Bahama Breeze, and still no call from Jerome. Whenever she stopped by his workstation, he was either repairing a broken down bus outside the depot or on a break. She thought his timing was convenient. How coincidental for Jerome to be away from the depot or out of sight when she was on the premises. He knew Taylor's bus schedule well and should have made himself available. Jerome wasn't even eating lunch in the lunchroom. He and his crew had been going to McDonald's or Burger King. "We need a change of scenery," one of his colleagues had told her one day.

She had driven by his house that night hoping to see him, but saw Renee instead. The buzz around the depot was that he and his wife were having problems and he was now staying with his brother. So why hadn't he called? Why was he hiding? Taylor was tempted to drive over to Brandon's house, but her reactions in the movie theatre and the restaurant now seemed silly. If Jerome wanted to see Taylor, he knew how to contact her.

Taylor changed into a grease-stained T-shirt Jerome had left behind and lay stretched across the couch. The *Batman Returns* DVD was playing, but her mind was focused on other things.

Lance had left her apartment fifteen minutes ago. He had stopped by after work, hoping to spend some quality time.

They watched a movie, all the time with her head nestled snugly on his chest. At one point, she looked up to ask a question and her lips brushed lightly against his. For a few seconds, she was caught up in the softness of his touch. Before things could get out of hand Taylor tried to move away, but Lance wanted to finish what she had started. When Lance was through, Taylor was numb. It had been months since Taylor had felt a kiss like that. She inched away before her hormones got the best of the situation. If it would have lasted just one minute longer, she may have been tempted to invite him to her bed.

They had continued to watch the movie as if nothing had occurred. But it had. The kiss awakened a part of her that she tried to keep hidden. The heat she was feeling was too much to bear, so Taylor had to come up with a way for Lance to leave. She pretended to be fatigued and suffering from a headache. She closed her eyes a few times then eventually kept them closed, occasionally breathing heavy for affect. Being the man that he was, Lance placed a bottle of Tylenol and a tall glass of water on the coffee table and crept out the door.

Taylor waited ten minutes before leaving her spot on the couch. She eyed the cordless on the floor and picked it up. Before she could really think about what she was doing, she dialed Jerome's number.

"Hello," a woman answered.

"I-I'm sorry," Taylor stuttered. "I was looking for Jerome Thomas."

"You have the right number. Who's calling?" the woman wanted to know.

Taylor thought about hanging up. Was it Renee? It didn't sound like her. But if it wasn't Renee, who was it? And why was she answering Jerome's cell phone? "I'm a driver from his job. I um . . . I have a question about something he did to my bus."

"Who is it, Jocelyn?" Taylor heard Jerome say in the background.

Jocelyn? Who the heck was Jocelyn?

"A woman says something's wrong with her bus," Jocelyn tried to whisper.

"Why are you looking at me like that?" he said, and took the phone. "Hello?"

Taylor couldn't answer. Had Jerome found someone new? Was he dating her while they were together? "Hello?" he repeated. Taylor stayed on the phone, breathing softly until Jerome hung up.

Taylor picked up the Tylenol bottle on the table. She wondered if she was infested with the same genes that made her mother give up her own happiness for a man; and one that didn't want her. She slammed the bottle of pills on the table and she screamed at the top of her lungs. Taylor shoved a popcorn bowl so hard across the coffee table, it hit the wall and shattered into pieces. The sound of the mess she made escalated her anger. "I hate men!" she shrieked and flung the only picture she had of her father at the door. The glass of the frame broke and Taylor dropped to the floor. As she lay there, the telephone rang, but she couldn't tear herself away from her current position. Through her moans, she could hear Kara's voice on the answering machine.

"Taylor, I know you're there. We need to talk. Please pick up." There was a few seconds of silence before she continued. "Okay, but you can't ignore me forever." Taylor crawled to her bedroom and into her bed. She was definitely in no condition to deal with Kara tonight.

Taylor strolled to her bus like she had all the time in the world. She was scheduled to depart the mall in less than two minutes and she hadn't boarded the round of usual passengers yet. She walked along the side of the bus and reached in the driver's window to open the door. "Excuse me," she alerted an anxious passenger trying to board. "I need to be on board first." The passenger rolled his eyes and stepped back. She could hear him stirring up the crowd as she walked around the bus. But Taylor didn't care that they were angry. She was tired of this job.

Taylor finished off the last drop of her strawberry milkshake, slurping loud enough to annoy everyone waiting to take their seats. Before she could get settled in her seat, the passengers made their way inside.

"Rough day?" Ivy asked, flashing her fare card.

"You can say that." Taylor shut the doors and sped out of the parking lot.

Ivy, a Community College of Philadelphia student by day, and Zan Zabar Blue bartender by night, came to the mall once a week. She loved to sit by the front door and talk about the latest designers and fashion disasters. She used the money she made as a bartender to fill her closets with the latest styles. Talking to Ivy inspired Taylor's own passion.

Traffic was backed up on the way into the city and the people on the bus were becoming agitated. "If you would have left on time, we wouldn't be in this mess," someone yelled from the back of the bus. Taylor ignored their grumbles and moans. There was nothing she could do.

"Let me off here," an older gentleman demanded.

"Sir, we should be moving in a few minutes," Taylor tried to tell him, but he would not listen. Taylor gave up and opened the door to let him out. If he wanted to walk, that was on him.

Taylor left the door open, taking in the fresh air. She looked at the stores lined along the street and sighed. "One day, I'll have my own boutique."

"What are you waiting for? I'll need a place to house my creations," Ivy said. "I hope your store won't be outrageous. I love clothes, but I can't afford the ones I *really* like."

As the bus inched to the stop light, Taylor noticed a *For Sale* sign in the Bedazzled window. She wasn't surprised that they had gone out of business. "I'd try to be reasonable. But sometimes it doesn't work that way." She pictured herself hanging a sign on the front door that read: Taylor's Boutique.

"Just don't forget about the little people," Ivy continued, "I like to look good, too."

Sherry used her spare key to let herself in Taylor's apartment. Taylor was still dressed in her driver uniform and was watching an old episode of Mash on TV. The living room was overtaken by candy bar wrappers, empty ice cream cartons, and half-eaten cookies. This was unusual for Taylor. Of the three friends, she was the most meticulous. Sherry hung her bag around the knob of the hall closet door and surveyed the apartment. The kitchen was not as bad, though there were a few dirty dishes in the sink. From the odor, Sherry had the impression that they had been there for several days. She walked to the bedroom. As she had expected, clothes were thrown around haphazardly and the covers on the bed were scrunched into a small ball. Sherry took a deep breath and walked back to the living room. She moved an open box of chocolate Teddy Grahams to the coffee table and sat down next to Taylor.

"So, I think we need to talk," Sherry said, using the remote to turn off the television. Taylor was silent, as she stuffed her mouth with sour cream Pringles. "Taylor, eating yourself to death is not going to change anything." Sherry snatched the container from her hand. "Now, tell me what's going on? You didn't answer my calls all week."

"My life is a mess," Taylor mumbled.

"Whose life isn't?" Sherry put her arm around her friend. "We just have to learn how to roll with the punches."

"I can't seem to get ahead. Jerome doesn't want me. Kara's not really my friend. I can't figure out how to start a boutique and Lance is great, but I don't like him," she rambled.

"Okay, let's think about each of these things rationally," Sherry offered. "Jerome may have feelings for you, but the timing is not right. He may divorce his wife in a year. Who knows? But for now, you have to let him go." Sherry looked around the room. "Especially if he's turning you into a slob."

"He's already with someone else," Taylor said solemnly.

"Then be glad it's over," Sherry said. "Now, as for Kara . . . she was in a sticky situation."

"You're on her side?" Taylor asked, her voice rising to a higher pitch.

"That's not what I'm saying. I think she should have told us *something*, but knowing her and her religious nature, I'm sure she didn't know what to do. And, I don't think she would share *any* information about you with Renee."

Sherry had a point. "Do you think I was too hard on her?"

"No, but I don't think you should end the friendship, either."

"You sound like Kara. She must be rubbing off on you."

"I don't think so," Sherry laughed. "But, back to you. As for the boutique, we have to come up with a plan, and as your best friend, I'm here to help. Once we clean up this mess, we'll do some research on the Internet. Now," Sherry paused, "as for Lance. Don't force something that's not working. If you're not ready for him, pass him along to the next girl. Does he know I'm single?"

21

Renee

Renee drove to Brandon's house in great spirits. When she dropped the boys off, she'd drive to the airport, park her car and then board an 8:05 am flight to Chicago. Today, she was scheduled to meet some of the people she'd be working with. Since Renee would be away for several days, she made arrangements for the boys to stay with their father. Jerome was standing on the porch when Renee pulled up to Brandon's house. It was six o' clock in the morning. He hadn't shaved yet, and his eyes were not as wide as they should be. Renee hoped he wasn't drinking again. He had a tendency to wallow in self pity when things weren't going his way. Although she was concerned, his addiction was no longer her problem. Against her mother and Elise's advice, Renee had scheduled an appointment with a divorce lawyer after her trip to Chicago.

"Okay, make sure your father gets you to school on time," she said as she helped them unload the car.

"I'll keep a record," Jerome Jr. replied.

"Okay, give me a kiss. I'll be back on Sunday."

Jerome Jr. kissed his mother and ran out of the car. Oscar ran behind him, stopping a few times to catch a "second wind." She was surprised at how responsible the boys had become about taking care of the dog. She had actually grown to love Oscar and his funny noises more than she expected. Maybe Jerome had finally picked the perfect gift after all.

Reggie lifted his book bag from the sidewalk and gave Renee a quick peck on the cheek.

"Just because I'll be away doesn't mean you don't need your teacher's signatures," she mentioned, reminding Reggie of the daily progress report she had created for his teachers to sign and comment on every day.

"I know, Mom," he said, clinging to his basketball.

"I'm just letting you know. You've been doing good so far, keep it up."

"Can I play ball this weekend?" Reggie asked with a spark in his eyes. He was praying his mother would reconsider her no-basketball-at-the-club-until-Christmas rule.

Renee hesitated, afraid that she would seem like a push over if she gave in. Just last week, she agreed to let him accompany Zora to a movie with her family. "You can go to the center this week, *only* if your father agrees to pick you up." Reggie smiled and gave her another kiss. "Be good," she said watching him bounce his ball up the walkway. "I'll call everyday!"

When Renee pulled off, she called Jocelyn. In case Jerome failed to pick up Reggie from the center, she wanted to make sure someone else would.

Everett was at the O' Hare airport when Renee's plane landed. She was surprised to see him. Originally, his assistant was scheduled to pick her up and carry her back to the hotel. Everett walked slightly ahead of her, carrying two of her heaviest bags. Even dressed casually in a crème linen pants ensemble, Everett looked good. Renee didn't understand why this man wasn't married. He was intelligent, had a stable career, no children, and fine. *Something must be wrong with him*, she thought.

He placed her Louis Vuitton luggage collection in the trunk of the rental car with little effort. "You sure you're not moving today?" he teased.

Renee found herself staring at the muscle definition of his arms. Even in high school, Jerome didn't have arms that perfect.

"Once you're settled, I thought I'd show you around Chicago. It's a beautiful city. Ever been?" he queried as he opened Renee's door.

"Only to the airport in between connecting flights," she said, enjoying his gentleman-like behavior.

Driving along the Dan Ryan expressway, Everett called out various neighborhoods. He grew up near the Garfield Park section of the city. "I have to give you a tour. I think you'll like it here. It's much bigger than Philly and has great culture, great food, many things to do, and the Navy Pier is incredible."

Renee listened to Everett sell the city and could feel something happening between them. "I look forward to the tour."

"I know I'm excited. But I'm glad to finally be able to work with you. You've done so many great things in Philly. With all of the resources here in Chicago, I can't wait to see what you'll do with this hotel."

The drive from the airport to the downtown hotel was long. Traffic was bumper to bumper, much more than what she experienced on the 76 expressway in Philly. When they finally reached Michigan Ave, Renee was awestruck. In her opinion, the infamous Rodeo Drive had nothing on the Magnificent Mile. The downtown streets were lined with many different theatres, restaurants, and designer stores. It was a shopper's paradise!

Everett turned off Michigan Avenue and onto a small street. At first glance, it looked isolated. One side of the street consisted of a huge parking garage and one restaurant. A Potbelly's was at the corner. Construction was taking place on the other side. It only took a minute for Renee to realize that behind the boarded walls, builders were working on Luxury Inn's grand hotel.

Everett parked in the car lot and they walked across the street, past the observers trying to peek inside the compound. People strained their necks to get an up close view of the new addition to the downtown urban experience. Others studied the life-size poster planted close to the corner. Renee and Everett wove through the crowd and entered the building through the employee only entrance. Renee was impressed. The hotel was massive! The new millennium-like exterior was sure to attract tourists and locals alike.

In the lobby, Renee marveled at the glass elevators outlined with tiny white lights. On the outside of the elevators was a waterfall whose water flowed into a small pond of tropical fish. "This is beautiful," she exclaimed.

"Then you've got to see upstairs," Everett stated softly.

Waiting for the elevator, Renee observed the men in hard hats and tank tops, diligently working on the stores that would outline the main floor.

"The suites are already done," Everett stated. "You'll be staying in one of them."

"I hope I won't be the only one on the floor," she said, giving him a concerned glare.

"No," he laughed. "We're all on the same floor."

The elevator arrived and they stepped inside. Everett pushed the number seven button and they cruised smoothly to the seventh floor. When the doors opened, Renee walked out first with her bags in tow. Everett ran in front of Renee and escorted her to the executive offices. "Your office is at the end of the hall," he said, pointing to a large door with chrome handles.

The other members of the team were seated in the conference room and came to the door when they heard Everett's voice. They all smiled and congratulated Renee on her new position as she slowly walked toward them. She felt like a movie star walking down the red carpet as she approached the door to her private office. She paused briefly to study her name and title engraved on the oblong chrome plate positioned in the center of the door. She pushed the door lightly and was overwhelmed by the space inside. Windows covered an entire section of the wall, giving her a fantastic view of Navy Pier and Lake Michigan. She walked further in and quickly estimated the room dimensions. The room was not yet decorated, but the possibilities were endless. The room was big enough to fit at least fifty people comfortably. *Is this for real?* she silently asked God.

Everett stood by the window and looked out over the lake. "What do you think?"

Renee moved next to him. Although there were people already enjoying the serene waters in their boats, the scenery was still amazing. "This is well beyond my expectations."

"Enjoy it, Renee. You've worked hard for this."

"Will you have an office here?" she asked, still entranced by the peaceful waters.

"No, I'll only be here until the grand opening. After that, I'm back in California."

Renee closed her eyes to keep from crying. After all that she had suffered with Jerome, she could tell that her life was finally coming back together.

The team of managers spent several hours reviewing the plans for the grand opening and hotel operations, leaving only enough time to grab sandwiches at the Potbelly's across the street. By seven o'clock, everyone but Renee and Everett were ready to enjoy the Chicago nightlife. Instead of joining their colleagues for a night of fun, they decided to walk a few blocks to the Grand Lux Cafe, a Cheesecake Factory subsidiary, where the meals were even more exotic. There, they could discuss work-related matters more intimately.

Renee ordered the Indochine chicken and shrimp entrée. The fusion of Chinese and Indian flavors captivated her taste buds. She savored every minute of the spicy sauce, plum wine, and ginger mixed with the meat and rice. She tried to focus on hotel business, but was more interested in her meal.

Renee glanced around the room, observing the unique architecture and atmosphere. With the exception of a few group of friends, the restaurant was filled with couples. It had been a long time since Renee enjoyed an upscale restaurant without numerous co-workers or clients. She noticed that Everett was enjoying his caramel chicken. He barely said a word since his meal was placed on the table.

"So, why aren't you married?" Renee decided to ask.

He swallowed the food in his mouth before speaking. "Women say I work and travel too much. And to think, I thought this job would put me in a better position with women."

"Oh, it is a bonus. We love a working man," she laughed. "You just need to find the balance between work and social life. Women love attention." Renee placed the last forkful of food in her mouth and pushed her plate away.

"I think I need a woman that can match my drive and work ethic."

Renee wiped her mouth and took a sip of water. "She's out there. You just need to be more observant."

"I'll keep that in mind," Everett responded and leaned back in his seat. "If you don't mind me asking, what's up with you and your husband?"

Renee paused. She was having such a good time that she had forgotten about Jerome. "We're separated."

"That's too bad," Everett simply said and Renee couldn't tell whether or not he meant it.

The waiter arrived with the check and they both reached for their credit cards. "I got this one," Renee insisted, handing the waiter her Master Card. "You can take care of dinner tomorrow."

Minutes later, the waiter returned and leaned in close to Renee's ear. "Excuse me, Mrs. Thomas. Do you have another card? This one has been denied."

"What? That can't be right," she replied, embarrassed.

Everett pulled out his wallet. "Don't worry, I'll take care of this."

"No, I have another card. I just don't know why this one didn't go through," she said, then remembered the suits and shoes she purchased for the meeting. *But, there should still be enough on the card.* Jerome must have gone over the limit. "This one should be good," she told the waiter, handing him a different card.

As if he could read her thoughts, Everett leaned in close and said, "Before you blame your husband, call the company to see if this is some kind of mistaken identity case."

It was too late to call the credit card company, so Renee hooked up her laptop and connected to the Internet. She navigated through the Master Card website. Right away she noticed that there was only twenty-four dollars left on a card that had a five thousand dollar limit. She hit the button for recent and archived purchases and discovered that Jerome recently used the card to pay a twelve hundred dollar gas bill. She slapped the desk with her hand and chipped a nail. With her finger in her mouth, she continued to investigate. Previous months showed Jerome's miniscule payments, as well as charges for the electric, gas, cable, and telephone bills—all the bills he was supposed to pay with his bi-weekly check. She clicked back to the month of December and couldn't believe her eyes. There were purchases for items that never made it into their home. Jerome had purchased a flat screen television, a stove, an entertainment center . . .

Renee slammed the laptop shut and dialed Jerome's cell. When he answered, Renee could tell he was at the bar. She could barely hear him through all of the loud music and conversations around him. "Do you want to explain the Master Card?" she bawled into the phone.

"What? What did you say? I can barely hear you," he said into the phone. "Let me go outside and call you right back."

Renee sat on the edge of the bed tapping her foot against the bedspring. The phone only had one chance to ring. "How did you manage to get the credit card up to five thousand dollars?" she yelled.

"What are you talking about now?"

"The Master Card. I tried to pay for dinner and the card was denied."

"If you didn't buy all those uppity clothes, that wouldn't have happened," he slurred in defense.

"Never mind my clothes, Jerome. I've been contributing to a bill primarily used to furnish your girlfriend's home."

"The card was doing fine until you ran it up."

"What part don't you understand? We didn't get this card to finance extramarital affairs."

"You don't pay *that* bill," Jerome stumbled though his words.

"So, I believe *my* money has been paying the bill."

"But, what about the budget? It was established based on the money *we* made."

"As you have repeatedly pointed out, you're the one making all the money. Think of this as charity."

Renee hung up the phone before their disagreement escalated. He was obviously drunk and in no condition to make any sense. She made a note to cancel the account in the morning. She'd also have to call and check on the other bills. She and the boys shouldn't have to live without utilities because he didn't have any money. She walked to the window and looked out into the night sky. Chicago's skyline was lit up in an array of colors. "Beautiful," she sighed. She placed her hand on the windowsill and looked down. *Very soon, I'll be a free woman.*

"Up for a boat ride?" Everett asked Renee, looking up from a pile of papers in his office. "I think we're done for the day."

"Sure, I'll be done in twenty minutes," she answered, typing notes into her laptop. Renee worked diligently all day, skipping lunch and declining dinner plans with their other team members to avoid thinking about Jerome. The best way for her to calm down after an argument was to dedicate her energy to work.

"Okay, but only twenty minutes. You need a change of scenery." Everett stood to his feet. "Have you left the hotel at all today?"

"No, I haven't. There's so much to do."

Everett walked over to where she was seated and moved her hands away from the computer. Renee was sensitive to his touch. He moved the mouse around until it reached the save icon. "This can wait until tomorrow," he told her as she saved the document she was working on. "You've gone above and beyond your tasks for the day. Now, shut down this thing."

Renee was motionless as he lightly brushed against her. The muscles in her stomach began to shudder each time he said a word. "Okay," she said, rationalizing that it was not polite to argue with the boss. Everett smiled and Renee couldn't believe she was blushing. She only hoped he hadn't noticed.

"Besides, it's a beautiful evening," he said. "I'll meet you in the lobby in fifteen minutes."

"Make it thirty, I need to change."

Renee got to see yet another side of Everett. When she met him in the lobby, he was dressed in dark jeans and a button down shirt; probably his best attempt at being "hip." Still, he wore the outfit well. The sound of her heels clicking on the marble floor alerted Everett to her arrival. The bottom of her sundress swayed from side to side as she walked toward him.

"Pretty dress," he commented, trying not to stare at her legs too long. "You're starting at a good time of the year. Early June weather isn't bad at all. But by September you'll need a wool coat."

Renee flashed a smile. "Please say you're exaggerating."

Everett grinned, pleased that he had gotten Renee to loosen up with a smile. "I am. But you will have to get used to cold winters. They don't call this the Windy City for nothing." He pointed toward the doors of the hotel. "Shall we?"

Rather than drive to the Navy Pier, they hailed a cab. It was cheaper than spending money on a garage and better than taking a risk of not getting a good parking space. They could've walked the seven or eight blocks, but Renee wasn't going to make it that far in her high heel sandals.

Seeing the Ferris wheel up close was even more spectacular than the view from her window. She felt like a kid going to an amusement park for the first time. Trying to contain her excitement wasn't easy. This was the first time she had been to a place like this without the boys. Tonight, she would actually be able to enjoy herself without Jerome Jr. whining for sweets, Reggie begging for money to play games, and Jerome getting sick from an upset stomach.

Chicago was known for its cold weather and monster winds, but the night was warm and comfortable with a slight breeze. Thousands of people were hanging out at the pier; laughing, enjoying rides and digesting good food. The line to the Ferris wheel was long, but Renee insisted they wait. The actual ride wasn't much faster as it was created more for sight-seers than for thrillseekers. The view from the top was amazing and only a professional picture could capture its true beauty. Being 150 feet in the air, overlooking Lake Michigan and the lakefront was magical. Renee felt it and was sure Everett did, too. He put his arm along the back of the car, his hand vaguely touching her shoulder while she was taking pictures, and she didn't mind. It felt good and in a strange way made her feel safe.

The boat ride was just as special. As they flowed down Lake Michigan on one of Chicago's sightseeing tour boats, Renee and Everett enjoyed the fireworks. They sipped fruit drinks and talked about their college days. Renee was surprised to learn that Everett belonged to one of the most prestigious black fraternities. They joked about the crazy things he had done as part of his initiation, and he performed a solo step show. Renee was impressed by this man and it scared her. She sensed that their business relationship was taking off in a different direction. And, her suspicions were right. At the end of the night, Everett walked Renee to her door and touched her hand. Renee knew a kiss was coming and didn't stop him. She didn't want to. But when their lips touched, guilt made her pull back.

"I know that was a little forward. It's just that . . . well, we had such a nice time," he said, his eyes soft and comforting.

"No need to explain. I had a nice time, too," Renee assured him, "but, I'm still married."

"You're right. It was wrong of me to put you in that position. I hope this won't affect our working together."

Renee could see that he was sincere. "We'll just pretend it never happened."

"Then I'll see you in the morning."

Back in Philadelphia, all Renee could think about was the kiss she almost shared with Everett. That night had not impeded on their working relationship, in fact, they had made great strides. The grand opening was still on schedule for December. She left Everett in Chicago knowing that if nothing else happened between them, they'd at least be good friends.

Renee was ready to see her children. She had called Jerome an hour ago to let him know she was back in town. Since it was late, Renee asked him to bring the boys home. She was too tired to swing by Brandon's to get them herself. Oscar was the first to realize she was home, barking and shuffling his feet in a frenzy.

"I missed you, too, little guy," Renee said, shaking his loose cheeks. Jerome was on the couch half asleep and watching a baseball game on TV. He acknowledged Renee with a head nod.

Jerome Jr. ran downstairs and nearly knocked Renee into the chair. "Did you find us a place?" he asked excitedly.

Renee reached into the shopping bag from Marshall Field's. "I saw a few possibilities. Where's your brother?" she asked, tossing him a Chicago Bears T-shirt.

"Cool," Jerome Jr. replied. "Reggie's in his room. He has a new hairdo," he tattled, holding the shirt in the air.

Jerome let out a huge sigh and Renee could smell the traces of alcohol. "Snitches get stitches," he said to his youngest son.

She rolled her eyes and walked to the stairs. "Reggie, I'm home.

Come let me get a look at you." In less than a minute, Reggie walked downstairs and Renee could feel her blood pressure jump several notches. Reggie's afro was now a series of tiny, intricate rows and twists of cornrows. "Who approved this?" Reggie looked at his father. Jerome was no help. Just that quick, he had fallen asleep, his head bent backward and mouth wide open. "Why didn't you call and ask me, Reggie? You know how I feel about braids."

"It's nothing wrong with the cornrows, Renee. Calm down," Jerome barked from the couch, half asleep.

Her head quickly spun around in his direction. "That's beside the point. I told him he had to wait until he was sixteen."

"Braids will be out of style by then. Let the boy be a teenager. All his friends have them," Jerome said, bothered that his sleep was being interrupted.

"Reggie, go upstairs and take the braids out. Wash your hair and when I come up there, I want to see the afro you had when I left on Wednesday." She threw the gift she had for him back in the bag. "Junior, take Oscar upstairs. Mommy will be up soon." Jerome Jr. used all the strength he had to lift Oscar and didn't waste anytime going to his room. He couldn't stand to hear his parents argue.

"Jerome, please get your things and leave," ordered Renee.

Jerome stretched. "I've been thinking. This is my house, too. I think I should stay," he said, ending the sleep he knew he wasn't going to get.

This man has lost his mind. "If you don't leave in ten minutes, I'm calling the police."

"Call the police? Have we come to this?" he questioned, struggling to sit up straight.

"I'm through arguing. I have an appointment with Diane, my divorce attorney, on Tuesday."

Jerome's boldness decreased. "I can't believe you want a divorce."

"What did you expect, Jerome? I come home to find you chillin' on the couch like you belong here, when I *told* you to bring the boys home and wait for me to get here. And to make matters worse, I can smell the alcohol. You know how much I despise that around my children."

"So now they're your children."

"Is that all you have to say?" Renee looked at him in disbelief. "My fourteen-year-old child has braids after I told him he had to wait. Add this to the years I spent taking care of this family *alone*. And, let's not forget the Taylor discovery. You know, the woman you don't know?"

"Oh, not again," Jerome flipped her off.

"Yes, you were involved in a serious relationship with another woman. And, that's all you have to say?" Jerome didn't move. Renee placed her Louis Vuitton luggage on the bottom stairs and walked to the front door. "It's over, Jerome. Now please, just leave."

"You made me this way, you know. I wouldn't be drinking if I felt like a man around here." Jerome was reaching, hoping Renee would have a change of heart.

Renee walked to the phone and picked up the receiver. "I'm calling the cops in two minutes."

Jerome's cell phone vibrated on the coffee table and he picked it up. He looked at the number and got up, straightening his clothes. "I'll be back for my things next weekend." Jerome stumbled onto the porch and checked his cell again.

"You might want to answer that. It might be Taylor."

Jerome rolled his eyes and hit the talk button, "Hello?" A few seconds later, he grabbed the railing to keep from falling. "What happened?"

Whatever happened, Renee didn't want to know about it. She prayed he'd get home safely, turned off the porch light, and went upstairs to spend time with her children.

Renee was awakened by the doorbell. She looked at her clock. 2:33 am. Someone had obviously made a mistake by coming to her house at that hour. She buried herself deeper under the covers and tried to go back to sleep. A minute later, the doorbell rang again. This time, she threw the sheet off her body. The bell rang again, this time three times in a row and followed by a series of thumps on the door. Renee jumped up and ran down the hall to check on her children. They were both still sound asleep. She stood at the top of the stairs, waiting for something else to happen. *Who could it be? Taylor again? Is she trying to hurt me?*

A crash from the side of her house made her leap at least two inches into the air. She was beginning to panic, but ran back to her bedroom to get the cordless and peek out the window. There was a car in the middle of the street. One she didn't recognize. Maybe Taylor was in a different car. The bell rang again and she could hear a male voice shouting curse words. *Who is this guy?* Renee went to dial 9-1-1, but was shaking so hard she could barely hold the phone in her hand.

"Mom?" Reggie muttered, scaring Renee as he entered her room.

She motioned for him to get back in his room. She listened intently for any movement or evidence of an intruder. Reggie noticed her shaky hands and took the phone. "I'll call the cops."

Renee didn't argue with him. She was glad he was awake. She slowly walked down the stairs, picking up an African statue along the way. She had to hold it with both hands for fear of dropping it. Her hands were still quivering uncontrollably.

Voices from the street caught her attention. She ducked and crawled to the front window, peeking just enough to get a good look. No sign of Taylor. Just two men arguing and pushing one another. One of them was her neighbor.

"Is this your car?" one man slurred.

"You're drunk," the neighbor shouted back. "Go back to the bar."

The man ran back up the shared driveway and kicked the neighbor's car. "Is this your car? You're in my spot, man. Move your car!" he roared, now pounding the car with his fists.

The neighbor realized that his side and back window was broken and flipped. "Hey, man, what's your problem? This is my driveway. You don't live here!"

Renee stayed low in the event the man had a gun or other weapon. Reggie came down the stairs and put his arm around his mother. "They're on their way."

Renee and Reggie remained hidden under the living room window, praying until red and blue flashing lights appeared. Renee could finally breathe. The man outside very clearly had one too many drinks and was unaware of his surroundings, not to mention overemotional about a parking space that didn't belong to him. Something like this had never happened on her block before. Tonight was a first, and it made her situation clear. She was paranoid about what Taylor could possibly do to her family and Reggie was now the man of the house.

22

Jerome

Jerome rushed to the hospital after receiving Sherry's call. Taylor had been in a car accident. Weaving through traffic, Jerome prayed he wouldn't get stopped by the police. He had a few Heinekens while waiting for Renee to get home from Chicago and would definitely fail a breathing test.

Through blurry eyes and ignoring several red lights, Jerome made it to Einstein hospital safely. He grabbed the mints from the glove compartment and popped five of them in his mouth. He tested the mints by blowing hot air into his hands, and then swallowed four more. He didn't want to take any chances.

At the front desk, Jerome explained that his girlfriend had been in an accident. "We got in a huge fight, and now," he told an uninterested guard, "I just hope she's all right." Jerome explained more than he should, causing a small hint of alcohol to creep into the air. The guard shook his head, but decided to give Jerome the necessary information anyway.

Jerome stood by the elevators and tapped the button nonstop. "What's taking it so long?" he griped aloud. Impatient, Jerome decided to take the stairs. By the third landing, he was out of breath and sweating. He leaned against the railing and took a few deep breathes. "Get yourself together, Jerome." He counted to ten and skipped two stairs at a time to the fifth floor. When he opened the doors he was tired, but too anxious to find Taylor. He started walking to the left and spotted Harold reading a newspaper in the waiting room. "How is she?" he asked, breathing heavy.

"Her leg was broken in two places, but she'll be fine," Harold told him.

"Where is she? I need to see her."

Harold put down the paper. "I don't think that's a good idea."

"Why not?"

Harold looked as if to say, "C'mon, man." Jerome backed out of the room and looked down the hall. "I don't care what you think, where is she?" Lance appeared in the hallway and Jerome became defensive. "Is he the reason I can't see her?"

Harold folded his paper and followed him. "Jerome, man, you need to calm down. This is a hospital."

"I'll calm down once I see Taylor." Jerome charged toward Lance who was now positioned in front of the door like a soldier. Jerome stopped in front of him and poked out his chest. "You need to move out my way."

Lance didn't budge. "I'm not looking for any trouble, man. Taylor isn't ready to see any visitors."

"You're here. If anybody had a right to be here . . ." Jerome said before Harold pulled him away by the arm and dragged him around the corner, pushing him up against the wall.

"Man, what's wrong—"

"How much did you have?" Harold questioned.

"What are you talking about?"

"You can't be serious. It's no secret that you've been drinking. And in case you weren't aware, there are a few people in Taylor's room that blame you for her accident."

"How is this *my* fault? We haven't been together in months!"

"We know, and Taylor's been an emotional wreck since."

Jerome smacked his forehead with the palm of his hand. "I have to see her," he blurted and charged back to her room. This time, Kara was blocking the door.

"Don't even think about it. You've done enough damage," Kara said. "How did you know she was here anyway?"

"Sherry called me," he noted. "Is she here?" Kara rolled her eyes. "I just want to see that she's all right," Jerome begged. He tried to peek inside, but Kara didn't give him any leeway. "Why are you doing this? I should be in there with her."

Harold stepped to Jerome once again and said, "Let's take a walk."

From the corner of Jerome's eye, he could see the nurses on the floor looking his way. To avoid any further embarrassment, he conceded to Kara's demands and walked away with Harold.

Harold and Jerome walked along the path leading to the street and settled on a bench hidden on the side of a tree. "Jerome, I mean this as a friend and a brother. You need to get your life together," Harold told him.

Jerome began to sob. For five minutes, he cried like a child. His shoulders heaved up and down and his nose released an ounce of liquid. And, Jerome wasn't ashamed. "Nothing in my life is going right." He wiped his nose with the sleeve of his shirt. "I guess my bad deeds are catching up with me, huh?"

Harold had been drawing pictures in the dirt with the tip of his Nike. "You can't keep doing the wrong thing and expect something good to come out of it. I've been in your shoes, so I know. My life became a mess when I started cheating on Kara. It took more than two years for us to patch things up."

Jerome wiped his eyes to clear any trace of tears. "Renee wants a divorce, and I think she's serious." Jerome kicked the rocks surrounding his feet. "Kara never asked you for a divorce, did she?"

"No, but then she was never confronted in a restaurant."

Jerome chuckled. "Only in my world does that happen."

"You're lucky they didn't kill each other."

"Yeah, or me."

"Seriously, man, it took Kara and I two years to work things out. If you and Renee really love each other, God can find a way to change her mind about the divorce. But you have got to be willing to change."

"That's a shameless plug."

Harold looked confused. "What do you mean?"

"You're trying to get me to come to church."

"Hey, it can't hurt. You see I'm back with my wife. Where have you been laying your head?"

Harold had a point. Jerome had been sharing a room with his nephew since Renee put him out. The twin bed he slept on was barely big enough for his two hundred and fifty pound body. "I really messed up," Jerome confessed. "I love Renee, I really do, but it's like . . ." Jerome looked away, "one day I woke up and she was this high powered professional."

"And, you're ashamed of that?"

"No . . . not really."

"Don't tell me you're one of those guys who is intimidated by women who make more money?" Jerome focused on the cars that whizzed by on Broad Street. "There's no room for an ego in marriage. You should be proud of Renee. She's worked hard to be where she is at the hotel," Harold commented. "I don't think Renee ever had a problem with you being a Septa mechanic. That's your hang up. The last time I checked, mechanics bring home a paycheck, too."

Jerome half smiled. "I am proud of her. Did you know she got another promotion?"

"Renee is going to own Luxury Inn one day." Harold smiled, "And if I was you, I wouldn't stand in her way. Some women were just born with a business-oriented mind. Don't penalize her for that."

"I guess my pride got in the way," Jerome admitted.

"Putting all that pressure on Renee isn't fair," Harold told him. "You have to work with her not against her."

Jerome got up and faced the busy street. "I hear you, Harold, and I appreciate this talk. But, I think it's too late for me and Renee."

"With God, anything is possible," Harold replied.

23

Taylor

For hours, Taylor stared at a tiny black stain on the ceiling of her hospital room. Taylor's unresponsive behavior concerned her friends. They sat next to her bed in shifts, praying she'd will herself out of what appeared to be a self-induced coma.

The sound of Jerome's voice is what snapped her back into reality. She'd heard the commotion outside her door, but lay silently in the bed. She wasn't ready to speak to anyone. On any other day, Taylor would have responded to his demands to see her. But today, she needed her space.

Kara had walked in once Jerome left the floor. "You think she heard any of that?" she whispered to Sherry.

"She hasn't moved, but it's possible." Sherry grabbed her purse from the windowsill. "Maybe you should have let him in. She might have responded."

"I told you not to call him," Kara stated. "She'll be very vulnerable when she decides to talk. His being here would just confuse her." Kara sat in the empty chair by the window. "We did the right thing by turning him away."

"If you say so," Sherry uttered and left the room.

From the bed, Taylor could tell there was still some tension between her two friends. She wiggled her toes quickly a few times while the girls weren't looking. They were itching and felt a bit stiff. Surviving the crash was a miracle. Her truck was completely totaled, yet the only injuries she incurred were a broken leg and a few scratches.

After work that night, she had planned to meet Sherry to discuss ideas for starting the boutique. Taylor had stopped by the Barnes and Noble just minutes from the bus depot to purchase books that would help them develop a strong business plan. Sherry promised to order pizza if Taylor made her famous pineapple upside down cake. In the midst of mixing the batter, Taylor realized she didn't have enough brown sugar. It was pouring outside, but she didn't want to let Sherry down.

On the way to the market, Taylor sat close on the wheel, straining to see the other cars on the road. *This wasn't a good idea,* she thought, cruising past Girls High. As she followed the curve around LaSalle University, the rain started to let up. Taylor was relieved, sitting a little more comfortably in the seat. Out of nowhere, a stray dog limped into the road, causing Taylor to slam on her brakes. The street was too slick to withstand the sudden force of the wheels, and Taylor's 4Runner skidded onto the sidewalk and into a tree in the middle of the park. When Taylor came to, she was laying in a hospital bed with Sherry and Kara sniffling by her side.

Taylor hated hospitals. The last time she had been in one, her mother died. Though she knew wonderful things happened in the hospital, like the birth of a baby or saving someone from a stroke, negative experiences were all she had. Until today. For some reason God chose to spare her life, and she had decided not to take that for granted.

Kara moved the chair closer to Taylor's bed. She looked at the machines above the bed and the tubes coming from Taylor's arms. The thought of losing Taylor before they had a chance to make up bothered her, and she began to cry. She closed the book in her hand and pulled a tissue from her purse. "Thank you, Jesus," she repeated over and over. She was well aware that the accident could have ended differently.

According to the doctors, Taylor's present condition was not unusual. It had only been eight hours since the accident. "Let's give her more time," the doctor told a concerned Kara. "Her body is still in shock."

Kara got up to turn on the television and paused to look at the bruises on Taylor's face. The nurse on duty said Taylor was lucky, but Kara chose to believe that angels had shielded her from any major damage. She rubbed Taylor's hair, trying to control a few stubborn strands. Slow-moving tears were still falling from her eyes, occasionally landing on Taylor's shoulder. Kara placed her other hand over Renee's and prayed. Halfway through, Kara felt the gentle rub of Taylor's thumb on her hand.

After a couple days of tests and observation, Taylor was released from the hospital on crutches. Minus the broken leg, Taylor was in excellent condition. She was not as talkative, but that was by choice.

Sherry moved in with Taylor to assist with everyday needs. Taylor didn't mind. Things that once took five minutes to do, now took thirty or more. Walking to one end of her apartment to the other was a chore. Taylor's hallway was narrow, so she had to inch down sideways, careful not to hit her cast on the wall. It was difficult, but Taylor was learning how to maneuver and adjust. Now all that was left to handle was her personal relationships. Starting with Lance.

Since the accident, not a day had gone by without seeing Lance. But today she had to put a stop his visits. As she looked at him putting fresh flowers in a glass vase in the kitchen table, Taylor couldn't believe she was about to end their budding relationship. He had been so supportive; more supportive than she imagined Jerome would've been. Not to mention the fact that he was handsome. The crème and gold Sean John sweats he was wearing hung well on him. It made his chubbier areas look flattering.

Behind him, Sherry was parked in front of the refrigerator, pulling out any and everything that smelled or appeared suspicious. Once she was satisfied with the food she kept inside it, she closed the door and tied two garbage bags.

"I'll leave you two alone," Sherry announced, twisting her micro braids into a ponytail. "Either of you need anything from the market?"

"I'm good," Lance said and joined Taylor on the couch.

"Okay, I'll be back in an hour," she said, grabbing the two garbage bags and heading to the front door.

"You sure you don't need any help with that?" Lance offered, seeing Sherry struggle to get out the door.

"Positive," Sherry asserted. "These aren't as heavy as they look," she said and left the apartment.

Taylor's palms and underarms were sweaty, as they always were when she was nervous. Lance sat comfortably on the other end of the couch clinging to the remote control. In just a few months, they had once again become good friends. That's what made this a difficult moment for Taylor. Lance was a good man. Much better than the ones she was used to dealing with, but she had to concentrate on taking care of herself.

"Can you turn the TV off?" she said a notch above the characters on the TV screen. Lance looked her way. He knew something bad was coming. "We need to talk."

"Uh-oh, that doesn't sound good," he said, hitting the mute button.

Taylor repositioned her body on the couch, careful not to whack her leg on the table. "You're a very nice guy . . ."

"I see where this is going," Lance sighed.

"You've been supportive from day one, and I really appreciate that . . ."

"But . . ."

"But . . . I need to focus on making my life better," Taylor said, wiping the sweat that had accumulated in her palms on her legs. "I've been so preoccupied with finding the right man, that I didn't make time for something I've wanted since I was ten." Taylor paused briefly, "I hope you understand. I really do like you, but I've been given a second chance at life. I can't afford to be distracted this time around."

Lance sat on the couch, tossing the remote from one hand to the other. "I guess there's nothing I can say," he said, eyes now fixed on a candle in the middle of the coffee table. "I have to respect your wishes."

"Lance, please don't make this hard on me. I still want us to be friends."

Lance got up to leave. "It's cool, Taylor. I understand, but forgive me if I can't go back to just being friends." Lance sat the remote on the table, gathered his belongings and walked out of the apartment.

Sherry returned from the grocery store, managing to carry several plastic bags up the three flights of stairs to Taylor's apartment, where she stumbled into the apartment with the bags in her hands. "You really need a working elevator in this building," she said, nearly our breath. "I think I bought enough food to last us until next month." Sherry dropped the bags on the floor and looked around the apartment. "Lance went home?"

"He left," Taylor said sadly, still stationed in front of the television.

"Something happen between you two?"

Taylor attempted to get up, but kept falling back into the couch. She lifted both legs and swung them on the couch instead. "I told him I wanted us just to be friends."

"Why'd you do that?" she asked. "And, why today? I could've used some help putting this stuff away," Sherry said, trying to make light of the situation.

"I need to step away from men for a while."

"Is this a new Taylor?"

"You can say that."

"Does this mean I'm getting the axe, too?"

"I could never break up with my best friend, but I do need to talk to you."

Sherry studied Taylor's face. "Should I pack my things?" she questioned, half joking.

"Of course not. I just want to get something off my chest."

"Oookay, can I at least put the groceries away?"

Taylor nodded in approval and patiently waited.

Sherry handed Taylor a cup filled with her favorite drink of the month, Minute Maid's *Cherry Limeade*. She cuddled in the corner of the couch. "So, what's up?"

Taylor turned off the television. "Thank you for being my friend."

"No need to thank me. I'm just doing what best friends do." Sherry pulled a decorative pillow from behind her and hugged it. "It's the least I can do after what happened. I mean, if you weren't going to buy sugar for a cake I really didn't need, you wouldn't be bound in that cast."

"What happened wasn't your fault," Taylor responded. "I think I needed a wake up call. Which is what I want to talk to you about." Taylor sipped the juice. "Kara asked me to go to a women's Bible study Friday night. I want you to come with me."

"You have changed," Sherry said, surprised. "But I don't know. You know how I feel about church people. And on a Friday night?"

"I'm not asking you to go for the people. I'm asking you to go as my friend, my best friend. I can't explain it, but I feel like God wants me to go," Taylor said, hoping Sherry would understand. Taylor wasn't sure what to expect when she got there, but she knew she had to go, and she wanted her best friend by her side. "You have something better to do?"

Sherry looked at Taylor strangely. "Doesn't Renee go to New Life?"

Taylor nodded yes. "As Kara explained to me earlier on the phone, we don't have to sit anywhere near her. She might not even show up."

"It's a good thing New Life is huge," Sherry said.

"Besides," Taylor began, "I'm going to see Jesus. I don't have time to think about Renee."

Sherry laughed so hard at Taylor's last remark that she almost choked on her drink. "Don't tell me I have another Kara on my hands." She sat her glass on the coffee table. "I'm not sure about this, but if you want me there, I'll go. You might have to owe me after this."

"Why? You should want to go to church."

"This is a women's Bible study. There won't be any men for me to meet."

24

Jerome

On his day off, Jerome sat in front of Taylor's apartment waiting for Sherry to leave. He overheard Kara telling a co-worker that she was staying with Taylor until the cast was removed.

When Sherry finally came out of the building, Jerome turned the radio off and held his head low. He waited until Sherry's car was out of sight before entering the building. Jerome took a deep breath and buzzed her apartment. He had his own set of keys, but thought it best to buzz first. What if she had company? Jerome waited a few minutes, and when there was no response, he hit the buzzer again.

"Yes," Taylor sang into the intercom.

"Taylor," he said nervously, "It's me. Can I please come up?"

Taylor hesitated, but pushed the button to let him in. When Jerome got to the third floor, her apartment door was open. Taylor was seated on the couch with her leg propped on the coffee table, and still in her nightclothes. She didn't shift her position once, not even to say hello. Jerome shut the door and placed the keys he had to her place in the bowl by the door, just as he always did. He looked around for any clue that another man had been there rearranging her space. With the exception of a few medicine bottles, tissue boxes, and candy wrappers, everything looked to be just as it was when he was there last. Jerome crouched above the seat ready to sit, but Taylor stopped him.

"Don't get comfortable," she said.

Jerome stood up tall. "How are you?"

"I can't complain," she said, surfing the channels.

"How's your leg?"

"Healing."

Taylor seemed so cold. Maybe he should have brought some flowers. "I tried to visit you at the hospital," he said, hoping she'd let down her guard a little.

"I know," she mumbled, clearly not in the mood for idle conversation.

It was clear that Taylor wasn't in the mood to talk. Jerome knew that he was to blame for her nonchalant attitude, but thought all that could change after she heard what he'd come to say. "I wanted you to know that Renee and I are getting a divorce." Taylor looked at him for the first time since he entered the apartment. "I know you probably don't believe me, but it's true. We're getting a divorce and she's moving to Chicago." Jerome put his hands in his pockets, trying to keep from trembling. "I know it's been a while, but you said I could come back when things were final."

"Did you ask for the divorce or did Renee?"

Jerome wanted to lie, but he couldn't. Lies ruined his marriage, and he wanted to begin his next relationship on a good note, that is, if Taylor was going to take him back. "Renee brought it up."

"So, you had to wait for Renee to bring it up?" Jerome started to explain, but Taylor interrupted him. "Jerome, I care about you. But what we did was wrong. When I think about the part I played in this, I'm disgusted with myself. You and Renee may have had problems before we met, but I certainly didn't make matters any better. I can't be with you. If you could cheat on your wife and your children, there's no guarantee that you wouldn't do the same to me."

Jerome was shocked. He hadn't expected to hear those words from Taylor. He thought the news would have made her happy. "I was wrong, Taylor. But I wasn't in this relationship alone. We have a strong connection. You can't deny that."

"That *strong* connection isn't love. The way you pulled away from me at the movies showed me that. You were afraid of what Renee might think," Taylor said sadly. "You still have feelings for your wife."

Jerome was desperate. He couldn't let Taylor give up on him this easily. "You're wrong, baby. I was protecting you. Renee found a card you gave me, and there was no telling what she might have done."

"I don't believe that." Taylor shifted her position on the couch. "That day made me think about our future. What if we got married and had children? Would you be there for me? Would you help with the dirty diapers, late night cries, or temper tantrums? Or would you only be around for basketball games and music recitals?"

"You know the answer to that."

"But that's the problem, Jerome. I couldn't answer those questions with confidence. And that's not how I should feel about someone I want to spend the rest of my life with."

Jerome stared at her, straight-faced and confused. Taylor didn't want him anymore. Not only had Renee walked away from him, but now so had Taylor. What was he supposed to do?

"Jerome, as much as I hate to say this, I have to. Please leave and don't call me anymore."

Jerome frowned, but accepted defeat. There was nothing else he could say. He wanted to cry, but didn't want that to be the last image Taylor remembered of him. He backed away slowly toward the front door. He went to scoop his keys out of the bowl and then realized he wouldn't need them again. He looked at Taylor one last time for a sign that she wanted him to stay, but he found none.

Jerome slowly backed out the door and drove to Sam and Pete's, the only place he felt wanted.

Jerome watched the kids run out of the school building, excited that the day was over, and summer vacation was near. Jerome leaned back into the seat as the kids ran up and down the sidewalk. After this year, he wouldn't have to pick up the boys at all. Once Renee moved to Chicago, seeing the boys would be reduced to some holidays and a few weeks in the summer. He never wanted this for his family. Jerome's birth father had abandoned him when he was nine years old, so he knew what it felt like to grow up without one. It was hard watching the fathers of his son's teammates cheering for their sons and offering knowledge of sportsmanship. There was also no one around to teach him what it meant to be a man. What he did learn about manhood came from observing his friends and their male relatives. Jerome's mother raised her children alone. For seven years, she worked double shifts and long hours to make sure her children didn't suffer. It wasn't until she met her second husband that life began to change. But by that the time, Jerome was seventeen and on his way to being an adult.

Jerome blinked his eyes a few times. *What if Renee meets someone else and they get married?* Although Jerome's stepfather was a good man, Jerome didn't want his boys raised by another man. That was his job. Jerome looked in the rearview mirror to see if the kids were coming and was startled by the reflection in the mirror. He was no longer looking at himself. Instead, the face of his birth father was glaring back at him. Jerome rubbed his face vigorously with his hands. Still, the image of his father stared back at him, this time saying, "You're just like your old man."

Jerome Jr. tapped the car door and Jerome rolled down the window. "Reggie's helping Mrs. Wagner in the gym. They should be done soon," he said, trying to open the passenger door.

Jerome unlocked the doors. "Okay, get in the car." Jerome Jr. hopped in the backseat, put on his seatbelt, and grabbed his Game Boy from the pocket on the back of the passenger seat. After three minutes passed, Jerome realized that he and his youngest son never had much to talk about. Their conversations often ended in, "Stop crying!" "Stop whining!" or "Stop acting like a baby!" As Jerome watched him, he thought about Renee's words, "If you spent more time with him . . ." He was definitely guilty of the accusation. By the time Jerome Jr. was old enough for school, the problems between he and Renee had escalated, and he slowly drifted away from home, spending more time at Sam and Pete's than with his own family. He looked at himself in the mirror again. *I am just like my father.*

Jerome could see Mother Wagner walking to the car and sat up in his seat. Zora and Reggie, with his basketball under his arm and two book bags on each shoulder, were following close behind.

"Sorry he's late," Mother Wagner told Jerome. "I needed some help putting away chairs."

"No problem. I knew he was in good hands," Jerome said.

Reggie stood close to Mother Wagner. "Dad, can you drop Zora off?"

Jerome observed Zora with a skeptical eye. "Something special go on here today?" he asked, referring to the fact that this was an all boys school.

Zora didn't recognize Jerome's cynicism. She smiled sweetly and answered him. "At the end of the year, the boy and girl schools have a big celebration together. I'm on the planning committee."

"Umm. Alright, get in," he replied, really wanting to say no. It wasn't that he didn't want to take Zora home, or that he didn't like her, Jerome was just upset at the amount of attention she was receiving. Though he initially gave Reggie permission to have a girlfriend, he had come to regret the time he spent with Zora. He should use any free time to practice basketball.

The young couple dived in the backseat, Reggie bribing

Jerome Jr. for the middle seat. Since he was getting taller, the space in the middle provided a little more space for him to stretch his legs.

Jerome could not keep his eyes off them giggling and poking one another. Most alarming was the basketball that never left Reggie's side. His once prized possession was tucked under Jerome Jr.'s feet. Although Jerome didn't approve of Reggie and Zora getting back together, it wasn't for the same reasons Renee had. He worried that Zora was affecting his game.

"He's doing good, Jerome," Mother Wagner said, as she leaned against the driver side door. "Every now and then you have to set kids straight. My kids are grown and I still have to check them."

"Thanks for looking out for him," Jerome said and started the ignition. Mother Wagner would talk to them until midnight if she could.

"Before you go," she continued, "How are you?"

"I'm making it," he said, and shifted the gear to drive.

"You got to be better than that. God has blessed you with a beautiful family. Oh, I know all is not perfect, but family is meant to stay together. And I know mistakes are made. I sure made a ton of them when my kids were young," she laughed. "But we are supposed to learn from our mistakes." She reached inside the window and pat his shoulder. "Well, I see my husband pulling up behind you. You guys have a blessed evening."

With the exception of an old Stevie Wonder CD playing in the background, the car was quiet. Jerome Jr. was tapping away on his electronic game while Reggie and Zora mouthed the words of a song they barely knew. Reggie didn't think Jerome could see his hands intertwined with Zora's. If Renee were driving, she would've pulled off the road and reorganized the seating arrangement.

When Jerome dropped Zora off, Reggie walked her inside. He had to speak to Zora's parents, just as Renee's parents made Jerome do when they were dating.

"Dad," Jerome Jr. said, finally lifting his eyes off the game he was holding. "Do you still love Mommy?"

Jerome's heart began to beat faster than usual. "Why would you ask me that?" he replied.

"You two fight more than me and Reggie and you live with Uncle Brandon now." Jerome closed his eyes. *What am I supposed to say?*

"You're not even coming with us to Chicago," Jerome Jr. pouted. Renee had talked to the boys a few days ago about the separation, but his youngest son didn't really understand what it meant. In his seven-year-old mind, mothers and fathers were supposed to stay together. After all, both sets of grandparents were still together, as was his favorite aunt and uncle.

Jerome felt like a bad role model. "You're mother and I care about each other a lot. We're just having some problems."

Jerome Jr. perked up. "Does that mean you're coming to Chicago?"

"No, son, I have a job here. The job in Chicago is something your mother has wanted for a long time, so she has to move." Jerome turned around, but Jerome Jr. had resumed tapping the keys of his game with a scowl on his face. Jerome could tell that he was upset, and that hurt his heart more than anything.

25

Renee

"Good morning, sleepy head," a cheerful Elise sang on the other end of the phone.

Renee checked the time and sat up, afraid that the alarm hadn't gone off. "Hey, Elise. Is it seven already?" Since the night of Renee's birthday, she and Elise had agreed to pray together twice a week in the morning.

"No, it's five thirty, but I have some news for you."

It had to be good news. Elise wouldn't have called so early otherwise. Renee swung out of her bed and turned on the lamp. "Did you have the baby?"

"Yes, I delivered a beautiful and healthy baby girl at 11:47 last night," Elise beamed.

Renee bombarded her with questions. "A preemie? How is she? What's her name? How are you? How much does she weigh?"

"Elise Marie Bennet, born on June 11th, is six pounds seven ounces and getting stronger every hour." From her voice, Renee could tell that the baby was nearby, and possibly in her arms.

"Six pounds isn't a preemie," Renee said, reflecting on Reggie's birth weight.

"It is when you deliver eight weeks before the due date."

"As long as she's healthy. That's all that really matters." Renee took her Bible out of the drawer and turned to Psalms 34. "I'm so happy for you. I can't wait to see her."

Elise blew kisses at her newborn daughter. "You know you have an open invitation. She'd love to meet her Auntie Renee."

"Well, I guess this is cause for celebration. Shall we pray?"

Renee read the entire psalm 34 verse, and when they were finished, Elise asked Renee about her trip to Chicago. Renee described the scenery and energy of the city with enthusiasm. She shared her ideas for the hotel and expressed her eagerness to begin the new position. As she talked, Renee could feel her spirit lift whenever Everett's name was mentioned.

"You and Everett seem to be getting along very well," prodded Elise.

"It's not what you're thinking," Renee said, glad that she hadn't told her about the night they spent at Navy Pier. "Besides, he lives in Los Angeles."

"I understand," Elise began sincerely, "but as your friend, I have to tell you to be careful. You're vulnerable right now. And as your prayer partner, I have to tell you what my grandmother always told me." Elise cleared her throat and mimicked her grandmother's voice. "Whenever you're tempted by your flesh, don't stick around because you'll lose every time. You've got to flee, child. Run far, far away." Elise burst into laughter before continuing. "As fine as you say Everett is, you better invest in some sturdy track shoes."

While the boys finished eating their breakfast, Renee sorted the mail. She sifted through the unwanted circulars and promotions and came across a manila envelope marked: *from the office of Diane Kelley.* The divorce papers had arrived. Once they were signed, she'd officially be a single woman again. The kids would be upset, but they would get over it in time. Although Jerome Jr. would miss seeing his father, he was excited about the move. Reggie wasn't quite ready at all. Yesterday, he asked if he could live with his father. Renee didn't mean to raise her voice when telling him no, but she couldn't believe Reggie had the nerve to ask. She suspected his query stemmed from his rejuvenated relationship with Zora.

Renee looked around the kitchen and shivered. The house would have to be put on the market soon, and it was nowhere near being ready. There was a lot of work to do. Thirteen years of stuff had to be sorted, thrown away, or packed in boxes. When the boys got out of school in a few weeks, she would take some time off from work to get things in order.

Renee looked down at the ceramic tile Jerome spent a year replacing. For months, she had to tolerate a half tile, half linoleum floor. Memories of the life she and Jerome shared in the house flashed through her mind—the day she brought Jerome Jr. home, the nights they spent remodeling the bathroom, the family cookouts. *Things weren't always so bad.*

"Put your plates in the sink. It's time to go," Renee told the boys, and put the manila folder in her new briefcase. "Don't forget your bags. You're going straight to Uncle Brandon's after school."

Reggie cleaned the table then handed Renee an envelope.

"What's this?" she asked.

"You forgot to ask me for my signatures last night."

She looked the paper over thoroughly. "These aren't fake signatures are they?" she joked.

"Mom," Reggie responded, half-smiling. Reggie picked up his overnight bag and held the front door open for his mother. "Can I have my cell phone back? I've been doing everything I promised."

Renee couldn't argue with that. Reggie was not only doing better in school, he also did extra chores around the house. "It's in my jewelry box upstairs. Hurry up so we won't be late."

Reggie kissed her and charged up the steps.

* * *

"Mrs. Thomas," Bianca called through the intercom.

Renee was removing the books she had accumulated over the years from the shelf. "Yes, Bianca," she said, hoping there wouldn't be another major distraction. Earlier, she was pulled away to settle a disagreement with a new client. It took two hours to settle on a date for a fundraising event.

"You have a call on line one. Should I put it through?"

Renee sighed, "Do you know who it is?"

"Mr. Coleman," Bianca responded.

Renee could tell she was smiling. "Sure," she said nonchalantly, careful not to sound too excited. "Put him through." Renee sat in her swivel chair, and put the receiver to her ear. "Hey, Everett. What's up?" Renee was glad he called. She hadn't spoken to him since they parted ways in Chicago. Since then she had dreamed about him a few nights, waking up in hot sweats. She felt guilty, but after the night at Navy Pier, she was longing for more; more romantic outings, exquisite dinners, and intelligent conversations. All things she and Jerome had not done since Reggie was small.

"Hey, lady, I was calling to see if you had a chance to read the final budget," Everett said, his deep voice sending chills through her body.

"You could've sent an email, Everett. What's really up?" she questioned.

He laughed. "There's no beating around the bush with you, is it?"

"You're a to-the-point kind of guy. So, tell me. What's going on?"

"I wanted to hear your voice." Renee started tapping her foot briskly against the desk. "To make sure you were all right," he continued. "You're going to be my right hand woman until the end of the year."

Renee swirled the chair around to face the wall. In case someone walked in, she didn't want them to see the grin on her face. *Stay professional, Renee.* "I'm fine. Just trying to get everything organized for my replacement." Renee moved the chair from side to side and knocked her briefcase over. A few documents and the manila folder containing the divorce papers fell out. Renee planned to have Jerome sign them when she dropped the boys off after work.

"I'll be in Philly next week," Everett told her. "Why don't we plan to have lunch, and not at Bahama Breeze."

"Oh you have jokes, do you?" Renee said, holding the manila folder in her hand. "Maggianos isn't far from here. How does that sound?"

"Sounds perfect. I'll see you soon."

Renee held the phone in her hand for at least a minute after they ended the call. "I'm not single yet," she reminded herself. Her mind was taking her places she wasn't yet ready to go. Renee jumped to her feet and finished packing. "There's no good thing in the flesh," she repeated, and laughed thinking about the conversation with Elise. *I may need those track shoes.*

Renee looked forward to going to Bible study all week. With little persuasion, Jerome agreed to keep the boys all night. When she pulled up to Brandon's house, Jerome's car was not in sight. Before Renee became irate, she asked Jerome Jr. to ring the bell.

Jocelyn came to the door with her two-year-old daughter in her arms. "He's probably at the bar," she said before Renee had a chance to ask. "Did he know you were coming?"

"I told him I wanted to go to church tonight," she called from inside her car.

"Oh yeah, I remember. Women's night, right?" Jocelyn said.

"Yep. Jerome said he'd watch the kids for me."

"Maybe he's on his way." Jocelyn tried to sound convincing. "The boys can come in though. Brandon will be home soon."

Renee didn't want to leave the boys. Jocelyn had four children of her own. Adding two more was enough to put anyone on the edge. "I'll just take them with me," she said. "You have your arms full already."

"You're kids aren't a problem. I'd trade you any day," she chuckled. "You go on to church. They'll be fine."

Reluctantly, Renee agreed and kissed the boys goodbye. All the way to New Life Baptist, she reminded herself that she'd soon be a free woman.

By the time Renee got to church, the Bible study had begun. She stepped quietly inside, searching for a seat in one of the back pews, but Mother Wagner spotted her, and waved Renee down to a space in the third row. This was the first women's Bible study she had attended since Jerome Jr. was born. From what she could tell, the structure had drastically changed. Both the main floor and the balcony were filled with women. The women's choir was dressed in their Sunday robes and not casual attire. All of the musicians were present, not just the pianist. This was a long way from the classroom sessions they used to have to discuss a specific scripture. But then, church had grown tremendously since Reverend Robinson became pastor.

"I Almost Let Go" by Kurt Karr was playing over the church sound system as liturgical dancers performed. Renee watched them interpret the words of the song and became one with the music. Her eyes gravitated to the lead dancer. With each delicate movement, she made the audience feel the pain and turmoil expressed in the song. The lyrics became personal for Renee:

"I almost let go. I felt like I just couldn't take life anymore."

All of the pain associated with her marriage surfaced, but Renee resisted the battle to let go. She kept replaying the things that weighed heavy on her heart. She was getting a divorce, not because she didn't love her husband, but because he stopped loving her, which made it hard to love him. Renee gave all she had to keep them happy, yet in the end, Jerome found pleasure in the arms of another woman and abandoned his family with his actions, leaving Renee to raise the boys alone. And, now Reggie wants to live with his father. With the exception of his basketball games and practices, Jerome stood him up on more occasions than she could count, and he still wanted to be with his father. Jerome Jr. was her pride and joy, but he was spoiled. And then there was Everett. What was she supposed to do about him? There was certainly more between them than business and friendship.

By the time the song was over, Renee was at the altar crying before the Lord. She knew that it was nothing else but God that had kept her sanity all these years. Even during the years she abandoned Him by not praying, volunteering her time, or attending Sunday services.

Other women in pain were stretched around the pulpit pouring out their hearts. Soon the music stopped. Only the sounds of desperate souls in need of a touch from God filled the sanctuary. Reverend Robinson came to the pulpit and prayed for the women kneeled below him. When he was through, Renee felt like a different woman. She stood up and turned to hug the woman standing to her left. "Everything will be all right," she whispered in her ear. Renee turned around to hug and encourage the woman on her right, but froze when she recognized who the woman was.

"I know the last thing you want to hear from me is sorry," Taylor cried. "But I have to apologize. I know what I did was wrong." She wiped the tears that were steadily rolling down her cheeks.

Renee looked down at the cast on her leg, not sure what to do. Kara was behind her, and next to her was Sherry. They grabbed Taylor and followed the remaining women leaving the altar. Renee was numb, as she watched Taylor hobble to her seat. Renee knew she was in God's house, so she had to behave, but the next time Taylor approached her in public, she would break her other leg.

"Some of you are sick because you're holding on to past hurt and anger. Somebody did you wrong. They lied on you at the job. Friends stabbed you in the back. Your man left you. Your husband cheated on you." Reverend Robinson was electrifying, but Renee couldn't concentrate on the message. She kept looking in Taylor's direction, trying to figure out what she was up to.

Reverend Robinson had hit a nerve and Renee directed her attention to the pulpit.

"Life is not always a smooth walk in the park. But we mess up because as Christians, children of God, we are supposed to forgive, not hold a grudge. Some of you act like you've never hurt someone's feelings. If we were honest, we'd have to admit, that at one time or another, we mistreated and cheated on God."

Renee felt like the message was designed specifically for her ears. She sat still, afraid to yell, "Amen!" or holler, "Halleluiah!" for fear that her shouts would expose what was happening in her life.

"And now you're ready to quit your job, leave your husband, and forget about God. Remember . . . God didn't just kick you to the curb," the pastor continued.

After the service was over, Renee sat in the pew confused. She had come to church positive that she was about to embark on a new life. She expected to shout and dance all night.

"Everything okay, Renee," Mother Wagner asked, realizing she was sitting there after most of the women had already gone home.

"I'm confused." Renee slid further down in the seat, and laid her head on the back of the pew. "I've been waiting for God to send me some answers."

Mother Wagner sat next to her. "I may not have the answers you want, but I'm here if you feel like talking."

"The divorce papers came in the mail today."

"And I take it you're having second thoughts," Mother Wagner responded.

She sighed. "That forgiveness message touched me."

"Well," she said. "It's not too late to change your mind. *If* that's what you want to do." Taylor stared ahead toward the pulpit. "Renee honey, is that what you want?"

Renee sat up and faced her. "I don't know. I thought divorce was the answer. We're not getting along." Renee paused. "And the woman he had the affair with keeps showing up. I think I even imagined she drove by my house one day."

"This woman knows you're his wife?" Mother Wagner asked, surprised at the woman's gumption.

Renee nodded. "She definitely knows."

"That makes this harder." she said. "That kind of woman won't volunteer to leave a man alone too easily." Renee sighed and Mother Wagner took her hand and balled it into a fist. "All that means is, you'll have to fight harder then. You still love him, don't you?"

Renee didn't answer her question. Instead she brought up her attraction to Everett. "And in addition to all this, I met an incredible guy."

"I see," Mother Wagner said. "Are you sure you're not attracted to him because of Jerome's mistake?"

"I ask myself that question everyday," sighed Renee.

"Don't make the same mistakes Jerome did. You don't have to cheat because he did." Mother Wagner paused for a moment and then continued, remembering her previous question. "Do you still love him?"

This time, Renee answered. "My head says no, but my heart says something else. Jerome isn't a bad man. I just don't know that I have the stamina to deal with all this . . . this mess anymore."

"Well, baby, what does your spirit say?"

In that moment, Renee realized that although their lives didn't run as smoothly as she would have liked, Jerome did contribute to her success. Life would have been different if he didn't pay the smaller bills or if he didn't agree to work a job he didn't really like. Renee had made some sacrifices for their family, but then, so did Jerome. "I think I'm afraid to admit what my spirit is saying."

26

Taylor

"What a night!" Sherry exclaimed once the girls were settled in Taylor's apartment. "Out of all the women there, I can't believe we saw Renee."

"She is a member of the church, although she usually doesn't attend Bible Study," Kara responded. "Did you at least enjoy the service?"

Sherry shook her head. "I actually had a nice time. That Reverend Robinson was off the chain."

Kara smirked. "Maybe you'll go to the prayer breakfast with me next weekend then."

"Here we go," Sherry huffed. "I knew this was gonna happen. Give me at least a month to digest tonight."

"I guess that means no," Kara giggled and turned to her other friend. "Tay, what about you?"

"I guess so," Taylor said, though not fully a part of the conversation. She wasn't in the mood to talk tonight. After hearing the sermon, she had even more things on her mind. When she saw Renee at the altar crying, Taylor knew she was responsible for her pain. Although Taylor couldn't erase the past, she wanted to at least say, "I'm sorry."

She hadn't expected to get to the front of the crowd, but as she hobbled forward, the semi-circle of women moved aside to let her through. Renee didn't see Taylor because her head was tucked deep into her arms. Listening to Renee's moans tormented Taylor's spirit. She knelt next to Renee, begging God to forgive her carelessness and insensitivity. And when Renee got up, Taylor wanted desperately to hug her. If her leg wasn't broken, she would have dropped down and thrown her arms around Renee's legs. But when Renee saw her, all she could do was apologize. Even if Renee didn't want to hear it.

Small beads of perspiration formed on Taylor's nose and at the base of her back. Uncomfortable with the sticky feeling, she decided to change her shirt.

"Need any help?" Kara asked, as Taylor wiggled out of her chair.

"No," she said, "I'm going to put on a tank top."

Taylor limped in her bedroom and headed straight for her nightstand. She shuffled some loose papers around until an old box was uncovered. A picture of Renee and the boys were on top of the small collection of photographs stored inside. She had taken it from Jerome's wallet one afternoon while he was in the shower. He had two others like it, so she didn't think he'd notice. Now that Taylor had apologized to Renee, there was no need to hold on it. She stared at the photograph for a few seconds then ripped it into tiny pieces. This chapter in her life was now permanently closed.

Taylor dumped the pieces in the trash can on the side of her bed. She was feeling a little lightheaded but continued to browse through the remaining pictures in the box, pausing on one of her mother. Tonight, she had forgiven her for giving up on life at such a young age. Taylor had also forgiven her father for not being around and let go of blaming him for her mother's death. As she rubbed the picture, she realized that it was thicker than the average photograph. She examined it and noticed that there was another photo stuck on its back. She carefully separated the two pictures, not wanting to ruin either one.

The other photograph was one Taylor had not seen in years. She almost forgot it existed. She was just a baby, about three months, nestled on her father's lap. Taylor ran her fingertips across his image. Back then, she gazed into his eyes as if he were a king. Until today, Taylor thought she only had one picture of her father. The one now cracked from the night she threw it across the room. It was taken at a family reunion when she was sixteen. He had made a quick appearance to appease her mother. Taylor had refused to be in the picture, but her mother insisted. And, although he was full of smiles, Taylor defiantly stood next to him with a scrunched face and arms straight as a board on her sides. She studied the photograph still in her hand. *How did our relationship get so bad?*

Kara poked her head into the bedroom, "You okay?"

"I'm just sitting here thinking about my life," Taylor said, "and about my father."

"When was the last time you spoke to him?" Kara asked, sitting on the edge of the bed.

Taylor was embarrassed to answer. "Since my mother's funeral."

"That is a long time. If you're thinking about him that much, you should probably give him a call," Kara reasoned.

Taylor looked away. "I said some pretty nasty things to him after the funeral."

"You might have, but you were extremely emotional, and not thinking with a clear head. People change in six years. Give him a call," she encouraged. "He's the only family you have right now."

"I don't know. I think I met my apology quota for the day."

"It took a lot for you to tell Renee sorry. Sherry and I were shocked. For a minute, we thought we were going to have another Bahama Breeze on our hands," she laughed. "But seriously, if you can apologize to her, your Dad should be a piece of cake." Kara looked through the pictures in Taylor's box, pausing at the one marked *Daddy and Me.* "The word tells us to forgive, no matter what, so . . ."

"God sure has a lot of rules," Taylor laughed, struggling to get up.

"Yes, but He also has our best interest at heart." Kara assisted Taylor off the bed as she struggled to get up.

"You know," Taylor said, "I do have one more apology left in me. I never said I was sorry for questioning your friendship."

"I was upset, but I understand. It's unfortunate you had to be in an accident for us to make up."

"Just know that I appreciate you," Taylor told her and grabbed a tank top from the middle dresser drawer.

"This is why people don't go to church," Taylor teased, "It makes you confess your faults and want to do right."

"That's the whole idea," Kara chuckled. "How long are you off from work?"

"I'm told this cast can come off in a few weeks, and then I can work in a booth collecting fares, but," Taylor positioned herself carefully so she could switch tops. "I don't know if I want to come back," she said, glad that she hadn't waived the extra disability insurance Septa offered its employees. Taylor had actually signed up for it in the event she became pregnant with Jerome's baby. *Crazy thought.*

"I presume you have an alternate plan," Kara quizzed.

"I've been doing some research and making some calls. I can't just sit here all day and do nothing," Taylor explained. "I'm finally going to turn my boutique into a reality. I've had my eye on a space that's been on the market for a while."

"Claim it and it's yours. And you know I'm here if you need me." Kara gave Taylor a hug. "I have to run. Sherry's already asleep, so, can I get you anything before I head out?"

"No, I'll be fine," Taylor replied.

Kara let herself out and Taylor sat on the bed. She sifted through her nightstand again, this time searching for an old letter from her father.

27

Renee

Instead of going home after church, Renee drove back to Brandon's. Jerome's car was still out of sight. Aretha Franklin was singing about the pain of breaking up with someone on the radio. Renee sat in the car until the song was finished. She could relate to the lyrics more than she cared to admit. She stared at Brandon's house, trying to decide whether or not she should go inside. She and Jerome needed to talk, but there was no telling what time he would return.

The light in Brandon's family room went out and Renee could see the kids' shadows running up the stairs. She looked at her watch and wondered where Jerome could be. There weren't many places he could be. Was he with Taylor? Maybe they had decided to be together after all? Renee hadn't exactly given Jerome any incentive to leave her alone. Taylor did say she was sorry, but sorry for what? For taking her husband? For the possible stalking and turning her into a paranoid woman? What exactly was Taylor sorry for?

Renee looked at the divorce papers lying in the passenger seat. She had read them three times since she left church. Reverend Robinson's sermon had strangely touched her heart. She turned her car back on and pulled off. Renee needed to find her husband, and she had an idea of where he might be.

As expected, Sam and Pete's was crowded. There were hardly any spaces left to park. Renee circled the neighborhood three times, hoping someone had left the bar early. No luck. The city was experiencing a wave of seventy-five degree weather. The customers had no intentions of going home before closing hours, especially on a Friday.

Renee eventually gave in and parked five blocks away. As she walked to the bar in her three-inch heels and Ellen Tracy suit, she prayed no one from New Life Baptist would drive by. The closer she got to the front door, she noticed that not much had changed since she stopped socializing there. People were still hanging around the outside of the building, rapping to the opposite sex in hopes of making a love connection. The same bouncer was at the door, eyeing the young ladies that entered. And from the look of people dressed in blue uniforms, Renee could see that Septa employees were still Sam and Pete's biggest customers.

Renee was uncomfortable when she walked into the sweatbox. The pungent odor of beer and cigarettes instantly gave her a headache. Although there was little room to move around, people seemed to be enjoying themselves. Renee definitely looked and felt like an outsider. Someone from behind touched her arm, and she jerked around.

"Hey, Renee," one of Jerome's co-workers shouted over the music. "Long time no see."

Renee said a quick and uneasy hello. "I'm supposed to meet Jerome. Have you seen him by chance?"

"Not yet," the man said. "But I'm sure he's in here." A girl standing next to him grabbed his hand and he muttered something in her ear. She couldn't have been more than twenty-five. He kissed her on the lips before turning back to Renee, "If I see him, I'll tell him you're looking for him."

"Thanks," Renee sighed, figuring she better leave before someone thought she was trying to take their man. *God, please help me.*

The lights were so dim, Renee could barely see, but she knew Jerome was there. From time to time, a waitress trying to squeeze by would ask if she needed any help. Renee didn't recognize any of them, but eventually decided to ask for Jerome by name. Not much to her surprise, the waitress knew him and pointed Renee in his direction.

When Renee found him, he was sitting alone in the back of the bar, leaning against the wall and caressing a Heineken bottle. Renee slid into the booth, counting the number of empty bottles on the table. Jerome looked as if he hadn't shaved in weeks.

His somber expression didn't change when Renee sat down. "I've been to Brandon's and I made sure the boys were fine before I left their house. You didn't have to track me down," he blurted right away.

Renee couldn't stand to look at him in this state. "You can't drink your problems away. They'll still be around in the morning," she told him.

"Why are you here?" he asked, annoyed. "It's over. Remember?"

"I wanted to talk," she coughed through the heavy smoke clouds drifting her way. "I knew you'd be hiding in here." Jerome lifted the beer bottle to his lips and gulped the remaining liquid inside. Renee waited patiently as he slurped it down. "The divorce papers came today."

"Is that why you're here?

"Yes," she said. "But I also want some answers." Renee moved the bottles to the edge of the table, hoping a waiter would take them away. "This is a major decision. I want to be sure this is the best thing to do." Renee twisted the wedding ring on her finger. "I heard a sermon . . ." she strained to talk over the loud music then realized Jerome wasn't really listening. His eyes were on the people dancing and mingling in the aisle. She tapped the table with the car keys that were in her hand to grab his attention. Jerome turned, but barely. Renee spoke louder. "Jerome, tell me, and please be honest. I promise I won't yell or judge or talk back." Jerome was looking at her head on now. "Why did you cheat? I mean . . . we always had problems, but to cheat . . ." She wasn't able to finish for the tightness in her throat.

Jerome lifted the Heineken and took a small sip, "You changed after your second promotion. And then you stopped loving me. I wasn't good enough for you anymore."

"How do you figure that?"

"You didn't have to say it, Renee. I could see it in your eyes."

"There may have been a point where I got frustrated, but I never stopped loving you. Nor did I ever think to cheat on you."

Jerome tossed the glass in his hand back and forth. He wanted to focus on something other than the look in her eyes. "You didn't need me anymore, Renee. You wouldn't even make love to me anymore."

"You were the one that decided to stay at Septa when I encouraged you to start the basketball league again. You were the one that chose to stay out late at the bars." Her voice raised an octave and she could feel Jerome's leg begin to shake. "You were the one that chose basketball with the guys over your family. And you were the one, Jerome, that decided it was okay to sleep with another woman. I gave my very best to this marriage." Renee couldn't catch herself before she started to cry, but she wiped at the tears before they could fall. "I supported you as best I could, but I guess it just wasn't good enough for you."

"I'm sorry," he said, eyes glossy. "I'm sorry," he said. "I know I messed up. It just seemed like the more you started doing good on your job, the more I hated mine. You were making all the money and I felt like I didn't have anything more to offer you."

"I never said you had nothing to offer. I needed you, Jerome. I needed more than your money. That's not why we got married."

Jerome laid his head on the table and started to cry. Renee got out of her seat and sat next to him. She wanted to forgive him; give the divorce papers some more thought, but was afraid. What if they couldn't fix what was wrong between them?

Renee put her arm around him. His shoulders heaved when he felt her touch. "You hurt me, Jerome," she cried quietly in his ear.

Jerome looked up, his nose running nonstop. "Renee, I'm so sorry. I'm sorry, Renee," he repeated. "My life is going to be nothing without you." He wiped his face with his arm and continued to beg. "Please don't leave me. I need you. I'll do whatever you want me to do."

"I don't know. It's not that easy. We have some serious issues. I mean . . . What about Taylor?"

"It's over," he cried. "It's been over."

"Are you sure about that?" Renee was thinking about the confrontations in the restaurant and in church. Not to mention the mysterious car that appeared in front of her door the day it rained.

"I don't think she'll be a problem anymore."

Renee and Jerome sat quietly, taking in the hip-hop music blasting through the speakers. They sat through three songs before Renee broke their silence. "I'm not saying yes, but . . . maybe we should try a marriage counselor."

Jerome threw his head back and a smile came across his face. "You know I'm not into that therapy stuff, but if it means we'll stay together, I'm willing to give it a try."

"Daddy's here!" Jerome Jr. shouted.

Renee finished feeding Oscar and waited for Jerome to come in. Since they started counseling last week, Jerome had been coming by everyday to spend time with the family. Renee noticed that the boys were happier when they were all together. Jerome Jr. wasn't as picky about things and Reggie had gone through an attitude adjustment. Renee was in better spirits too.

Jerome came into the kitchen looking like a new man. He had

a fresh hair cut and had finally shaved the beard that was growing out of control. "What time should I bring them back?" he asked.

"Noon should be good."

"I was thinking . . . maybe we could drive over to the Camden waterfront when you're done. They're having some kind of festival today."

"I'd like that," Renee smiled. "I should be back by noon." Renee picked up her purse from the couch and placed it on her shoulder. "Ready to go?"

Jerome and the boys scurried to the door and they all walked out together. The boys went off to the park with their father and Renee to a prayer breakfast.

Renee sat at her assigned table beaming. This was the first women's breakfast she had attended since Elise moved to Florida. She looked around the banquet hall, critiquing the angel decorations and streamers hanging from the ceiling. She was sure she and Bianca could've come up with something more suited for the event. But this breakfast wasn't about appearances. It was about bonding with other women and receiving a good Word, something she hadn't done in a very long time.

One of the coordinators of the event stopped by the table to say hello and Renee placed a business card in her hand. "Next year, I insist you use the Luxury Inn," Renee smiled.

"Good morning, ladies," a familiar voice interrupted. Kara and her friends, including Taylor, were taking seats at the table.

"Good morning," the coordinator said back. "Renee, I'll definitely be in touch." She patted Renee's shoulder and walked to the next table. "I hope you enjoy yourselves, ladies."

"Hi, Renee," Kara said. "Seems like we've all been assigned to table 33."

"Good morning," Renee muttered, trying not to ruin her pleasant mood. *This can't be happening.*

"Mind if I sit next to you?" Kara asked.

Renee stared at Kara trying to keep a straight face. "No," she said and wrapped her hands around her glass of cranberry juice.

Taylor sat on the other side of Kara. "We keep running into each other," she said cheerfully in Renee's direction. Renee pretended her words were meant for someone else. "The food smells good. I can't wait to eat." Renee saw Taylor's arm reach for the basket of biscuits in the middle of the table. "Renee, did you try these yet?"

Renee could feel her blood boil. *How dare she pretend we're friends?* She turned around quickly, trying hard to appear calm. "Just because we're both in church doesn't mean we have to be nice to each other. I haven't forgotten that you slept with my husband."

"This is Jerome's *wife?*" a woman Taylor had come to the breakfast with questioned.

"Be quiet, Chairese!" snapped Kara.

Taylor looked around the table and almost burst into tears. She pushed herself away and walked as fast as she could in the cast.

With the exception of Kara, Taylor's friends rushed behind her. Kara started talking to Renee when they were gone, vaguely concerned that the other women at the table could hear. "I realize that we may never speak to each other again, but I feel the need to say something about this situation." Renee turned in her chair, facing the stage, leaving Kara to talk to the back of head. It was childish, but Renee had had enough of this crew. If she and Renee were going to try and start over, they'd need to find a new church.

Kara continued despite Renee's behavior. "You might not know that Harold is my second husband. My first husband was very abusive, both mentally and physically. I told myself that I would never tolerate a man who didn't respect me again." Kara removed her glasses and sat them down. "When Harold admitted his affair, I was ready to leave. There was nothing he could do to change my mind. But then, God reminded me that I had married this man for better or for worse. Lord knows it hasn't been easy, and I still struggle from time to time, but I had to test my faith and really trust God." Kara poured some orange juice in a glass. "Forgiving Harold wasn't the hard part for me. I also had to forgive everybody that participated in the charade. And I had to do it in my heart. It was the only way I could truly mend my marriage."

Though Renee didn't want to admit it, Kara was making sense. She was dealing with Jerome's affair well today, but next month or next year might be a different story. If she didn't forgive and let go of the pain, the bitterness she felt would eventually creep back in.

"For better or for worse," Reverend Robinson had said last week. *It can't get any worse than this.* Renee bit her bottom lip and excused herself from the table. She headed for the restroom, where she found Taylor dabbing her eyes with a paper towel. Taylor's friends were on each side of her, providing words of comfort in her ear.

Renee took a deep breath. What she was about to do made no sense, but Renee knew this was an opportunity to exercise her own faith. "Excuse me," she said to the friend she hadn't seen before today. Kara had called her Chairese and she had apparently known about Jerome's affair.

Chairese cautiously moved aside, eyeing Renee's every step. Renee couldn't look Taylor in the face, but she gave her a hug. "Everybody makes mistakes," she whispered in her ear. "God bless you." With that, she walked away. If she would've turned around, Renee was sure the women's mouths would've been wide open.

Mother Wager surprised Renee when she came out the rest room. "Kara told me what happened. I was coming to make sure you were okay. How do you feel?"

"Like I did the right thing," said Renee.

"You did, sweetie." Mother Wagner put her arm around Renee, "And, God will reward your effort."

*   *   *

Renee met Jerome and the boys at the Camden waterfront after the prayer breakfast. She was surprised that she had managed to get through an entire morning seated near her husband's mistress, ex-mistress she hoped. After the encounter in the ladies room, the tension between all of the women was significantly reduced, and they were able to really enjoy the meal and the sermon.

It was hot and humid for such a sunny Sunday afternoon, but Renee was glad they had decided to spend the day someplace other than in the house or in a store. She and Jerome cruised the waterfront, exploring the different vendors that lined the curvy path, while the boys occupied their time in the activity zone. Renee hadn't even noticed that they were holding hands.

"Taylor was at the breakfast," she mentioned and could feel Jerome's grip tighten.

"We're having a nice time. Let's not ruin it by talking about Taylor. Remember what our counselor said."

"Oh, now you approve of therapy," she said, not sure why she was becoming upset.

Jerome stopped walking. "I thought we had put all our cards on the table. We're not supposed to keep bringing up the past. Besides, you'll be in Chicago soon."

"It's just that she's a very beautiful woman. If we start fighting again, you might run back to her, or maybe another woman."

"Stop anticipating the worst. I'm not thinking about any woman but you. You're a handful." Jerome lifted her chin with his hand and pecked her nose with his lips. "And, for the record, you've got her looks beat by a long shot."

Renee blushed. "I'm sorry. I guess I'm still harboring some bad feelings."

"I know this is hard, but, I'm going to try and make up what I've done to you."

They started walking toward their children playing in a marked-off area. It was getting late and Renee was hungry. "I was thinking . . . After our session tomorrow, why don't we catch a movie?"

Jerome smiled. "Like a date?"

"You can say that."

Renee and Jerome held hands as they watched their children. Jerome Jr. was having his face painted like one of the characters from his favorite video game and Reggie a basketball on his upper arm. In that moment, Renee was happy.

Everett was definitely in the building. Women at the front desk who normally came to work free of makeup had faces covered with foundation, eye shadow, lip gloss and blush. Since Everett showed up for the big meeting a few months ago, the female employees went to great lengths to present themselves available to him. Bianca was no exception. She sat at her desk dressed in her Sunday best and sporting a fresh perm. "Good morning," she said in a tone unfamiliar to Renee.

"You look nice," Renee smirked. "Special occasion?"

Bianca gave her a look that said, "You know the deal."

Renee gathered her mail and went into her office. Although there were plenty of women longing to see Everett, Renee was not one of them. At least not today. She and Jerome were on the road to recovery, there couldn't be any interference at this point. And Everett would definitely be an interference. If she would have left Jerome at the bar, Renee was sure he would have drunk himself into a slow death. That would hurt the children, and Renee wouldn't have been able to live with herself. Despite their troubling years, she did love Jerome. He just needed to change. Their marriage needed to change, and in order for that to happen, Renee and Jerome had to be willing to make sacrifices.

Last night, after the boys finished eating and had taken their baths, Renee and Jerome watched old movies and talked well into the morning, just as they used to when they were first married. Since Jerome was not yet officially moved back home, at Renee's request he left before the boys woke up.

Renee opened the top drawer where she kept the divorce papers hidden. She stared at the first page, contemplating whether or not the time was right to shred them. A still voice whispered in her ear, "Trust me," and Renee looked toward heaven and said, "I'll try." She browsed through the papers one last time.

"Always hard at work," Everett said, startling Renee. She stuffed the papers, now jumbled in her hand, in the drawer quickly and looked toward the door.

Everett could have been a famous model with the way he fit into his clothes. Renee looked at her wedding ring, reminding her of the commitment she made to Jerome and to God. "Good morning," she said, careful not to smile too much.

Everett leaned against Renee's empty bookcase. "How are things?"

"We need to talk," she said before she lost her nerve.

Everett looked concerned, "Should I have a seat?" he asked in a more professional manner.

"I'll get to the point," she said, mimicking a phrase they both used to laugh about. She looked for a smile, a smirk, or any response that would make what she was about to say easier. "My husband and I are trying to work things out." Everett was silent. "I just thought you should know."

"So, he's going to Chicago with you," he said, more as a statement to himself. Renee could see the muscles in his face tighten.

"We've been together a long time," she said, feeling the need to explain. "I owe it to my family." She paused, waiting for Everett to say something, hoping he would say something. When he didn't, she continued. "We never really tried to fix our problems. But this time is different. He's really making an effort."

"And this is what you really want?" he questioned, his eyes suggesting she should change her mind.

Renee turned away. "I have to do this."

"I thought . . . well, I hoped we'd get to know each other better," Everett responded, not once taking his eyes off her.

"Professionally," she said, her heart fluttering, "professionally, we'll get to know each other."

Everett was direct. "I think you and I both know what I mean."

Renee looked up, but she still couldn't look at him directly. "I'm sorry, Everett. But, the timing is bad. I want to give this thing with Jerome a try."

"And, if it doesn't work out?"

"Then we'll cross that bridge when we get to it."

Everett leaned over Renee's desk. "Jerome's a lucky man." He remained fixed, staring Renee in the eyes. She held her breath, afraid that any movement could lead to a kiss. When he leaned back, Renee slowly released air from her lungs.

"Excuse me, Mr. Coleman," Bianca said as she appeared at the door. "Mr. Kotlarczyk would like to see you in the conference room."

"I'm leaving Philly tonight. I guess the next time I see you will be in Chicago."

Everett glided out of the office.

Bianca gave Renee "the look." "Did I interrupt something?"

"I think you're needed at your desk," Renee said, unable to hide her true feelings.

Bianca backed out of the office slowly, giggling softly. When all was clear, Renee dropped her head on the desk. *God, I hope I'm doing the right thing.*

Reggie and Zora were hugged up on the couch when Renee came home from work. They were too involved in the comedy on TV to hear her come in. "Where's your father?" Renee asked.

Reggie jumped and Zora sat up, moving down some, but not enough for Renee's comfort. "He's in the back grilling steaks for dinner," answered Reggie.

"How was work, Mrs. Thomas?" Zora asked.

Renee sat her briefcase on the stairs and slid into her house shoes. "I can't complain." But, the truth was that she had spent the whole day avoiding a man that made her temperature rise and keeping an inquisitive intern busy with unnecessary tasks to eliminate having a discussion about him. "You have plans for the summer?" Renee asked, still uncomfortable about their seating arrangement.

"I'm going to Europe with my parents for a month," Zora replied.

"So, you and Reggie won't be together for five whole weeks," she teased, masking her pleasure.

"I have a cell phone now," Zora responded.

"Well, I hope you'll have access to email," she said, looking at her son slumped in the couch as if he paid rent. His long legs stretched well into the middle of the floor, and his arms easily stretched across the width of the sofa. Renee pulled a pillow from under him and he frowned. "These are for decoration. They lose shape when you lay on them."

"My Dad has a laptop," Zora let Renee know, grinning from ear to ear.

"The joys of modern technology. Are you staying for dinner?" Renee asked.

Reggie perked up, afraid his mother would say no. "Dad said she could."

"Okay, I was just asking," she said, realizing Reggie was growing into a young man faster than she wanted.

Renee could hear laughter in the backyard as she approached the door. Jerome Jr. was playing Catch with Oscar and his father. She stood behind the screen door, not wanting to interrupt their time together. Jerome had called while she was at work to ask if he could cook dinner tonight and she agreed immediately.

Jerome saw Renee standing at the door and winked. Renee blushed.

"Keep an eye on the steaks," he told Jerome Jr. and jogged to his wife, happy that she was home. "How was your day?"

"Pretty good," she said, "I think you need to have a talk with Reggie."

"What'd he do?"

"He and Zora seem to be getting along *very* well," she stressed.

"I thought you liked Zora?"

"I do. I just want them to like each other a little less."

"I think they're fine, but," he threw his hands in the air as a sign of surrender, "if it bothers you that much, I'll talk to him."

"I'd appreciate that."

"I know we were waiting for our next session, but I think we should talk about Chicago. The boys will be out of school soon and I need to be in Chicago after Independence Day. I know it's late in the game, but . . . would you come with us?"

"Of course." Jerome was excited. "You deserve that job, Renee. I was actually hoping you'd ask me.

"There's going to be a lot of long hours, especially in the beginning," she said. "Do you think we'll be okay? I mean . . . I don't want to deal with anymore drinking or cheating again. I don't want to mess up what we've got going on now." Jerome smiled. Renee could tell that he wanted a kiss, but she didn't pursue it.

"Dad!" Jerome Jr. shouted. "It looks like the steaks are burning!"

"Neither do I." Jerome kissed his pointer and index fingers, then pressed them against the screen. Renee did the same.

"I guess you should move back in then," she told Jerome, grinning like a school girl.

Oscar ran over to Jerome and circled around him. "I'd like that," he said, picking up a small rock and throwing it. Oscar took off, moving slightly faster than a tortoise. Jerome looked back at his wife. "Dinner should be ready in fifteen minutes."

28

Jerome

Reverend Robinson stood behind the podium and looked across the congregation. "The doors of the church are open. No matter what you're facing, God is in control. All you need to do is surrender."

Jerome made his way down the aisle, trembling, but confident he was doing the right thing. He had never taken this journey before. In high school, he told Renee's parents that he was saved, just so he'd be able to date their daughter. Once they were married, he only attended church to please Renee. Though he believed there was a God, His presence wasn't real until the day Renee showed up at the bar.

When Jerome reached the altar, Reverend Robinson was ready to pray with him. The pastor placed his hands on Jerome's shoulder. "Help me be a better man so I can be a better husband and father. And please Lord, take control of my drinking. I don't want to be an alcoholic anymore."

When Jerome opened his eyes, he turned to see Mother Wagner and Renee in tears behind him. Reggie and Jerome Jr. stood behind their mother, choked up from the emotions that circled the sanctuary. Jerome reached out for them. "I promise I won't leave you guys again."

Reverend Robinson asked Jerome to come back to the altar. "There's only one more thing left for you to do," the pastor said. Jerome nodded in agreement. "Good, then repeat after me."

With the support of his family standing behind him, Jerome confessed the prayer of salvation aloud for the very first time.

It had been a long day. After church, Mother Wagner invited Jerome and his family over for dinner in celebration of Jerome's new life. He had never felt so special in all his life. And, Jerome had moved his things back in the house the night before. Jerome only hoped he would not let God or his family down.

He nestled between the pillows on the bed, taking deep breaths and enjoying the soft mattress. No more of the futon or twin bed where he could easily feel the loose springs. Jerome was finally home.

He flipped to the other end of the bed, something he warned Jerome Jr. about, and spread his legs apart. He laid in the middle of the king size bed pretending he was in snow making an angel. He heard Oscar barking outside and rolled onto the floor. Renee and the boys would be back from walking Oscar any minute. He rushed into Renee's bathroom and turned on Anita Baker's greatest hits. Renee loved her deep sultry voice.

"Time for your bath," he heard Renee tell Jerome Jr.

"Why do I always have to go first," he complained.

"Don't give your mother a hard time," Jerome said, walking down the steps. "Go ahead and get ready for bed."

Jerome Jr. poked out his lips and stared in Renee's direction. "Don't give me that look. You heard your father." Renee blew a kiss at Jerome in approval.

Jerome Jr. crawled up the stairs mumbling softly, "I always go first. This isn't fair."

"Stop whining. We only have two more days of school," Reggie mentioned.

"YIPEE!" Jerome Jr. shouted as he ran into the bathroom he shared with the other two males in the house. "Then I can stay up as late as I want."

While he waited for his turn, Reggie ran to his room to talk to Zora on the phone. With the living room cleared, Jerome whispered to his wife, "I've got a surprise for you."

"What kind of surprise?" Renee said anxiously.

"I'll meet you in your bathroom in five minutes," he said and danced up the steps. As he walked past Reggie's room, he poked his head inside. "You have fifteen minutes. It's a school night."

Reggie wasn't used to being disciplined by Jerome in this way. Renee always kept them in line. He was only used to Jerome telling him what to do on the court. "Awwight," Reggie shrugged him off.

Jerome's voice became a little more forceful, "Awwight? If I come back after fifteen minutes and you're still on the phone, you won't use it for a week."

Reggie straightened up, "Okay, Dad."

"That's more like it." Jerome closed the door just enough so he could still hear Reggie's movements.

Inside Renee's bathroom, Jerome tested the water he prepared with the tip of his fingers. When he started running the water ten minutes ago, he made sure it was piping hot. He knew by the time Renee was ready to relax, the water would be at the right temperature. He added a few more rose petals to match an advertisement he'd seen in one of her magazines. Jerome didn't see the point, but thought it might be romantic.

He heard Renee come up the steps. He lit the candles already around the tub and dimmed the lights. Renee said a few words to the boys then headed down the hall. Jerome was nervous. More nervous than the first time they had sex on their wedding night.

When Renee finally walked in, the gaze in her eyes told Jerome that he had done a good job. "It's been a long week. I thought you'd like to end it with a milk and honey bath." Jerome prayed he chose the right combination. There were so many bath ointments to choose from in Target.

"You thought right," Renee said, still beaming. "Thank you."

Jerome held his wife's hands. "About Chicago."

"I thought we settled that already," she sighed.

"Baby, this is your dream job. I'm okay with it. Really, I am." He kissed her forehead.

Renee dropped her hands. "Are you about to tell me something I don't want to hear?"

"Well, I was hoping the boys and I could stay in Philly for the summer."

Renee was puzzled, and Jerome explained his idea in more detail. "I took some initiative and pulled a few strings with some buddies of mine. They want me to assist them with an NBA juniors camp. Reggie could go. It would be a great opportunity for him . . . and me."

Renee's face was starting to light up again, and Jerome loved it. "And, I have an interview with the Bulls in a few weeks." Renee looked at him strangely. "Not as a player, though I *can* still play."

"If you say so," she joked.

"I'll be part of their Community Relations team. I don't know what I'll do yet, but I'm willing to give it a try."

Glaring deep into Jerome's eyes, Renee said, "I'm proud of you."

"I know we still have a lot to pack, but I think the boys and I can handle that, too. You just go to Chicago and find us a home." Jerome pointed to the bath tub. "The water's getting cold. You better get in."

"Thank you," Renee said, and then hummed the melody of Anita Baker's "Sweet Love."

Jerome kissed her cheek. "Okay, enjoy your bath."

"Where are you going?"

"I need to make sure the boys get to bed."

"Well, when you're done, come back and join me."

29

Taylor

Six Months Later

"Happy holidays," Sherry said, welcoming customers into the store.

Taylor had finally accomplished her dream. Second Chance consignment shop was opened one week before Christmas. After the accident, Taylor joined New Life Baptist and joined the Women Entrepreneurs ministry. Through the ministry, she acquired the knowledge needed to open the boutique, and was linked to a mentor who guided her through the process. It was challenging, but Taylor was dedicated.

Taylor's leg healed a lot better than expected and during the healing process, she developed a plan for her business idea. After the cast was removed, she decided to go back to work, but only for a few months. During that time, she was approved for a business loan and immediately purchased the space Bedazzled once occupied.

Once the loan was approved, she switched to part-time hours in order to concentrate on the store. With the help of friends, the store was ready for business faster than anticipated.

Plans for the urban boutique were well underway until the day Taylor bumped into Ivy, her favorite passenger, in the grocery store. Seeing Ivy again reminded Taylor of the conversation they had concerning fashion. Ivy loved trendy and expensive clothes. But like many women, she couldn't afford to dress like she lived in Beverly Hills every day. Taylor went home that night and prayed about ways to make a difference in the lives of men and women like Ivy. And in her dreams, God planted the vision of opening a consignment shop. Taylor would provide upscale clothes, slightly used and in good condition for a discounted price.

Opening day was better than Taylor had dreamed. Sherry, Kara, and members of the Women Entrepreneur ministry volunteered their time to help decorate and organize the shop. Taylor was able to secure seven racks of clothes—three for women of all sizes, and two each for men and children. As customers browsed the racks, they enjoyed holiday jazz and moderate refreshments.

Taylor watched the customers, looking for their reactions to the garments on display.

"Mary J. wore this in her video, didn't she?" Ivy asked excited, trying to maintain the clothes hanging over her arm.

Taylor inspected the caramel faux fur vest that she was waving in the air. "She may have had a black one, but you're right, that is the same style," Taylor corrected.

"Cool," Ivy said, and ran to the fitting room.

Taylor replaced the empty Dunkin Donuts boxes and refilled the pretzel and potato chip bowls. She reached under the refreshment table and pulled out a basket of napkins. Grabbing a stack, she placed them on the table then stepped back to make sure the snack area was clean. *I need more spoons.* Taylor surveyed the room for Kara. She was in charge of replenishing supplies. Taylor's eyes roamed around the small gathering of people and stopped on a man she'd only recently seen in pictures.

He stood by the front door holding a bag filled with professionally wrapped gifts. He was older now, but looked the same.

He walked over to Taylor with a slight limp; the effect of a stroke he had a few years ago. "This is a nice place," he said.

"Hi, Dad," said Taylor, not sure if she should smile. It had been a while since they last talked and even longer since she'd seen him. The moment felt strange, like they were old acquaintances seeing each other for the first time in many years.

"I got your letters," he said, shifting the shopping bag he was holding to his other hand. "I didn't write back 'cause I'm not so good at writing anymore."

"Thanks for coming," she said, wanting desperately to hug him.

"You look exactly the way I pictured you. Only a little bigger," her father teased. "You've done good for yourself."

The accident had softened Taylor's heart toward her father. He was the only family she had. And today, more than ever, with all that was going on in her life, she needed to feel the comforting and protective arms of her father.

"I'm praying it'll be successful."

"It will be," he added. "You're mother would be proud." He paused for a moment to take in her mother's memory, then said, "I'm proud of you, too."

"Well, don't just stand there." Taylor reached for his arm. "Let's take a walk around. You might see something you like."

"I'd like that, but first," he said, handing Taylor the shopping bag, "my wife and I got you a few things."

She put the shopping bag behind the counter and gave her father an abbreviated tour of the store. As Taylor and her father walked, they updated one another on their lives. Taylor was excited to learn that she had siblings and made plans to meet them soon.

Once back at the register, Taylor could feel her feet swelling. She was going to rest in the back, but persuaded her father to hang around for a bit. She picked up the shopping bag of gifts and said, "I'm going to hide this bag in the back room." She watched as a small group of carolers prepared to sing. "You still have a great voice?" she asked her father.

He looked surprised that she remembered. Taylor was a toddler when he sang soft melodies in her ear at night to help her sleep. "I'm not too bad in my old age," he prided.

"Go join them. It'll be fun."

Her father checked his watch. "I think I will," he replied. Then, to Taylor's surprise, he moved in close and hugged his daughter.

Taken off guard, Taylor allowed the hug to erase the many years of pain. She closed her eyes to keep from crying.

"I love you, Taylor," he whispered into her ear and then released his arms without looking into her face. He walked away, singing "Silver Bells."

Taylor dabbed at her eyes, careful not to ruin the fancy makeup Sherry had spent hours applying.

When she entered the employee room, Kara was sipping on a cup of hot chocolate and reading the latest *Essence* magazine. "Someone brought you gifts?" Kara asked, referring to the bag in Taylor's hand.

"You'll never believe from who," Taylor replied, smiling uncontrollably.

"Well, don't keep me in suspense."

"My father is here."

Kara sat her cup on the table. "Isn't God good?"

"And guess what?" Taylor said, hiding the gifts under her desk. "I have a brother and two sisters. Can you believe that?"

"So, your baby will have a family after all," Kara said, rubbing Taylor's round belly. "I bet they can't wait to meet you."

Taylor had her legs propped on top of her desk, her hand softly rubbing her stomach. It had been a long day, but she was happy. The opening was very successful. She relaxed while her friends cleaned up the store. There wasn't much to do, but everyone insisted she rest.

She looked at the shopping bag her father had given her and pulled out one of the presents. The red and gold wrapping was so pretty, she hated to open it. She unraveled the specially tied bow and removed the pine cone that sat in the middle. She lifted the box and shook it lightly. She could hear a few loose pieces inside and tried to figure out what it could be.

She unwrapped the gift neatly and cried as soon as she recognized the jewelry box her mother had given her for Christmas when she was just five years old. She thought it had been misplaced when she and her mother moved into their last apartment. It wasn't anything spectacular. The wooden sides were worn and the lock hung loosely on the side. If there was a key, she wouldn't of been able to use it. When she opened it, a ballerina popped up and twirled around in a tiny circular stage. Music used to play as she spun around, but that must've been broken, too.

The inside of the box was empty, but Taylor could see a piece of a chain hanging from one of the smaller boxes inside. She pulled it out and opened it. Attached to the chain was a heart-shaped locket, the same locket her mother had given her many years ago. When Taylor opened it, she was glad to see a picture of her mother. She was ten years old. On the other side of the locket was an empty space, one she supposed she would reserve for her unborn child.

"I hope you're having a girl," a voice said from behind.

Taylor turned quickly, surprised to see Lance. Since the talk they had months ago, he had stopped communicating with her. She put the box on the desk and started to get out the chair. "Don't get up," he said, and hugged her. "You and the baby had a long day."

"I guess Kara told you, huh?" she sniffed, wiping her eyes with the sleeve of her sweater.

"You can't hide behind oversize sweaters forever," he laughed, then leaned against the wall across from her desk. "How are you?"

"I've been busy with this shop and, well . . . the baby," she said pointing to her stomach.

Lance looked around. "Nice place you have here. It's a nice size, too." Lance took off his leather jacket and placed it on a chair. "So, you ready to be a single parent?"

Taylor stood in front of the mailbox shivering and afraid to put the letter she was holding inside. She had given up hope that she and Jerome were going to get back together, but felt he needed to know about the baby. She also didn't want to carry such a big secret into the New Year. Soon, there would be no denying her pregnancy.

The last time Taylor saw Jerome, it was mid-August and he had stopped by the depot to finish clearing out his locker. He looked really happy. She hadn't expected to see Jerome later that night, but he showed up at her door unannounced. "I was in the neighborhood," he told her. But, Taylor knew that was a lie. "I wanted to say goodbye without so many people around. You deserve at least that after all we've been through," he stated once inside her apartment.

It was either pain medication or her overactive hormones that kicked in at that moment, but the thought of never seeing Jerome again saddened her. And before she knew it, tears were falling from her eyes and Jerome's hands were caressing her body. Making love to him was a blur, but somehow they had managed to work around the cast on her leg. When they were done, Jerome cried, and for once, it was Taylor that dried his tears. No words were exchanged. They barely even looked at one another; both feeling guilty about what had occurred. They both knew they had some serious repenting to do.

Jerome left Taylor's side in order to get dressed. And then, with one gentle kiss on her cheek and a soft goodbye, he was gone. Forever. Or so Taylor thought. Weeks later, she found out she was pregnant.

She thought about telling Jerome's brother about her pregnancy many times. He was the only line of communication left between her and Jerome. She often saw Brandon in church with his family. They always seemed so happy together, causing Taylor to dream about her life with Jerome. Maybe, just maybe if he knew she was carrying his child, they could be happy, too. But, her dreams didn't matter now. Jerome was in Chicago, starting his life over with Renee. Still, she felt compelled to tell him. It had just been eating away at her soul.

Taylor pulled down the lever and took a deep breath. Her hand was shaking, so much so that the letter slid out of her grip and inside the box. There was no turning back now. If Jerome had forwarded his mail to Chicago, he would receive the news by New Years. *God, forgive me if I'm doing the wrong thing.*

30

Renee

December 30th. Just two days before the end of the year. And what a year she had had. Through all the highs and lows, she was grateful God remained by her side. Had it not been for his intervention, she and Jerome would've been divorced.

Renee walked backstage after the ribbon cutting ceremony was over. She was exhausted, but there was still work to do. The musical concert was next, followed by remarks from distinguished guests and employees.

Renee couldn't wait to get home and enjoy her family. The last month had been so overwhelming, that she barely had time to spend her first Christmas in Chicago with them. But it was all worth it. Thus far, the move to the Midwest had been a wise decision. When Renee moved without her family in July, it only took two weeks for her to settle on making Oak Park, a suburb just west of Chicago, her new home. Once Jerome and the boys arrived, they smoothly transitioned into their routines—making new friends and participating in sports and music. Jerome was so busy enjoying his new life and career, that drinking took a back seat. Renee hoped that they had seen the worst of their marriage.

Renee glanced at her watch. *Only two hours left.* Backstage, Jerome was waiting for her, holding a dozen roses in one hand, and her favorite Enzo mules in the other.

"I figured you'd need these," he said with a smile. "You did a fantastic job. You're speech was great." He kissed her lightly on the lips. "I'm so proud of you."

Jerome handed Renee the roses and she sniffed them. "Thank you, baby. They're beautiful." Renee sat in a portable chair behind her and kicked off her favorite four-inch heels. Usually, she'd be able to work in them all day without a problem. Jerome bent down and massaged her aching feet.

Elise walked in, pausing long enough to pull out her camera. She took a picture of the happy couple and the flash caught their attention. "You two act like newlyweds," Elise said.

"It feels like it," Jerome replied, now deeply rubbing Renee's ankles.

Elise took her left foot out of her shoe and wiggled her toes. "I wonder if my hubby will massage my feet."

Jerome slid Renee's mules on her feet and excused himself. Renee's eyes followed him until he was out of sight.

"Look at you two. And to think, a few months ago you were ready to give all that up."

"He was a different man then." Renee stuffed her heels in the tote bag beside her. "And I guess I was a different woman."

"You're a strong and special woman," Elise confirmed. "Forgiving an affair is a whole new level of faith."

"Tell me about it," she said, watching the crew set up the stage. She was tempted to step in and direct them. "But you know I can't take the credit for this." Renee paused, reflecting on the past. "God is truly able."

Elise beamed, "Yes, he is," and pulled out a picture of her daughter. "Look at that smile."

An anxious crowd interrupted their moment. Elise put the photo away and pulled the curtain back. "I can't believe you put all this together. There are so many people here."

Renee joined Elise at the curtain. "I'm sure they're here to see the celebrities. They could care less about me."

"You'll make a name for yourself here. You're good at this. Don't underestimate yourself."

"Thanks, girl," Renee replied. "I'll be glad when I can go home and rest."

Renee and her crew worked overtime all week to make sure everything ran smoothly. This was an important moment for Mr. Engleton. Renee wanted him to leave feeling confident that he had made the right decision. She also wanted to make Mr. Kotlarczyk proud. He had traveled across a time zone to support his prized pupil. There were over two hundred guests in the hotel for the grand opening, including her parents, Jerome's parents, Brandon, Jocelyn and their children. Elise and Mother Wagner's families had also flown into town to support the launch of Renee's hotel.

Jerome had been a big help with entertaining everyone while she was preparing for the big day. There was so much she had to coordinate. From the special guest speakers to the new store owners, Renee had her hands full, but it was all worth it. Everyone was having a great time. Jerome had convinced a few Chicago Bulls players to stop by and christen the new sports lounge on the west wing of the building. Since Everett had ties in California, he was able to schedule a few celebrities as guest speakers. There was music, dancing, and plenty of food to welcome Luxury Inn to Chicago.

"Mrs. Thomas!" Bianca cried frantically. "Is there an extra mic somewhere? This one doesn't work and our first artist is ready to go on stage."

Renee was glad Bianca had chosen to relocate. She was a little high strung at times, but she was an excellent worker. Renee convinced Everett to bring Bianca on as her assistant. She was sure Bianca would exceed those expectations in no time, just as she had done when she started.

"There should be one in the box over—" Renee turned around

and almost lost her balance. Bianca ran up behind Renee and held her waist to keep her from falling. "Somebody get her some water quick!" she yelled to a nearby employee.

"Are you okay?" Elise gasped.

Everett was on the other side of the stage and quickly ran to Renee's aid. "Do you need me to call the hospital?"

"Please everybody, I'm fine." Renee said, wiping the sweat from her brow, "Really, I'm fine. Just a little tired."

"I don't know," Elise said, slowly shaking her head. "You look a little flushed. I'm going to find Jerome."

Renee quickly grabbed her, "Please, Elise. Don't worry about this. I just turned around a little too fast."

An employee came back with a bottle of water. "Thanks," Everett said, taking the bottle and removing the cap. "Renee, you've been working hard. Why don't you sit back here and relax." He gave her the water and helped her to a chair.

Renee sipped on the water as Elise and Bianca fanned her with loose papers. "Wait a minute!" Renee jumped up. "Did you get the mic?"

Bianca pushed her back into the seat. "I asked someone else to take care of that. You just relax."

"It's time to introduce the first performer," an employee yelled to Bianca. She acknowledged him by holding up one finger then turned to Renee. "Mrs. Thomas, I'll make an appointment for you in the morning, okay?" Renee agreed. "I really think I should tell Jerome," Elise said, still fanning Renee. "What if this happens again while you're at home?"

"This really isn't a big issue." Renee pulled Elise closer to her, "And please don't tell my mother. She'll have me hospitalized."

Everett grabbed her hand, "Renee, I can't leave Chicago until I know you're all right."

Renee slid her hand out of his and said, "You don't have to worry."

"I can't help it. You're important to this franchise."

There was an awkward moment of silence as Everett and

Renee's eyes locked. They forgot Elise was present. She coughed quietly to break their stance. Everett pretended to check the time on his watch. "Let me know what the doctor says," he said.

Thank God he's going back to California, Renee thought, watching him walk away.

Renee sat in the examination room waiting for the results of the blood tests. She was ready to get back to the office to review the grand opening evaluation report. The surveys in the report would let her know what changes, if any, she needed to make for the New Year's soiree. She looked at her watch and yawned. Thirty minutes had already passed. Dr. Belahmira had asked her too many questions. *How do you feel? Have you eaten today? When was your last period? Was it normal? Have you experienced any dizziness?* Renee leaned down and pulled her day planner out of her briefcase and flipped it to December. No record of her period. *Maybe I forgot to mark it. I have been extremely busy.* Renee turned back a page to the month of November. No record. *It is possible that I forgot to mark it.* Renee closed the planner and stared at the ceiling. *This can't be happening!*

Since she and Jerome were having problems, she had stopped taking birth control. There was no point in taking them. When they got back together, the thought to renew the prescription never crossed her mind.

Dr. Belahmira walked in with Renee's folder tucked under her arm. "What's the verdict, doc?" Renee questioned, not sure she was ready for the answer.

"You're pregnant."

Jerome was sitting down at the kitchen table sorting the mail when Renee came home. "Hey, babe," he said without looking up. "How was your day?"

"That depends."

Oscar wobbled down the steps as best he could and charged toward Renee. Jerome got to one envelope in particular and looked at it strangely. Renee didn't pay his expression any mind. She rambled on about her day, easing key words in, hoping Jerome would pick up the clues.

"Jerome," she said, "I said I had a doctor's appointment today. Don't you care about what happened?"

Jerome opened the envelope and started reading the letter inside. "Yeah, babe, I'm listening."

"Then did you hear me say that I missed my period." Renee waited for a response.

In slow motion, Jerome looked her way. "Are you saying we're having another baby?"

"That's what the doc said," Renee smiled.

Jerome left his chair and folded the letter before placing it in his pocket. "Maybe we'll finally have a little girl," he said, kissing his wife.

"Maybe. Who's that letter from?" she asked, slightly concerned.

Jerome wrapped his arms tightly around Renee. "Just an old friend," he said, kissing his wife on the forehead. "Just an old friend."

Although Jerome didn't say it, Renee knew Jerome was hiding something, but the chemistry between them had been too good since they moved to Chicago that she didn't want to make a big deal out of the letter.

Renee put her husband's hands on her stomach and then placed her own over his. Gently, they rubbed her belly. Though they didn't exchange any words, their eyes revealed that the rough patch of their relationship was over. This was their chance to prove to themselves and to God that they could be better parents, better husband and wife.

Renee hugged Jerome and closed her eyes. She no longer had to wait for her happily ever after ending. She was finally happy now.

Reader's Group Guide Questions

1. Renee and Jerome got married right after they graduated high school. Do you think they were too young to get married? Was marrying young one of the reasons for the problems in their marriage?

2. Do you think Renee should have filed for divorce, or did she make the right decision? Why or why not?

3. Jerome had strong views about belonging to and attending church. Do you think a lot of men feel the way Jerome did in the beginning of the story?

4. Do you think Jerome felt threatened by Renee's professional success? What are some pros and cons about women making more money than their husbands?

5. Who was more to blame for the affair and why? Jerome, Renee, or Taylor?

6. Why do you think women become involved in relationships with married men?

7. Taylor and her friends had a discussion about sex before marriage. As Christians, we are supposed to wait until marriage before having sex. Do you think this is a realistic standard for living in the new millennium?

8. Did Renee accept the job offer for selfish reasons (she wanted to get ahead), or was she truly concerned about the welfare of her family?

9. Everett entered Renee's life at a very vulnerable time. How do you feel she handled her attraction to him? Should she have pursued their budding friendship?

10. Did Taylor take advantage of Lance, or did she really care about him?

11. Was mailing the letter to Jerome at the end of the story the right thing for Taylor to do? How do you think Jerome will respond?

12. Do you believe Jerome is really over Taylor?

13. Compare and contrast Renee and Taylor's personality. What are some of the things Jerome loved about both women? What are some things he disliked?

14. If you were one of Taylor's friends, how would you have dealt with her relationship with Jerome?

15. Discuss how Renee and Taylor's family and/or friends influenced their lives and relationship with Jerome.

Exerpt from *Someone to Love Me*
A novel by Nicole S. Rouse

This is the last time I'm going to work in this store on a Saturday. I have better and more exciting things to do on the weekends. My mother was always late when she knew I had something important to do. But if I miss my date with Markus, she'll regret it. If she thinks I'm the problem child now, she's in for a rude awakening.

I tried to occupy my time by changing the clothes on the mannequin, but that got boring quick. My mother was the fashion diva. She knew how to coordinate and make a plain pair of shorts look like they belonged in *Vogue*. More often than not, I preferred subtle outfits. Jeans and a simple but cute top worked just fine for me.

Linda, or Ms. Linda, as my mother makes me call the lady, (even though she's only three years older than me), was in the back room watching television, or more than likely, polishing off the pineapple upside down cake my mother baked last night. She was my mother's star employee. Mostly because she personally brought in new customers each week. If I left, I'm certain Linda could handle everything by herself. It's not like there was a crowd of people in the store.

Entertaining myself and the three customers searching for clothes, I bobbed and weaved up and down the center aisle pretending I was on a basketball court. I loved the game, but after five minutes, even that was boring. I went to the window at the front of the store, praying my mother, along with my little sister, Leah, would bounce down the street any minute. This was torture for me. The big clock on the building across the street reminded me that I was going to be late. I became more and more aggravated as each second passed.

Strolling to the counter, I turned on the computer next to the register. In the background, Kirk Franklin's latest hit was softly oozing from the speakers. I wanted to change the station to something more suited for my mood, but my mother would chop my fingers off if I touched her top of the line stereo system. After waiting five minutes, the computer was finally booted and I began to play advanced solitaire.

"What time do you close?" one of the customers asked, interrupting my intense computer game.

"In two hours," I told her without looking in her direction.

"Could I ask you to hold these items until I come back?" She dumped a hand full of clothes on the counter. "I need to run to the cash machine."

I stopped playing and grabbed a pen from the side of the register. "What's your name?"

"Chairese. Chairese Gunter. That's C-H-A-I-R-E-S-E. I promise I'll be back in a few minutes," she said and rushed out the door.

I folded the clothes to waste time and put them in a plastic bag. My mother had ten minutes to get back to the store or I was going to leave. Linda wouldn't mind, and I was certain she'd take good care of the merchandise. Markus and I had plans to go skating and then back to his place for a movie. We did this most Saturdays without my parents' knowledge. If they knew I was dating a sophomore in college, I'd be grounded until I turned twenty-one.

"Joi!" my little sister called through the store. She ran behind the counter and threw her arms around my neck.

"What's up, Leah." I said, tickling her plump waist. She tumbled over in laughter and placed a Limited Too bag in a cabinet underneath the counter.

"What'd you get?" I asked curiously.

"Mom bought me lime green capris and flip-flops to go with my bathing suit," she gloated. "I'm going to Wildwood next weekend."

I was a little surprised. Just last week I had asked for a new pair of tennis shoes. I needed them to play ball at school. My mom told me I had to wait until school was over. Supposedly, she didn't even have money to put gas in her car.

Leah was clearly my mother's favorite child. By the time she was five, Leah could coordinate the color of her sheets with the paint on her bedroom walls. She was also able to verbalize which outfits to match with her growing collection of shoes and jewelry. At five, I could have cared less. I was more into playing street games with the neighborhood kids and getting dirty in the backyard. Leah hadn't changed much over the years. Now at ten years old, she did a better job at accessorizing and redesigning the window displays than me and my mother combined.

I don't mind that Leah gets all the attention. She's a great kid and an even better little sister. I just wish Mom wouldn't make it so obvious all the time. Last year I came home excited about making the varsity basketball team. I was the only freshman in my high school to make the team that year, so it was a big accomplishment. "That's great news," she had said, while running a hot comb through Leah's thick hair. That same week, Leah announced that she wanted to be in a fashion show and my mother bent over backwards to express her excitement, practicing different runway walks with her every night before bed.

"Where's your mother?" I wanted to know. She was already cutting into my personal time.

"Outside talking to some lady."

I looked through the glass window and saw my mother laughing like she was at a comedy show. I tapped lightly on the window and motioned for her to come inside. Markus would be around the corner in five minutes and I didn't want to keep him waiting. I tapped the window a little harder and she finally got the hint. She said goodbye to her friend and marched inside.

"That was rude," she said, straightening a few clothes on a nearby rack.

"I'm meeting Rayven at the library in twenty minutes. We have a big math test coming up," I lied.

"We're going to Bible study tonight. You and Rayven can study after church tomorrow."

When did I agree to go to Bible study? She always made plans with my time. "I never said I was going to church *tonight*."

"We're all going. It's family night and your father's ushering."

"I can't go," I said, and gave her a stare that meant I wasn't playing.

She looked around the room and noted how many customers were present. Since the store wasn't empty, she couldn't say things to me she'd repent for later. Instead, "Don't play with me, Joi," came out her mouth. "We're all going as a family. It's family night!" She picked up a belt that had fallen off a floor mannequin. "I thought I told you to tidy up a bit."

"You're always telling me to do something," I mumbled under my breath, praying she'd go in the back to talk to Linda, because as soon as she was in the employee room, I was heading out the front door. Until then, I grabbed the broom hidden behind the counter and started to sweep the floor. My cell phone vibrated against my leg and I jumped.

"Is that your boyfriend?" Leah said playfully. She was the only member of my family that knew about Markus, and it was going to stay that way.

I winked and she giggled as I walked to a corner for better reception and privacy. "Hey," I said in a sultry voice. Markus liked when I sounded older than my actual years.

"What's up, Boo? I've been sitting out here for fifteen minutes. When you coming out?"

Markus was impatient, so I used my feminine power to calm him down. I suggested that tonight could be *the night*. When I hung up the phone, my mother was staring me in the eye. I knew she was on to me, but I kept my cool. "What's wrong with you?" I asked, slipping my cell phone in my pocket.

"Who was that?"

"Rayven," I snapped. "Why?"

She grabbed my arm so tight I couldn't move. "Rayven, huh?"

Before I could answer, Chairese Gunter, the woman who had been in earlier and put her merchandise on hold, walked into the store. "Taylor?"

"Hey, Chairese," my mother replied, a little surprised and loosened her grip. "How are you?"

"I'm good. I was in town for the weekend and bumped into Sherry at the mall. She told me you still had the store, so I had to come check you out," Chairese said.

Chairese talked so fast my head was spinning. My mother didn't have a chance to respond to anything the woman was saying. I tried to back away, but my path was blocked by my mother's foot and I almost lost my balance.

"I was in earlier and I saw some nice clothes," she continued. "This cute young lady put my stuff up . . ." Leah must've heard the fast talking woman and joined us. "Oh, is this your daughter?" Chairese asked, looking at the striking resemblance between them.

My mother finally got a chance to get in a few words. "Yes, this is my baby, Leah."

"She is beautiful. How are your other children? You had twins and—"

"The twins are with their father," she told her, then pointed to me. "That's my oldest daughter, Joi."

Chairese slapped her hands on her face. "She looks just like Jerome. You've grown up so pretty. Do you go visit your Daddy much in Chicago? I hear he and Renee—"

"Chairese!" my mother interrupted, startling everyone around her. "You said you left some clothes up front?"

I thought I was hearing things. Did this Chairese Gunter say I looked like my father? Did she say his name was Jerome?

"What is she talking about?" I asked my mother, who tried to ignore me but I wasn't letting up. I followed her to the register. "Mom?"

She wouldn't give me an answer and the look on Chairese's face told me that she had said something wrong. But I didn't care. The cat was already out of the bag. "Mrs. Gunter, what did you say about my father?"

"She said his name was Jerome," Leah replied, "but Daddy's name is Lance."

And on that note, both Leah and I stood staring at mother, waiting for answers. She could stall all she wanted, but sooner or later, I was going to find out all I needed to know about this Jerome.